P9-BZX-025

"Do you always get what you want?" Chloe murmured,

trying to put her thoughts in order but failing miserably. All she could think about was the feel of his mouth against hers.

Sloan DeWilde reached out and cupped her cheek in his palm, his brow arching sardonically. "I wanted a pet iguana once when I was a kid and didn't get it."

"I meant with women, not lizards," she said, pulling her arms from around his neck. She let her fingers slip through his silky dark hair along the way, then clasped her fingers in front of her, stilling the impulse to skim her palms along his chest, as well. It had been a long time since she'd touched a man. She'd nearly forgotten how unsettling the whole experience could be.

A devilish grin curled his firm mouth. "Well, maybe... yeah, now that I think of it, I guess I do. But it's not my fault that women never say no to me."

"I did," Chloe countered.

He shrugged. "I'm still trying to figure out where I went wrong on that one. You and the iguana. My only failures."

He glanced down at his watch and shook his head. "I have to go. I'm expecting a call at the office."

"Wh-what about dinner?" she asked.

"You said yes," Sloan replied. "I guess I'm going to have to be satisfied with that much for now. But I'll warn you, it took six months before I accepted defeat on the iguana."

Weddings by De Wilde™

Weddings by DeWilde™

PREVIOUSLY AT DeWILDES

GRACE IS BORN...

- Still smarting at the separation from her husband of thirty-odd years, Grace DeWilde is determined to make her own retailing mark in her hometown of San Francisco.
- She's hired a savvy executive assistant, Rita Shannon, and a money man, Erik Mulholland, to set her plans in motion.
- She could hardly know that she would play unwitting matchmaker to Rita and Erik, whose past, tempestuous history had ended in betrayal and pain....

With her new venture, **Grace**,
off the ground, it's off to
DeWildes, Fifth Avenue

ISBN 0-373-82539-0

DRESSED TO THRILL

Dressed to Thrill
KATE HOFFMANN

Harlequin Books

TORONTO • NEW YORK • LONDON
AMSTERDAM • PARIS • SYDNEY • HAMBURG
STOCKHOLM • ATHENS • TOKYO • MILAN
MADRID • WARSAW • BUDAPEST • AUCKLAND

MEMORANDUM

DATE: June 15, 1996

TO: Sloan DeWilde
General Manager
DeWildes Fifth Avenue

FROM: Miss Edna Crenshaw
Executive Assistant to the
General Manager
DeWildes Fifth Avenue

Please be advised that Chloe Durrant has been hired as Director of Visual Merchandising and Advertising. She comes highly recommended by our merchandising manager, Mr. Simpson-Davis, who conducted the search and interview process per your instructions.

Since you did not choose to take advantage of the opportunity to meet Ms. Durrant before she was hired, I would suggest meeting with her during your next visit to the store so that you might evaluate her rather untraditional approach to visual merchandising as it applies to DeWildes Fifth Avenue.

Please contact me regarding the date and time of your next store visit so that I may arrange your schedule accordingly.

CHAPTER ONE

"I WANT HER, MASE. I don't care what it takes. Money is no object. Just make it happen, all right? By tonight."

Sloan DeWilde held the car phone away from his ear and stared out the tinted window of the limo while his older brother vented his spleen all over the cellular airwaves. Good old Mason! His idea of a good risk was ordering the fish for lunch at Lutèce. The man had no imagination when it came to enterprising investment—or fine dining.

"Mase, look at the damn photos before you say no," Sloan shouted into the phone. "Have you ever seen anything more beautiful? Look at those legs, and that chest. And she's got everything I've been looking for. She's absolute perfection."

Sloan placed the phone next to him on the seat and, with silent curse, flipped open his briefcase. As he looked up, his eyes met Lew Antonucci's curious gaze in the rearview mirror. He raised a brow and grinned at the silver-haired chauffeur. "Mason does not trust my judgment in the acquisition of fine breeding stock."

Lew nodded stoically and chomped on the stub of an unlit cigar. "Sorry about the delay, Mr. Sloan. We should be there in ten minutes, tops."

Sloan glanced out the window. The limo was stopped dead in bumper-to-bumper traffic on Fifty-Ninth between Lexington and Park. This did not bode well for a productive morning. Even so, arguing with Mason while caught in

the midst of a Manhattan gridlock was infinitely preferable
to the task he had waiting for him at DeWilde's Fifth Avenue.

He grabbed a stack of photos from his briefcase and
handed them to Lew. "Take a look and tell me I'm wrong."
The chauffeur flipped through them, keeping one eye on the
traffic as he nodded in appreciation.

"She's called Sheba's Prize," Sloan continued. "Her
bloodlines run right back to Secretariat. Her little brother
won the Preakness last year. We could breed her with Paragon. Who knows what a colt by those two could do?"

"She's a beaut, Mr. Sloan," Lew said.

Sloan snatched up the phone and interrupted his brother's
harangue. "Lew says she's a beaut, Mason. And you know
Lew's been around our family long enough to be an excellent judge of horseflesh. Don't forget, he's the one who advised you to buy Seven Sins." His brother raised another
protest, but Sloan cut him short. "If you won't listen to me,
Mase, listen to Lew. Buy the damn mare before someone
else does!" With that, Sloan clicked the phone off and
tossed it impatiently into his briefcase. "If I ran the farm,"
he muttered, "we'd have winners in every stall."

"But you don't run the horse farm, Mr. Sloan," Lew
said. "Mr. Mason does. You run the store."

Leave it to Lew to so succinctly state the obvious. "Mason may run the farm now, but he's about to get himself a
not-so-silent partner very soon," Sloan muttered under his
breath. As soon as Sloan divested himself—and the family—of the DeWilde legacy.

He still wasn't quite sure how and why he had been stuck
with DeWilde's Fifth Avenue, but he'd run it for the past ten
years. After all, there were six other siblings to choose from,
all of whom probably would have shown more initiative
than he had. Sloan had suspected it was simply because his

family admired his impeccable taste in clothing. If he had known he was going to be saddled with the store, he would have started wearing cheap suits, ready-made shirts, and ties made of something other than the finest silk.

At least he had the art gallery in SoHo for amusement. He'd purchased a controlling interest more than a year ago and since then had enjoyed dabbling in the business of avant-garde art. Art was infinitely more stimulating than designer bridal veils and men's custom-tailored formal-wear. But if all went according to plan, DeWilde's Fifth Avenue would soon become a part of his past.

"Mr. Henry gave his life to that store," Lew went on, shaking his head.

"And my father loathed that place as much as I do," Sloan replied. "He always preferred his planes to the family business. I can see why."

Sloan sank into the plush leather seat and tipped his head back. He had been just sixteen when his father had died in a small plane crash. Henry DeWilde had been fifty-eight, leaving behind a wife and seven children. The only solace the family could take was in the knowledge that he had died doing something he loved, not closeted in some poorly lit office poring over sales reports and merchandising plans.

After Henry's death, nearly all relations with the De-Wilde family had been severed—except for the store. But even before his father's death, the relationship with the Royal Family had been strained at best.

Sloan smiled to himself. *The Royals.* That's what he and his siblings called the rest of the DeWildes, scorning their unflagging attention to propriety and decorum and family duty. He could imagine what they whispered about the American cousins—reckless renegades who played hard and worked as little as possible, possessing not an ounce of the DeWilde passion for retailing. The tensions were hard to ignore, but Sloan did his best to live up to their expectations.

"His heart never really was in that store," Lew said, interrupting Sloan's musings. "I could see it every day when I drove him into the city. That store was Dirk's dream, not Henry's."

"Or any of Henry's sons," Sloan murmured.

Sloan's Uncle Dirk had founded the store in 1938 as a small but exclusive stateside version of the London store. Over time, DeWilde's Fifth Avenue, as it was known, had managed to carve out a respectable niche in the wedding market, as well as maintain a strong presence in the jewelry business—a feat due largely to the celebrated reputation of the Paris and London stores. But the Fifth Avenue store had become the weakest link in the retailing empire—which now included branches in Monaco and Sydney—mostly because of its size and well-established local competition.

The store had been open barely ten years when Dirk disappeared without a trace. Sloan's father had steadfastly refused to take over the operation, until his brother Charles had thrown a substantial block of stock his way—and made him sign a deal that inextricably linked Henry and his heirs to the DeWilde family business.

Until now.

Now, with sales on the steady decline for the past two years, Sloan and Mason had finally found the American DeWildes a way out, a way to sell their five percent in the corporation and rid themselves of any interest in the business of retailing.

All that was needed was just one more quarter in the red and it would be done. The doors would finally close for good on DeWilde's Fifth Avenue and the last connection to The Royals would be severed. And Sloan would get exactly what he wanted—a full partnership in the family horse breeding operation. He smiled silently.

The deal was nearly a fait accompli. After all, Sloan DeWilde always got what he wanted.

"We're coming up to the store, Mr. Sloan."

Sloan snapped his briefcase shut. "Pick me up at noon, Lew. I've got a lunch date with Cassandra Talbot down at the Tribeca Grill and then I've got to stop by the gallery with her and check on the installation of the new show."

"Looks like somethin's goin' on up there," Lew commented. "On the sidewalk in front of the store."

Sloan squinted through the front window. "It's not those fur people, is it? We closed the fur salon over a year ago. I have neither the time nor the inclination to deal with them today."

"I don't think that's it. But it's a pretty big crowd. They're all standin' in line and lookin' at somethin' in the windows."

Lew double-parked the limo next to the loading zone in front of the store. He hopped out and circled the car, but before he could open the rear door, Sloan stepped out. Lew stood beside him like a bodyguard, his arms crossed over his considerable girth, his chauffeur's cap pulled low and threatening over his eyes.

The store looked much the same as it had nearly sixty years ago, an imposing gray marble facade ornamented with faux columns. Above the shiny brass revolving door, the familiar *D* and *W* intertwined, glinting with reflected light from the nearby skyscrapers.

Sloan frowned. He'd stood in front of the store on countless occasions in the past and he couldn't recall ever seeing pedestrians giving even the slightest notice to De-Wilde's windows. The windows were, in a word, unremarkable. But in front of each of the six wide display windows that flanked the entrance, a small line had formed.

As he watched, the first person in the line would step up, press their face against the glass and, a few seconds later, turn around with a satisfied smile, only to join the end of the next line.

"Whaddya s'pose they're lookin' at?" Lew muttered, shifting the cigar to the other side of his mouth.

"I'm about to find out." Sloan handed his briefcase to Lew, then wove through the crush of pedestrians. He joined one of the groups, taking a place at the end of the line. The huge windows in front of him were painted black from top to bottom with only a small rectangle left open at eye level. Next to the rectangle, elegant three-inch gold letters spelled out the words Lingerie, Fifth Floor.

When he reached the head of the queue, he leaned over slightly from his six-foot-one-inch height and looked through the peephole. The sight inside the window was both shocking and tantalizing. Lifelike mannequins, bent in seductive poses and dressed in sexy underthings, lounged in a boudoir setting worthy of a sultan's harem. The display dripped with sensuality, and Sloan found himself unnerved by an overwhelming sense of voyeurism. For a long moment, he was unable to tear himself away from the sight.

"Hey, buddy," a voice called from behind him. "You plan to gawk all day or are you gonna give the rest of us a chance?"

Sloan stepped back from the window and returned to Lew's side.

"What's in there?" Lew asked.

"Ladies' lingerie. Very... provocative."

"Looks like the crowd is enjoyin' it," Lew commented.

Sloan watched the proceedings for a long minute. "I wonder what's possessed Millie? This is not one of her typical windows." He frowned. Since when did a woman of Millie Carmichael's considerable retailing experience deem a peep show an appropriate concept for a DeWilde's window? She usually stuck to the traditional—a bridal gown and appropriate attendants' attire.

"Minnie," Lew corrected him. "The windows are dressed by Minerva Carmichael. Your father hired her in '58."

Sloan waved his hand distractedly. "Right...Minnie," he repeated. He turned back to the crowd.

"Customers ain't gonna like this," Lew said.

"True," Sloan said. The word was barely out of his mouth before a slow smile touched his lips. Lew was right again. This was precisely the type of display DeWilde's typical conservative customer would find appalling. And what better way to alienate the clientele and drive down sales? Minnie—Millie—whoever had designed these windows had inadvertently played right into his hands.

He glanced down at his watch. The employees would all be lined up inside, Robert Simpson-Davis and his minions, ready to fill him full of his monthly quota of DeWilde sales highlights—or lowlights, as it had been lately. It was a ritual he had hated ever since he'd been put in charge of the store, so properly British, like servants welcoming the lord of the manor home. But tradition ran deep at DeWilde's, and this was one of those traditions that began before Sloan was born, first with Dirk and then with Henry.

Sloan reached for his briefcase, then clapped Lew on the shoulder. "I'd better get in there and find out who's responsible for this outrage," he said. *And thank her,* he added silently.

As he predicted, they were all lined up, awaiting his arrival. He began with Simpson-Davis, DeWilde's merchandising manager, then slowly made his way down the line. He barely paid attention to the introductions, merely pasted a benign smile on his face and nodded, well versed in detached social interaction. He'd almost reached the end of the line when a soft, husky voice broke through his distraction.

"I'm Chloe Durrant, Mr. DeWilde. I'm the new director of visual merchandising and advertising. It's a pleasure to finally meet you."

He lowered his gaze from somewhere over the top of her head, past hair the color of flax to a pair of alluring green eyes and a heart-shaped face. He stared at her for a long moment, focusing on the enigmatic smile that curved her bow-shaped mouth. "Ms..."

"Durrant. Chloe Durrant."

Her voice was like raw silk, better suited to a bedroom than a boardroom. "And you are..."

A frown furrowed her smooth brow and she blinked in surprise. "I'm the new director of visual merchandising and advertising." She said it as if it were something he should have known, as if his lack of this knowledge had inadvertently caused insult.

He looked down at her delicate fingers clasped in his, his practiced eye searching for a wedding band that wasn't there. For an instant, Sloan was tempted to pull her hand to his lips and kiss it, to press the silken skin below her wrist to his mouth. The move had completely charmed countless women before, and he was curious to see if it might melt a bit of the icy look Chloe Durrant had fixed on him.

But now was not the time or the place to launch another conquest. He had a job to do, and regardless of how much he might want to have a little fun, this was one time that business took precedence over pleasure. Instead, he gently shook her hand. When their gazes met again, she was staring at him, a questioning arch to her brow.

"Ah, yes. Ms. Durrant," he said, quickly recovering. "You are the one responsible for that...unusual window display out front?"

She nodded. "Yes," she replied. "What do you think?" The question was more a challenge than a request for a compliment.

His gaze locked on hers and he forced back a seductive grin. "In my office," Sloan said, his tone even. "One hour." He turned and, without another word, strode toward the elevators. As the elevator doors closed, he blinked hard, trying to drive her image from his mind. But, as if he had stared at the sun for too long, it remained, burned indelibly into his consciousness.

"Chloe Durrant," he murmured to himself, a smile quirking his lips. "Very nice to meet you, too, Ms. Durrant."

"HE HATES THE WINDOWS," Chloe said in a matter-of-fact tone. "And he hates me. 'In my office,'" she mimicked in Sloan DeWilde's emotionless tone. "'One hour.'" She glanced over at her best friend and DeWilde's advertising director, Gina Calafano. "So, do you think I should pack up my things now or later?"

"Don't you think you're overreacting just a little bit?" Gina asked. "You only just met the man."

Chloe grabbed a wad of pink tulle from her worktable and began to twist it into a rosette. "It was a very portentous encounter," she replied.

"Portentous? Yikes, there's a twenty-dollar word if I ever heard one."

Chloe tossed the tulle back onto the table. "It was on Audrey's spelling list. Portentous. P-o-r-t-e-n-t-o-u-s."

"Wait, wait," Gina cried, waving her hand excitedly. She jumped off the tall stool she sat on. "I'll use it in a sentence! If Chloe Durrant doesn't lay off the cheesecake at Roxy's," she began, "her thighs will take on *portentous* proportions."

Gina laughed at her own joke, a warm, unfettered chuckle that echoed through the cavernous space, loud enough to carry through the thin walls that separated the workroom from the sales floor. Like many department stores, De-Wilde's was built like a Hollywood set, with all the gorgeous architectural detail on the customer side. Behind the pretentious mahogany-paneled walls and elegant carved moldings and beveled mirrors, the storerooms, workrooms and offices of DeWilde's seemed downright rustic.

Chloe shook her head. "It means ominous, foreboding...menacing. Not good at all."

"Hmm." Gina sighed dramatically as she stared down at her legs. "I've always aspired to have menacing thighs." She looked at her chest. "Not to mention intimidating breasts. And a cunning nose. In fact, I've always aspired to look exactly like you."

Chloe fixed her with an impatient glare. "My breasts have never intimidated anyone...except maybe me. And you're changing the subject!"

Gina folded her hands in front of her. "Go ahead," she said with a contrite look in her huge brown eyes. "I'm listening. Pour out your troubles and I promise to be sympathetic like a proper best friend."

"I just expected him to be older," Chloe said. "With graying temples and a country club tan and—and monogrammed cuff links. A real stuffed shirt."

"There's one shirt *I* certainly wouldn't mind unstuffing," Gina commented. "In a candlelit bedroom...with Frank Sinatra on the stereo and a bottle of Chianti between us."

"How do you know he's worth unstuffing? You were late—you didn't even see him."

Gina grinned. "I was hiding behind the pillar in perfume, between Givenchy and Guerlain. I couldn't resist. He is so..." She searched for the right word. "Suave. I actually thought he was going to kiss your hand."

An image of Sloan DeWilde flashed in Chloe's mind—nearly black hair that brushed his perfectly starched collar and fell across his smooth forehead, riveting hazel eyes beneath dark brows. A firm mouth and a body that any male model would covet. His suit, probably Armani, fit him to perfection, accentuating his broad shoulders and narrow waist and a chest that...

Chloe dragged on the reins of her imagination. Good grief, where was her mind going with this? She shouldn't be attracted to the man. He was her boss, her superior... her very charming, breathtaking, sophisticated superior. Any attraction to him was entirely improper, and dangerous to boot.

"So what did *you* think?" Gina asked.

"I—I thought he seemed... intelligent," Chloe said. "Shrewd and self-possessed. In complete control. The kind of man who gets exactly what he wants and settles for nothing less."

"I could live with that," Gina said. "I also like a man who takes charge in the bedroom."

Chloe's gaze snapped back to Gina. "We are not discussing sex here, we're discussing Sloan DeWilde's management style. I think the man is... dangerous."

"Definitely dangerous," Gina replied. "Come on, Chloe. You have to admit, the guy is a real hunk."

"All right, he's handsome. To use an expression of my eleven-year-old daughter's, he might even be classified a bodacious studmuffin with a bod to die for."

Gina giggled. "I'm beginning to think I've been hanging out with the wrong Durrant. Audrey has a much more healthy attitude toward the opposite sex than her mother."

"If you value your life, Angelina Maria Calafano, you will not mention the word *sex* and my daughter's name in the same sentence."

Gina picked up a stray arm from a mannequin and pointed it in Chloe's direction. "What about sex and *Chloe* Durrant?"

Chloe crossed her arms over her breasts. "That's even more unsettling."

"Is it?" Gina asked. "You know, one of these days you're going to have to find a cure for your little testosterone allergy. Maybe you just need a shot of Sloan DeWilde."

"Just because I mention in passing that he's handsome does not mean I'm sexually attracted to him. It's a casual observation. Besides, he's my boss." Chloe smoothed her fingers over her hair. "A relationship with my boss would be a lethal mistake. I've got a daughter to support. I've got her school tuition to pay and her music lessons to finance. And what about the impending orthodontics? I'll have to sell my body on the streets just to give her straight teeth."

Gina patted Chloe on the shoulder with the mannequin arm and nodded sympathetically. "I guess poor Audrey will just have to live with that nasty overbite."

Chloe brushed the plaster arm away and, when Gina persisted, grabbed it and tossed it into a bin of limbs in the corner. "What are you saying? Plenty of men find me attractive. I've had lots of dates." She shifted on the stool. "I could date Sloan DeWilde...if I wanted to...not that I want to, because I certainly don't...or wouldn't, if he asked, which he won't. Besides, I'm a mother. I have to set a good example for my daughter. I told Audrey she couldn't date until she was thirty, so how can I?"

"You're thirty-four, Chloe. You've dated five men in the last ten years and managed to remain celibate throughout. You're setting such a lofty example, your daughter's going to choose the Sisters of the Perpetually Repressed over NYU."

"A convent would be good," Chloe said. "Is eleven too young to sign her up?"

"I went to convent school," Gina said, "and believe me, Audrey would not do well there. She's too much like her mother. Opinionated, stubborn and way too creative for her own good."

"I don't feel very creative right now," Chloe said, a worried edge creeping into her voice. "In fact, I think I might have gone a little over the top with the peep-show windows. But Simpson-Davis gave me complete creative autonomy, so I took it and ran."

Gina shrugged. "Well then, Sloan DeWilde can't fire you. Besides, people have been talking about those windows all over town. One of the window dressers at Bendel's was pressing his nose up against *your* glass yesterday morning. And Bendel's has the best windows in the city."

"Someone from Bendel's was here looking at my windows?"

Gina picked up a foam head they used to store mannequin wigs and held it next to her face. They both nodded.

A smile of relief curved the corners of Chloe's mouth. "Bendel's," she murmured. "Maybe if Sloan DeWilde fires me, they'd hire me."

"How can he fire you once he sees what's been going on in the store? Traffic has increased at least twenty percent since you've started doing the windows. We're attracting a younger, hipper crowd. I've seen more men shopping for gifts. And my ads look so fresh and trendy, they're bound to draw in the nontraditional customer. Before long, we're going to see a nice rise in sales, too."

"Even if he hates my windows, he can't discount a rise in sales," Chloe said hopefully. "That hasn't happened in this store for nearly two years. We're the ones who are making it happen. I dare him to fire us."

"There you are!" Gina cried. "That's the Chloe Durrant confidence I've come to depend on for a weekly paycheck."

Gina was right. She'd just have to be more confident in her abilities and her instincts. In her heart she *knew* she was a good designer, and she was more than able to translate that into displays that appealed to the eye and the imagination. She might not be a "real" artist anymore, but she was the best visual merchandiser DeWilde's would ever have.

It had taken a long time to rebuild what Julien had demolished, and she wasn't about to give it all up now. Julien. Even his name still had the ability to dredge up all her deepest insecurities.

She'd been just twenty-two when she arrived in New York, fresh from four years at the Chicago Institute of Art and Design and ready to set the art world ablaze with her painting. She'd met Julien Moreau at a gallery opening, and he'd charmed her with his seductive European manner and his devastating charisma. A month later, they were living together in his messy, paint-spattered loft in the Village.

At first, their life together was wonderful. Chloe became an inspiration and even the subject of a series of paintings. But then their relationship crumbled. Julien had his own confidence problems, and the only way he could bolster his considerable ego was to destroy hers. He was devastating, all right, but not in the sensual way she'd first thought. Instead, he belittled everything she did, but most of all, he belittled her art.

When she had nothing left to offer him, he moved on to a fresh, young and nubile "muse," leaving Chloe with her passion to paint destroyed, her trust in men shattered. A month later, she found herself pregnant with Audrey. A courtesy phone call to Julien to inform him of his impending fatherhood was all it took for her to realize she'd be raising the child on her own. He planned to return to France within the month, choosing his art over her and their child.

From then on, she'd worked at any job she could get. Her brushes and paints had been stored away in a closet while she turned all her energies toward her daughter and making a stable life for them both. Gradually, she put together a respectable résumé as a free-lance window dresser, finding plenty of work in the designer boutiques and showrooms that lined Madison Avenue. She'd met Gina three jobs ago and they'd immediately become fast friends.

When the position at DeWilde's had opened up, it had seemed like a dream come true—a regular paycheck, an insurance plan and a salary large enough to pay tuition at a prestigious private day school for Audrey. And a job at which she could actually prove her talents—to her superiors and, more important, to herself.

DeWilde's needed her as much as she needed the store. Before she'd started, the windows and in-store displays were dressed by a sweet old lady who had been with the store for years. To Minerva Carmichael, bridesmaids' dresses in any fabric but taffeta were considered a bold fashion statement, and any bridal dress that didn't look good with pearls didn't appear in the front windows. To make matters worse, the ads were so lacking in spark that they nearly disappeared on the page.

Simpson-Davis had been anxious to bring Chloe on after Minnie had retired. But beneath his enthusiasm she sensed a desperation, as if he—and everyone else—might soon be out of work if her efforts didn't turn sales around. Convincing him to embrace her somewhat radical ideas hadn't been hard, though some of the veteran salesclerks put up a fuss. And she had managed to get Gina hired to revamp their ads.

"It's about time someone made some changes around here," Chloe said. "In almost sixty years, DeWilde's New York hasn't strayed one inch from its original merchandising strategy. The store has been so exclusive people are afraid to shop here. It's no fun."

"You're absolutely right," Gina said, taking aim at another bin across the room. She lofted the foam head into the air and it dropped inside with a thud. "Absolutely!"

"We have to create a new identity. We have to make this store the place to come for everyone who loves romance—not just brides."

"I agree!" Gina cried.

"But what if *he* doesn't agree? What if he hates my ideas as much as he hated the windows?"

"Flirt with him," Gina said.

Chloe gasped. "What?"

"The guy's a notorious womanizer, Chloe. All the salesclerks gossip about his social life. If you want him on your side, just flirt a little. String him along. The way he was staring at you, I'd say you've already attracted his attention. Now you just have to take advantage of his weakness for beautiful women."

"I can't do that!" Chloe cried. "It's . . . unprofessional. Besides, he doesn't find me attractive. No, absolutely not. I couldn't do that."

"Suit yourself," Gina replied. "But it certainly would make your meeting more interesting."

Chloe's eyes widened. "What time is it?"

Gina glanced at her watch. "Eleven o'clock."

"Good grief, I'm already late." Chloe smoothed her pencil-thin skirt, then reached to tuck an errant strand of hair behind her ear. "Do I look all right?" She spun around in front of Gina.

"You look absolutely ridiculous," Gina said.

"What?" Chloe cried.

"The suit. And that little schoolteacher bun at the back of your head. It looks like you're going to a funeral."

"I thought Mr. DeWilde would be impressed with a more businesslike look."

"The last time you wore a suit was when you were trying to get Audrey into the Wellton Academy."

"It worked, didn't it?" she said, grabbing a stack of reports from her desk in the corner. "Besides, I couldn't very well show up dressed the way I normally do. They'd never have taken her."

"I'm sure you'll charm Sloan DeWilde just as easily as you charmed the headmaster."

"I don't intend to charm Sloan," Chloe replied defensively. "This is business, and if he can't see how good my ideas are for DeWilde's, then he's not much of a businessman." She drew a deep breath and forced a smile. "Wish me luck."

"You don't need luck," Gina teased. "Just bat your eyes and the man will melt at your feet."

"THERE *WAS* A MEMO. Tell me, Sloan DeWilde, are you under the mistaken impression that I type memos for my *own* enjoyment? They're meant to be read."

Sloan glanced up from the teetering stacks of reports on his desk, his gaze meeting the steely blue glare of Miss Edna Crenshaw, executive assistant to the general manager of DeWilde's Fifth Avenue—in other words, his right-hand person and the bane of his existence.

At first glance, one might expect a kind, grandmotherly nature from a woman of her age. But upon further association with Miss Crenshaw, it became abundantly clear that if Edna was a doting grandmother, it could only be to a pack of snarling rottweilers.

"I don't recall getting the memo," he said.

She stiffened. "July 15. I sent it out to the farm by messenger, along with the second-quarter sales report."

Petite, yet with the bearing of a battlefield general, Miss Crenshaw always dressed in proper corporate uniform—a painfully tailored suit that did nothing to detract from her starchy nature, and an old-fashioned white blouse devoid of any impractical decorations, ruffles and such. Her silver-streaked hair was pulled back into a tight knot at her nape, and Sloan was nearly certain this was the cause of the perpetual grimace on her face, a grimace that became much more pronounced when he was in the general vicinity.

She had started working for his father in 1955, three years before Sloan was born. Prior to Edna Crenshaw, Henry DeWilde had gone through at least two assistants in each of the preceding seven years, all of them more willing to resign than deal with his lackadaisical disregard for the business of running the store.

But Edna had stayed, rising to every new challenge Henry placed in front of her. Before long, she was tacitly running DeWilde's, calling on Henry for only the most sensitive of decisions. After Henry died, she continued to be the liaison between Sloan's family and a succession of hired general managers.

Sloan suspected that Edna's career at DeWilde's was her entire life. She never mentioned family, a husband or children, or any outside interests. She arrived at the store at 7:00 a.m., three hours before the front doors were unlocked. She stayed at her desk until the store closed at six—eight on Wednesdays—and was customarily the last one out the door before the security guards locked up and began their nightly watch.

Of course, Sloan had no direct proof of this. He himself barely ever arrived before ten and was usually gone by three, taking care to spend no more than one day each month in his office. But he did know that Edna Crenshaw was not the type to alter the order and organization of her life, certainly not for him, and probably not for anyone.

"I understand Millie Carmichael has retired. So what do you know of this new person... Chloe Durrant?"

Edna pursed her lips, as if she'd just been forced to suck a lemon. "She comes very highly recommended." The words were meted out like a miser's gold. She was only repeating what she'd been told by others, for Sloan could tell Miss Crenshaw was not a fan of Chloe Durrant. "You did give Mr. Simpson-Davis carte blanche to hire whatever merchandising staff he wanted. I was not consulted on the matter, so what I think makes no difference at all." There was a definite "I told you so" tone in her voice.

"I get the sense that you don't care for Ms. Durrant's work, Miss Crenshaw," he said, stating the obvious.

"I don't recall saying that."

"Come on, Edna. Give it to me straight. What do you really think about Ms. Durrant?"

She tugged on the cuffs of her blouse until both showed a perfect quarter-inch of white. "I think her ideas are entirely wrong for DeWilde's. We are an institution in this city, steeped in tradition, a tradition that *she* seems determined to flout. If it were my decision, I would fire her immediately. Her visual merchandising can only hurt sales *and* our reputation for discriminating good taste." The last was said with a haughty sniff.

Sloan chuckled and the two spots of color in her parchment cheeks intensified. "I guess I don't have to ask what you thought of the windows."

"It doesn't matter what I think. It matters what our customers think. What mother would ever bring her daughter here to buy a wedding dress or trousseau after seeing that window?"

"So you believe Ms. Durrant's unconventional ideas might hurt sales?"

"Not might. *Will.* You can depend on it. This increase in floor traffic is merely a result of late-season tourists."

Sloan frowned. "There's been an increase in floor traffic?"

Edna nodded curtly.

"I'll have to discuss this new development with Ms. Durrant. We have a meeting scheduled in five minutes."

"A meeting?" She scowled and shook her head, as if scolding a wayward child. "Why was I not informed of this? How am I to oversee your schedule if you don't let me arrange your appointments?"

Sloan shrugged. "This was a spur-of-the-moment thing. But I would like you to call Cassandra Talbot at the gallery and cancel our lunch date. Tell her I'm buried in work here, then call the floral department and have Mr. What's-his-name send her a nice bouquet."

"Mr. Elvin is our florist," Edna corrected him. "And *I* am your executive assistant, Mr. DeWilde, not your social secretary. I will not become involved with your personal life or with the numerous women you seem to keep dangling."

"Then get me a cup of coffee and I'll do it myself," Sloan grumbled.

Edna held her ground, her arms akimbo. "Nor have I ever had any aspirations to be a waitress. The coffeepot is where it's always been," she said. "You're reasonably fit, so I'm certain you can handle both the distance and the weight of the cup."

With that, she turned and walked out of his office, leaving Sloan to wonder why he put up with her prickly attitude. "Because Edna knows this store better than you do, idiot," he muttered to himself. "And without Edna Crenshaw, you might actually have to spend more time in this mausoleum of an office."

Five minutes later, after he'd broken his lunch date with Cassandra, called Mason again to make sure he planned to buy Sheba's Prize, and phoned the in-store floral department, Edna appeared at his office door once again.

"Ms. Durrant is here for your eleven o'clock."

Sloan glanced at his watch, noting she was five minutes late, then smiled. "Show her in, Miss Crenshaw. And please, hold all my calls."

Edna snorted. "I don't expect the switchboard to be flooded, but I'll try to handle anything that comes up."

"You always do, my dear Miss Crenshaw," Sloan said. "I don't know what I'd do without you."

"Neither do I." She pushed the door open wider and turned her gaze to the outer office. "Ms. Durrant, Mr. DeWilde will see you now."

An instant later, Chloe Durrant appeared in the doorway. She paused for a moment, clutching a stack of reports to her chest, as if not sure whether she should enter. "Hello," she said at last.

She looked even more beautiful than he remembered, tall and slender, long-limbed and graceful. His gaze was drawn to her face. Her delicate features, high cheekbones and wide eyes were accentuated by her severe hairstyle, which was softened only by the tendrils of silver blond hair that escaped the knot at her nape.

Sloan slowly came to his feet, never taking his eyes from her. "Hello," he replied. "Come in...Ms. Durrant. Please, sit down."

She fixed her attention on one of his guest chairs and quickly crossed the office, sliding the reports onto his desk as she sat. Sloan watched her as she stared at her fingers, twisting them together nervously. Over the past hour, she'd lost a good measure of her temerity and seemed properly amenable.

From the doorway, Edna cleared her throat and shot him a disapproving look, then stepped out of the office and closed the door behind her. The sound of the latch clicking left them entirely alone, a state that seemed to increase Chloe Durrant's uneasiness. He heard her draw a deep breath as if she were about to speak, and he waited. She glanced up at him, then slowly released the tightly held breath.

"If you're going to fire me, you might as well do it now and get it over with," she said, her words containing that subtle hint of challenge he'd heard upon their first meeting.

Sloan was completely taken aback. He lowered himself into his chair. "Fire you?"

Her spine stiffened. "I know you don't like the windows. And that's fine. After all, you are the boss. But when I took this job, I was given complete creative control over all visual merchandising and advertising. I believe the windows work. They've created a lot of attention on the street."

"I can see that," Sloan said dryly. "People are lined up to see them."

To his surprise, his cynical tone didn't rattle her in the least. "I know DeWilde's has always been very conservative in its approach to retailing, but with so many stores out there competing for the same business, we can't continue to depend on an outdated image and lackluster visuals. Our research has shown that the traditional customer base is shrinking. We need to appeal to a younger demographic, the same customer who thinks of lingerie as more than just fancy or frivolous underwear."

"But isn't that what lingerie is?" Sloan asked.

Chloe slid forward on the edge of her chair and rested her arms on his desk. "Oh, no!" she replied, her voice now animated, intense and alluringly husky. "It's so much more. When a woman wears sexy lingerie, it changes her whole attitude. She becomes a more sensual being, more aware of her sexuality, more confident."

She looked even more beautiful in her excitement, her color high, her green eyes bright. "But why paint all the windows black?" he asked.

"I wanted the people on the street to be able to look at the scene as long as they wanted to, in private, without having to turn away or be embarrassed by their interest. I wanted them to recognize the voyeur in all of us. I wanted to create a level of sexual intimacy, to draw them in."

"Sexual intimacy," Sloan repeated, staring into her wide eyes.

She cleared her throat and a subtle blush crept up her cheeks. "Metaphorically speaking," she replied. With a restless smile, she flipped through the pile of reports in front of her and held one out to him. "Here," she said. "This is a floor traffic report. Since those windows have been up, we've seen a twenty percent increase in store traffic. And we've seen a seventy-five percent increase in the number of men shopping at DeWilde's."

"An increase?" Sloan asked. "That's...surprising news."

"And most of them head straight to the lingerie department," she continued, "which, as you know, is a high margin department."

He raised a brow, still not reaching for the report. She watched him expectantly, as if waiting for him to congratulate her on her efforts. For an instant, he saw a vulnerable look flash in her eyes, but then it was gone.

"We've counted the number of customers who've entered the store for a three-hour period every day for the past month," she continued, her voice now reserved. "All the figures are in the report. And I'm sure the month-end sales report will confirm what the daily flash reports have hinted at—a small increase in sales. Nothing big, but a move in the right direction."

"An increase in sales?" Sloan asked. He grabbed the report and flipped through the pages. But he'd never learned to decipher the endless computer reports that seemed to end up on his desk. "That can't be. We haven't had an increase in sales in nearly two years."

"I know," she said, sounding quite pleased with herself. "But, as I said, this is just a beginning. We need to retool the basic merchandising strategy, go after a younger customer, expand our image to include more than just jewelry and bridal. I want DeWilde's Fifth Avenue to be synonymous with...romance."

Sloan leaned back in his chair and linked his hands behind his head, considering all she had told him.

"And you know a lot about romance?" he asked.

The color rose in her cheeks again. "I know much more about merchandising. So, I really think it might be premature to fire me at this point," she continued. "If I were *you*, I'd give *me* at least another three months to prove what I can do for this store. It's the only prudent course of action."

"You've presented a very strong case," he said.

She tipped her chin up. "I didn't realize I was on trial."

Sloan grinned. "I wasn't planning to fire you, Ms. Durrant."

Relief flooded her expression and she smiled. Suddenly, he found himself transfixed by her luminous beauty—a sensual beauty that seemed at odds with her conservative suit and hairstyle. His mind drifted to the lingerie in the windows and he wondered what she might look like dressed in something more revealing.

"I just wanted to get to know you better," he added.

"Good. I'm glad, because I really enjoy this job. De-Wilde's is a wonderful store with outstanding potential. This traffic increase is just the beginning of a whole new era for DeWilde's."

He nodded, his thoughts drawn back to this unexpected twist in his plans. A sales increase was definitely not part of *his* delicate plan for DeWilde's Fifth Avenue. And all because of some rather provocatively placed mannequins and some lacy underwear. Chloe Durrant was dangerous, in more ways than one.

He quickly stood and held out his hand. "Yes . . . well, welcome aboard, Ms. Durrant."

She jumped to her feet and took his hand. "I look forward to working for you, Mr. DeWilde."

"And I look forward to working with you also, Ms. Durrant." He reached out and placed his other hand over hers, the need to touch her suddenly overwhelming.

They stood that way for a long moment. Then she slowly disentangled her fingers from his. "I'd better get back to work," she said. "I'll see you next month."

She hurried out his office door, closing it behind her. Sloan rubbed his palms together distractedly as he stared after her, trying to quell the strange tingling in his finger-tips.

A month. A month was far too long to wait. From now on, he would have spend much more time at the store—just to make sure everything went as smoothly as planned.

In six months, he wanted to be out of the retailing business and into the horse breeding business, and he would allow no one to stand in his way. Not even the lovely Ms. Chloe Durrant.

If she did, he'd have only one choice. He'd have to fire her.

CHAPTER TWO

CHLOE CRAWLED ACROSS the bedroom floor on her hands and knees, then stuck her head under her daughter's bed. "Good grief!" she called. "Audrey, have you bothered to look under this bed lately? You could outfit a small European nation with the clothes you've got under here."

"Mom, you're supposed to call me Madeline," Audrey called back.

"Your name is Audrey," Chloe replied as she wriggled under the bed. "That's what I put on the birth certificate, and until you go to court and change it, that's what I'm going to call you."

"But Madeline is my stage name," she said.

"Ima Pain-in-the-backside would be a better choice for this particular stage, don't you think?" Chloe asked.

"Ha, ha. That was so funny I forgot to laugh. What about my boot?" Audrey hunkered down beside her. "I have to wear my combat boots with this skirt. Nothing else goes!" The last remark climaxed in a whine that could have shattered fine crystal.

Fighting through a swarm of dust bunnies and the missing companions to half of Audrey's precious sock collection, Chloe reached for the object of their early morning search. "Heaven forbid you wear the wrong shoes," she said with a grunt, dragging herself from under the bed. "Life as we know it would surely cease to exist if you showed up at school in a pair of tennies."

Audrey gave Chloe "the look," the all-too-familiar expression that marked every adult, but Chloe in particular, as the intellectual equivalent of a sponge mop. "Get real, Mom," Audrey scoffed, pulling the boot onto her left foot. "Like tennies would even go with this outfit."

"I've raised a fashion monster," Chloe muttered as she watched Audrey stomp from the bedroom. She glanced over at the bedside clock and groaned. If they weren't out the door in ten minutes, Audrey would be late for school and she'd be late for work—again. Strange how her daughter always managed to walk out the door a picture of sixth-grade fashion perfection, while Chloe went to work looking as if she'd just rolled out of bed.

Clambering to her feet, she hurried to the bathroom, only to find that Audrey had commandeered the mirror and Chloe's hairbrush. In the interests of her own schedule, she snatched the brush from Audrey's fingers and quickly drew it through her daughter's long, dark hair—hair the exact color of Julien's, a rich mahogany that bordered on black.

Audrey munched on a piece of toast as she stared at herself in the mirror. "I don't look like you, do I?" she commented.

"No, not much," Chloe said.

"Do I look like my dad?"

Chloe blinked in surprise, then glanced down at her daughter's reflection in the mirror. "Yes, you do," she murmured. She held her breath, waiting for Audrey's next words, trying to anticipate what she might ask. The subject of Julien had come up more frequently as of late. For some reason, Audrey suddenly needed to know more about her father. But Chloe didn't know what to tell her.

"Did he have blue eyes like me?" she asked.

"Yes, he did," Chloe said.

What could she tell her? That the man had never even set his startling blue eyes on his beautiful child, that he had never shown the slightest interest in knowing his daughter? In many ways, Chloe was glad. She didn't have to share Audrey with anyone—especially not the irresponsible but infinitely charming Julien.

Life wasn't perfect, but it was close. There were the ever-present hassles with child care and schooling and after-school activities—and boys. But within their tiny two-bedroom apartment in the Village, life was happy and satisfying. She barely even noticed the lack of male companionship.

Her mind flashed an image of Sloan DeWilde, but she brushed it away as quickly as it had appeared. Fantasies were fine, but now was not the time to contemplate any type of relationship with a man. It could only complicate things, especially if the relationship didn't work out.

Audrey was at a vulnerable age, longing for a father figure, needing the security of a two-parent family. Before Chloe risked her daughter's fragile feelings, she'd have to be very sure that the man would be a permanent fixture in their lives. Though she found herself mildly attracted to Sloan DeWilde, she wasn't naive enough to believe he would be interested in a full-time position as Audrey's daddy.

"Mom? Are you all right?"

"What?" Chloe said distractedly, glancing down at her hands, which had stilled in the midst of brushing Audrey's hair.

"You look kinda sad," Audrey said. "I'm sorry I mentioned my father."

Chloe forced a smile. "I'm not sad. And whenever you want to talk about your father, you just go ahead. Now, go collect your books, Claude," she said, using their pet nickname for each other, a mixture of both their first names. "I'll be dressed in two minutes."

Audrey gave her a sideways glance in the mirror. "Are you going to wear your hair like that today?" she asked. "'Cause if you are, you can't come into school when you drop me off."

Chloe stared at herself in the mirror. She'd showered nearly an hour ago, right before she ironed her daughter's outfit, searched for lunch money in the bottom of every purse she owned and set off on her quest for the missing combat boot. Now there was no fixing the mop of ash blond tangles that fell to her shoulders, short of declaring a bad hair day and staying home.

"I guess not," she said as Audrey skipped from the room. "You have ten minutes," she called out after her. "If you're not ready...tough noogies."

Chloe braced her hands against the edge of the sink and breathed a long sigh of relief. Sooner or later Audrey was going to ask the inevitable—she'd ask to see her father. Chloe dreaded that moment, for she hadn't yet figured out what to tell her. The truth was too painful, but a lie would only cause more problems. Julien wanted nothing to do with his daughter.

She stared at her reflection in the mirror, then ran her fingers through her tangled hair. She'd deal with the situation when it arose, but meanwhile, she'd have to come up with a positive way to tell Audrey the truth.

With a sigh, Chloe opened the bathroom closet and pulled out a short-cropped black wig from her pile of spare hair. She'd always loved wearing wigs, having the ability to change her looks at will, from demure to outrageous. She had never quite outgrown her dress-up phase, a quality that working in the fashion industry only perpetuated. Clothes were an adventure, an expression of her personality, her own subtle rebellion against the strictures of society.

She'd always been a bit of a rebel, from the time she was a child. Her single-minded pursuit of a painting career had gone against everything her parents had wanted for her—a suitable husband, a house in the suburbs and a life spent raising perfect children.

But after art school, Chloe had run away to New York with less than a hundred dollars in her pocket. Moving in with Julien had been yet another rebellion. And then she found herself pregnant. Her decision to keep the baby was viewed by her parents as another slap in the face of propriety.

But Chloe knew better. From the moment she learned that Audrey was growing inside her, she had wanted her daughter. She'd never considered an alternative. To hell with what everyone said and thought. She had been determined to make a place in the world for them both. No sacrifice was too large. The lack of a regular social life and its resulting celibacy were a small price to pay for Audrey's happiness.

No one at the store, short of the personnel manager and Gina, knew about her daughter. This worked to her advantage, for no one bothered to keep track of the late mornings spent ironing Audrey's school clothes or the early afternoons occupied with school plays. She breezed in and out of the store, a competent and dedicated "single" professional whose first priority *seemed* to be DeWilde's... rather than a missing combat boot and a distraught eleven-year-old.

Twisting her hair on top of her head, she tugged the wig in place then quickly ran a brush through the long bangs and straight blunt cut. Satisfied with the faintly Oriental style of the wig, she quickly finished her makeup and pulled on an embroidered Chinese silk jacket in bottle green and a pair of baggy black crepe pants. She found her own shoes under her bed and, true to her word, was waiting at the door for Audrey ten minutes later.

Audrey's school was on Bleecker, only five blocks from the apartment, a distance they usually covered at a brisk jog. Today was no different. When they arrived at the front gate, Chloe distractedly smoothed her daughter's hair.

"Now, you remember the plan?" she asked.

Audrey put on a pout. "I don't see why I can't stay home by myself after school. Lots of kids do." She gave Chloe "the look" and sighed dramatically. "I take the subway uptown with Mrs. Barrington. We get off at the Fifth Avenue station and I come directly to the store. I know what I'm supposed to do."

"And you'll hold Mrs. Barrington's hand when you're on the subway?"

"I can ride the subway by myself. I don't need any old teacher's aide to show me how."

Chloe plucked at a tear in the sleeve of Audrey's over-sized denim jacket. "We're very lucky that Mrs. Barring-ton has agreed to do this for us. Lucky for us she lives only a few blocks from the store. And it will only be for a few days, just until I can find another after-school sitter."

Audrey snorted. "I don't need a baby-sitter. And I don't need Mrs. Barrington, either. She's always making that funny sound with her nose and calling us darlings and blowing her stupid whistle on the playground."

"Come on, Claude," Chloe said. "Just bear with me for a few days. Things will be back to normal soon. Do you remember where you're to go in the store?"

"Sixth floor, ladies' can."

"Bathroom," Chloe said. "You're to stay there and do your homework until five, and then I'll meet you at the front door of the store. If I'm going to be late, I'll come up and let you know." She stepped back, then shook her head. "Look at that jacket, Audrey. Must you wear that thing?"

Audrey glanced down at the tattered denim jacket, then grinned at Chloe. "Grunge is cool, Claude. The grungier the better."

"You look like a bum," Chloe murmured. "Don't you worry what the other kids at school think?"

Audrey shrugged. "All the other kids wish they had a mom that let them dress the way they want. Besides, I wouldn't talk, Claude. Geez, nobody's mom dresses like you do... unless they work in a circus."

"What about your teachers?"

"They're supposed to encourage our creativity. Besides, it's unconstitutional for them to force us to follow a dress code. One of the kids' fathers brought a lawsuit a few years ago when his son got his ear pierced and they wouldn't let him wear an earring."

"Are you sure you don't want a new jacket? We could go to Macy's after work and pick out something nice."

Audrey gave Chloe a long-suffering look. "Mom, I like my jacket. Just lay off, okay?"

Chloe reached out and straightened the black beret Audrey had borrowed from her closet that morning. "All right, I'll lay off. Just remember what we talked about. Sixth-floor ladies' lounge, and make sure you stick with Mrs. Barrington on the way there."

"I'm cool," Audrey said, pushing up on her tiptoes to kiss Chloe's cheek. "See ya on the flip side, Mom." With that and a quick wave, she ran through the gate to join a group of friends waiting in the school yard.

Chloe smiled and watched her daughter for a brief moment, before turning and setting off at a brisk walk for the subway station at Washington Square. One of these days, they'd get their morning routine on a schedule. They'd only

been trying for eleven years. Sooner or later they were
bound to get it right.

AN HOUR AFTER LEAVING Audrey at the front gate of the
school, Chloe was in the midst of wrestling a stuffed tiger
into the middle of her workroom, when Gina wandered in.

"Can I get you a whip, or do you have that musty old
thing under control?" Gina inquired.

Chloe dropped it on the floor and a cloud of dust ex-
ploded from the animal. Waving her hand in front of her
face, she sneezed twice, then stepped back and slipped her
hands into the pockets of her smock. "It was hanging from
the ceiling in the storage area behind china and crystal. This
will be perfect for that jungle display we're doing in luggage." She crinkled her nose. "If I can clean him up."

Gina took a long sip of her morning coffee and stared at
the snarling beast speculatively. "Poor thing. One of those
old DeWildes probably shot it on safari and had it stuffed.
Rich people don't go to Coney Island for their stuffed animals like the rest of us. They go to Africa."

"I'm sure they didn't shoot this tiger. It's not real, it's just
made to look real." Chloe bent down and stared at the
tiger's yellowed fangs and glass eyes. "I think." She
straightened and brushed the dust from her hands. As she
crossed the workroom, she caught sight of her reflection in
a nearby mirror.

It was only 9:00 a.m. and already she was a mess. She
plucked at the cobwebs sticking to the short, dark wig, then
gave up. She should really let her staff of assistants do the
dirty work. But Chloe had learned over the years that if she
wanted something done right, it was best to attack the
problem herself.

"I like the wig," Gina said, seating herself on a stool.
"I'm glad to see your little meeting with the boss hasn't

turned you into a replica of Miss Crenshaw, Stepford secretary.''

Chloe smiled. The suit had served its purpose, creating a good first impression on Sloan DeWilde. Thank goodness she wouldn't have to put it on for at least another month. In fact, she was glad he wouldn't be back for a while. Having Sloan DeWilde around full time could pose a real problem for her. She couldn't deny the glimmer of attraction she felt for him. But then, who wouldn't be attracted to a man like Sloan. He was handsome, sophisticated and—

"Have you ever wondered what it would be like to be as rich as the DeWildes?'' Gina asked.

"Never. I don't like to spend time depressing myself.''

"Do you think you'd spend your money on safaris?'' Gina pushed her bottom lip out thoughtfully. "Or would you spend it all on shoes?''

It didn't take Chloe more than an instant to consider her answer. "I'd buy myself a nanny for Audrey, and I'd pay her loads of money so she wouldn't up and quit on me with barely a day's notice. After that, if I had any money left, I'd buy a few hundred pairs of Manolo Blahniks.''

"Audrey's sitter quit?''

"Two days ago,'' Chloe told her.

"Gee, you've been going through sitters like I go through chocolates and Kleenex on a dateless Saturday night.''

Chloe crossed the workroom and rummaged beneath a pile of paint-spattered drop cloths until she located the shop vacuum. "I don't know what the problem is. I simply need someone to be at the apartment when she gets home from school in the afternoon. An hour. Two or three at the most, if I have to stay late at work.'' She grabbed the vacuum hose, hoisted it over her shoulder and dragged the industrial-size canister to the center of the room. "I'm not asking for much.''

"Why don't you have Mrs. O'Malley look after her?"

Chloe shook her head at the mention of her building manager's name. "I tried that yesterday afternoon and it was a disaster. Mrs. O'Malley is a little dense when it comes to preteens. By the time I got home, Audrey had convinced her that she was my little sister and not my daughter."

Gina blinked in surprise. "Audrey lied?"

"She said it was an exercise for her acting class, but I think it was more."

"What?" Gina asked.

Chloe rested her hands on her hips and considered the question for a long moment. "I think Mrs. O'Malley asked Audrey about her father, and rather than tell her the truth, Audrey fabricated some silly story that we were really sisters and our parents had been tragically killed in a bus accident in Mexico, where they were on an archaeological dig for a *Tyrannosaurus rex*. Something about a puppy in the road and the bus hurtling over a cliff. Of course, Audrey added all the flourishes, including a huge explosion and a state funeral attended by the president. Poor Mrs. O'Malley felt so sorry for the both of us, she baked a pan of brownies and brought them over for a nice long chat."

"So what did you do?"

"I made Audrey tell Mrs. O'Malley the truth. Then I sent her to bed and ate the whole pan of brownies myself." Chloe sighed. "They were frosted, with caramel in the middle."

"It's not like Audrey to lie," Gina said.

"Madeline," Chloe corrected her. "Audrey now wants to be called Madeline. And this goes a lot deeper than acting lessons. At first I thought it was a phase, like when she wanted a dog last year and a ferret the year before, but it's more. She's moved on to a full-fledged Homo sapiens. She's working up the courage to ask to visit Julien."

"But Julien doesn't want to see her."

"I know, but I haven't the heart to tell her that. I should have bought her that dog when I had the chance, Gina, and none of this would have happened. To top it all off, Miss Madeline Mature thinks she doesn't need a sitter."

"She is nearly twelve, Chloe. Maybe you should give in on this point."

"Absolutely not. If no one was there to make sure she came home on time, she'd be all over Manhattan. My daughter knows this city so well she could serve as a tour guide on the Circle Line."

"But if you don't have a sitter, what are you going to do with her?"

Chloe lowered her voice and slipped onto the stool next to Gina. "I have a temporary solution. One of her teachers at school lives over on Fifty-seventh and Lex. They're going to ride uptown together on the subway after school, and Audrey's going to spend the last hour or two of the afternoon studying in the ladies' lounge on the sixth floor."

Gina wagged her finger. "You're lucky Sloan DeWilde only shows up once a month. If he found out you're using DeWilde's as a child-care center, you'd be out of here at light speed, peep-show window or not. You know the rules. DeWilde's first, DeWilde's second, family third."

"I have no choice right now. And it's only until I line up an after-school sitter. As long as Audrey stays put, we'll be just fine."

Gina took a final sip of her coffee then tossed the paper cup into a tall cardboard barrel. "I've got to check the proofs on tomorrow's *Times* ad. Do you want to come along?"

Chloe shook her head. "I've got too much to do. And with Audrey coming here after school, I need to make sure I can get out of here at five sharp."

Gina waved as she walked out of the workroom, and
Chloe turned her attention to the stuffed tiger. Yes, it was
definitely good that Sloan DeWilde wasn't around. Past
experience had proven that most employers didn't want to
hear about child-care problems and bills that had to be paid.
And she certainly didn't want to give him yet another reason to fire her.

"Well, Simba," she muttered, "let's see if we can clean
you up." She grabbed her glasses from the worktable and
slipped them on, then flipped the switch on the vacuum. The
noise filled the room.

As she worked, her mind wandered back to Sloan De-
Wilde. What was it about him that made him so fascinat-
ing? She'd known several wealthy men in the past, but not
one of them had worn his money more comfortably than
Sloan did. It was as if the money made no difference to him
at all, as if he could separate who he was from what he possessed.

He exuded confidence and utter control. There was
something in those qualities that Chloe found incredibly
intriguing. A woman could feel safe with a man like him,
knowing that she wouldn't have to mortgage her own needs
to feed his ego—as she'd had to do for Julien.

Cursing her errant thoughts, she turned her attention
back to the stuffed tiger and tried to drive Sloan DeWilde
from her head. It wouldn't do to become to preoccupied
with the man. After all, he was her boss. And rumors of his
active social life ran rampant through the store. He probably had swarms of women in the wings, each one hoping for
the chance to spend a little of the DeWilde family fortune.

After several valiant attempts to focus her mind else-
where, she finally gave in to a brief daydream—Sloan
DeWilde in a pair of tight jeans, Sloan DeWilde without a
shirt, Sloan DeWilde with . . .

A tap on her shoulder startled her out of her reverie. With a cry of surprise, she jumped up and spun around, the vacuum nozzle clutched in her hand. "Gina! You scared the—" Chloe's mouth snapped shut. It wasn't Gina standing in front of her but Sloan DeWilde, fully dressed.

What was *he* doing here? In the store, in her workroom, in the middle of her daydream, looking so incredibly cool and sophisticated. He smiled at her in the same remote way she'd seen him smile yesterday when he had greeted her in the line of employees.

"I'm sorry to have startled you," he shouted, "but I was..." The last of his words were drowned out by the roar of the vacuum cleaner.

She leaned forward. "I can't hear you!" she cried.

The vacuum cleaner suddenly screamed with a high-pitched whine and Chloe stepped back, only to find the entire length of Sloan's expensive silk tie firmly in the clutches of the nozzle.

He stared down at the vacuum hose, then glanced up at her. Heat flooded her cheeks as she fumbled to release his tie. But the vacuum refused to give it up. Finally, with no other recourse, she handed him the nozzle and turned to flip off the switch. The whine gradually wound down to a deafening silence and Chloe slowly turned back to him.

"I'm so sorry," she said, hurriedly retrieving the nozzle from his hands and avoiding his startled expression. She tugged on the nozzle, but it still wouldn't give. Standing up on tiptoe, she tried to get a better look at the situation, but this brought her perilously close to Sloan DeWilde's body.

"Ms. Durrant?"

His breath was soft and warm against her temple. She jumped back, then glanced up at him. His brow furrowed into a confused frown, as if he had just now recognized who she was. She touched her trendy, black-rimmed glasses, then nervously reached to smooth her black wig. No wonder! She wasn't exactly dressed like the conservative businesswoman he'd met yesterday.

She swallowed convulsively. "Yes?"

A smile curved the corners of his mouth and he chuckled, plucking at a strand of her dark hair. "It is you. For a moment there, I didn't recognize you."

She gave another hopeful tug on the vacuum nozzle, unable to think of a single witty reply. Right now, she wished that he hadn't recognized her. Mortification was so much easier to take when one was incognito.

"Maybe you should try scissors," he suggested.

She spun around, grateful for the diversion, leaving the vacuum hose dangling from his neck as she rummaged through the mess on the worktable. "I know there's a pair of scissors here somewhere," she murmured. "This is a workroom, so we have to have scissors. We cut things all the time." After a long search, she managed to locate a utility knife. "I guess this will have to do." She stepped back in front of him, the razor knife clutched in her hand. But now what?

"Cut it," he said, as if he could read her thoughts.

"Don't you think we should try to save it? It looks like a very expensive tie."

"Cut the tie, and try not to do the same to me, please."

She heard the impatience in his voice and quickly stepped closer. But in order to cut the tie away safely, she realized that she'd have to touch him first. In fact, she would have to practically press her body against his. "Maybe you should do it," she suggested. "You have a better angle."

"I can't see a damn thing." With that, he grabbed her around the waist and pulled her along the length of him, crushing her breasts into his hard chest. Her pulse raced and her senses spun. If not for his strong arm around her waist, her knees would have collapsed then and there and she would have tumbled to the floor.

He patiently held the vacuum nozzle out from his throat, giving her a clear shot at the tie. Biting her lower lip, she plucked at the starched collar of his shirt and sliced through the silk tie in one swift movement. The hose clattered to the floor, along with the remains of his tie, and Chloe scampered out of his arms.

Sloan twisted open the top button on his shirt and let out a tightly held breath. "I guess I should have called first. It would have given you a chance to put that thing on its leash."

"I really am—"

He held up his hand to stop her apology. "No need." He gave her a sideways glance and a crooked smile. "I'm sorry I didn't recognize you at first. You look... different. The glasses... and the clothes... the hair."

She forced a smile of her own and tugged the smock closed in front. "I'm sorry, but—"

"No," he interrupted again, his gaze drifting appreciatively down the length of her body. "You're perfectly free to dress however you choose. And I like the hair."

"Thank you, Mr. DeWilde, but—"

"What *are* you doing in here?" He glanced down at his tie, then eyed the now silent vacuum cleaner. "Don't we have a custodial staff to do the cleaning?"

"I'm vacuuming this tiger I found."

"Tiger?" Sloan stepped around her, then bent down to look at the dusty cat. He slowly shook his head. "I can't believe it," he said in a soft voice. "Where did you find it?"

"In one of the storerooms. It was hanging from the rafters. That's why it's so dusty."

He reached out and ran his hand along the tiger's back, then rubbed his dusty hands together slowly. "My Uncle Dirk got this tiger on safari. He used to be a real adventurer."

Gina's words came back to her. *That's what rich people do for fun.* Suddenly, she felt as if a great chasm had opened up between them, as if they came from totally different worlds. His family traveled to Africa, she was a Coney Island kind of girl. He came from money, her father owned a hardware store. "He sounds like an interesting man," Chloe said.

"I wouldn't know," Sloan replied, his gaze still caught by the tiger. "I never met him. He disappeared before I was born."

Her curiosity was piqued. "Disappeared? Where?"

Sloan shrugged. "No one is sure." He turned and glanced over at her. "You know, this tiger used to stand on top of that tall mahogany diamond case in the jewelry department. I remember visiting the store with my father and my brother Mason. Mase and I would stand at the counter and watch it. We were so sure its eyes followed us as we moved. Gee, I must have been four or five years old, but I can remember it like it was yesterday."

She tried to imagine Sloan DeWilde as a child, but she couldn't picture him as anything but a full-grown man. Sloan DeWilde had never been "cute," he'd always been devastatingly handsome. "Some—some memories from childhood remain very vivid right into adulthood." Chloe groaned inwardly. Could she have thought of anything more stupid to say? A woman who quoted Dr. Benjamin Spock was not what Sloan DeWilde was accustomed to.

His hazel eyes locked with hers. He seemed surprised, even intrigued by her observation. "Yes, they do, don't they. And what do you remember from your childhood, Chloe?"

His grin was disarming, and at that moment, the chasm between them closed.

Chloe felt a flood of warmth rush through her as his penetrating gaze slowly dissolved her reticence. "I remember the first set of watercolors I got," she replied. "I got them from my aunt for my fifth birthday. She was an art teacher. And I remember opening that long black box and seeing all the little pots of perfect color inside—red, blue, green. And a brush that had its very own spot inside the box."

"And you knew right then that you wanted to be a painter?"

She shook her head. "That was just a childhood fantasy. I didn't have the talent."

"Well, you have quite an imagination, Ms. Durrant, as proven by your windows. And an unusual eye for color and design," he added, giving her outfit a meaningful look. "I suspect if you really wanted to be a painter, you would have made it happen."

In all the time she'd lived with Julien, he'd never given her one ounce of encouragement. And now, with just a passing remark, her employer, a complete stranger, had shown more faith in her talent than she herself possessed.

"Maybe," she replied, her unease returning. She smoothed her hands along her thighs and took a deep breath. "So, why are you here?" she asked. "I mean, usually you only visit the store once a month."

He levered himself up from beside the stuffed tiger and brushed the dust from the knees of his perfectly pressed trousers. "I've decided to devote more time to DeWilde's. And to that end, I came here looking for you. I thought we might walk the sales floor together. We could discuss your merchandising ideas."

Chloe hesitated. "Don't you think you should do that with Mr. Simpson-Davis? He is the merchandising manager."

"Mr. Simpson-Davis is scared to death of me. He tells me what he *thinks* I want to hear."

"And I don't?"

He pushed his jacket back and braced his hands on his hips. "Yesterday, you dared me to fire you, Ms. Durrant. I don't think you're scared of anyone, especially not me."

"You may be right, Mr. DeWilde," she said with false bravado, knowing full well that this man had the power to rattle her composure with just a smile.

"Sloan," he said.

"What?"

"Since we'll be working closely, you can call me Sloan."

She shifted uneasily on her feet. "Closely? How closely?" A hint of suspicion crept into her voice.

Sloan raised his brow. "I plan to take more interest in the day-to-day business of running the store," he explained. "In fact, I'll be coming in every day. And I want to hear much more about your ideas for increasing sales. I'd like you to copy me on all your reports. You don't have a problem with that, do you?"

She shook her head, her suspicion gone. "No. That would be fine, Mr.—Sloan."

He stepped behind her and helped her out of her smock, allowing his hands to rest for a brief instant on her shoulders. "Good. So why don't we get going. We can stop in the men's department and you can pick out a new tie for me."

Chloe winced. "We don't carry neckties."

His dark brow shot up. "We don't?"

She shook her head. "Just formalwear."

Sloan frowned, then cleared his throat. "Well, then, we'll have something to discuss, won't we." He casually grabbed her elbow and steered her toward the door. She stumbled once, her attention riveted on the warm brand of his fingers on her flesh.

He paused for a moment to stare at three naked and headless mannequins with a tangle of wires protruding from their necks. At the trio's feet sat three small television monitors. Sloan sighed and shook his head, as if he didn't really want to know about her latest display concept for cruisewear.

Shaken by his touch, she drew a long, fortifying breath and tried to marshal her thoughts for an explanation. But with his hand on her arm, she'd be lucky if she could put together a coherent sentence, much less expound on the artistic statement mannequins might make dressed in cruisewear and given television monitors for heads.

There was absolutely no doubt about it. Having Sloan DeWilde around was going to cause problems.

CHAPTER THREE

"MOTH-*ER*! I CAN FOLLOW directions. We've been doing this for a whole week now and I haven't set foot out of this dumb lounge."

Geez, sometimes parents could be such pests! Audrey brushed at her mother's hand impatiently. "I'm supposed to stay right here until five o'clock unless you come and get me before. I'm not supposed to talk to anyone. And if there's any trouble from the security guards, I'm to tell them that my grandmother is shopping and I'm supposed to meet her in front of the store at five. Duh! I'm not a dummy."

Chloe gave her a warning look, a look that meant Audrey was nearing the edge of her mother's patience. "I know you're not a dummy," her mother said. "I don't want you to move from this spot. If Sloan—I mean, Mr. DeWilde— finds out you're coming here after school, I could get into big trouble."

"You wouldn't have to worry if you let me stay at home by myself," Audrey challenged.

Her mother bent down and kissed her on the cheek. "When pigs fly, Claude. I'll see you at five."

"The name's Madeline," Audrey said, putting on her best sulky face.

Her mother shook her head. "I was there when you were born and I distinctly remember naming you Audrey." With that, she turned and walked out of the ladies' lounge.

Audrey waited patiently, watching the door. After the first few days, her mother had stopped checking up on her and she was left with an hour and a half of boring solitude, broken only by old ladies traipsing in and out of the bathroom. But now it was safe to venture out.

Audrey shoved her books beneath the couch, then stood up, straightening her denim skirt and yanking up her sagging tights. She'd only toured DeWilde's once, a few weeks after her mom got the job. They'd come on a Sunday, when the store was closed and everything was dark and kind of spooky. Even the escalators had been turned off. But they'd walked through the whole store, her mom showing her the different displays she'd done.

DeWilde's was just about the coolest place her mom had ever worked, even though the clothes they carried were pretty lame. But the jewelry was hot and the candy counter was awesome. That's the first place she'd go. She was starving to death, and with the lunch money she had saved over the week, she'd buy something to eat.

Keeping an eye peeled for her mom and the dreaded security guards, Audrey made her way down to the fourth floor. Her presence caused more than a few curious scowls from the salesclerks, but she ignored them. After all, it was a free country.

The candy counter was right where she remembered it to be. She slowly circled the glass cases, reading the delicious descriptions clipped onto the front of each gold tray. Her decision was made as soon as she spied the dark chocolate Turtles.

"May I help you, young lady?"

Audrey dug into the pocket of her jacket and pulled out the change she'd saved. "I'd like one of those Turtles," she said, pointing to the candy in the case. The salesclerk watched as Audrey picked through her change, then turned to pluck the candy from the case and place it in a pretty peach-and-navy paper bag.

"That will be two dollars," she said, dangling the bag in front of Audrey's nose.

Audrey looked up and blinked. "Two dollars? For a Turtle?"

The salesclerk nodded, a condescending smile on her face.

Audrey slowly counted her change out onto the glass counter. In the end, she was eleven cents short. The clerk pursed her lips and shook her head. "I'm afraid that's not enough," she snapped.

"Maybe you could give me a smaller one?" Audrey suggested.

"I am not going to pick through those turtles to—"

"Give her the candy." The deep-voiced command came from the man who stood next to her. "I'll pay the difference."

The smirk disappeared from the clerk's face and Audrey watched her complexion turn as purple as an ugly old beet. "Y-yes, sir," she stammered. "Right away, sir."

"In fact," the man said, "give us a bag of those Turtles. And throw in some of those Chambourd truffles while you're at it."

As the clerk scurried to follow orders, Audrey gave the man a sideways glance. He was tall, so tall she had to scrunch up her neck to look up at him. He was dressed in a navy blue suit and a red tie, so she was pretty sure he wasn't a security guard. But he did act pretty important. She smiled to herself. It served that stuck-up clerk right! He was probably some senator or congressman or maybe even the mayor of New York.

After he paid for the candy, he turned from the counter and handed Audrey the bag. She fell into step beside him and dug out a Turtle. "That was pretty cool," she said.

He looked down at her and frowned. "Cool?"

"The way you shot down that old sourpuss behind the candy counter. She was being a major league snot!" Audrey handed him the bag.

"I agree," he said.

"All the clerks in this store are really mean. I don't know why anyone would want to shop here. Someone should really fire them all."

"Really?" he asked. "I never noticed. Do you shop here often?"

Audrey shook her head and made a face. "No way!"

"Are you here with your mother?"

Audrey hesitated before she answered, not sure how much she should trust this stranger. She stopped in the middle of the aisle and stared up at him. "You aren't some kind of pervert, are you?" Her voice carried in the hushed atmosphere of the store and she saw a salesclerk's head pop up from behind a rack.

Her question seemed to take him by surprise. He scowled down at her. "Pervert?" he repeated softly.

"Yeah. One of those disgusting creeps who lure kids in with candy. They taught us about guys like you in school."

His frown gave way to a grin, and Audrey realized for the first time how cute he was. Much cuter than Mr. Dolan, her math teacher. And definitely better-looking than Tommy Sheridan, who acted like he was the cutest boy on planet Earth and the whole solar system. This guy was *really* cute.

"No," he said. "I'm almost certain I'm not a pervert."

"A kid can't be too careful," Audrey said with a shrug.

He handed her the bag again. "Have another Turtle," he suggested, resuming their stroll.

She snatched one up and gobbled it down, then grabbed another. "Turtles are my absolute favorite."

"I can see that," he said. "So, Miss Turtle Lover, what's your name?"

"You can call me Madeline," Audrey replied between chews. Madeline was a much more grown-up name, much more elegant and refined. Audrey sounded like something you hooked up to your stereo system. Her mother had told her she'd been named after some actress who had been in a movie about Tiffany's, but that didn't make her name any more glamorous. None of her friends had ever even seen the movie. "It's not my real name," she explained, "but it's what I'd like to be called. It's French, you know. I'm half French."

He nodded. "Madeline's a lovely name."

"What's your name?" she asked.

He considered her question for a long moment. "When I was younger I wanted to be called Jack."

She studied him, then nodded. "You look like a Jack." She wiped her sticky hand on her skirt, then held it out. "It's nice to meet you, Jack."

"The pleasure is all mine, Madeline." He peeked into the bag and retrieved a truffle. "So, Madeline, do you live near here?"

"Not really," she said.

"Does your father work in Manhattan?"

She shrugged again. "I don't have a father. Never have. He took off before I was born."

"What about your mother?"

Audrey stared at him suspiciously, weighing the merits of telling him the truth. "She was killed . . . in a bus crash in Mexico. Are you planning to rat me out to the security goons or are you just naturally nosy? It's a free country, you know. I can walk around in this store if I want to and there's nothing you can say about it.'' She shoved the bag of candy back at him. ''I gotta go,'' she said. She started toward the escalator at a brisk walk. Glancing over her shoulder, she saw him standing in the middle of the aisle, his arms folded over his chest.

''Come on, Madeline, wait,'' Jack called. ''I'm not going to rat on you! Come back here.''

But she kept walking. Even though she wouldn't mind hanging out with Jack for a while longer, she'd already spent too much time outside the ladies' lounge. And if she didn't have her math homework done by the time she met her mother at five, she'd have a lot of explaining to do.

When she reached the safety of the ladies' lounge, she retrieved her books from under the sofa and sat down, crossing her legs beneath her. She smiled to herself. Overall, she'd had a pretty interesting afternoon . . . even better than staying at home alone. And maybe, if she got lucky, her mother wouldn't find a new baby-sitter for at least another month or two.

By then, she'd know every nook and cranny of De-Wilde's. And maybe she'd run into Jack again.

''A CUP OF COFFEE WOULD go great with this candy, Edna,'' Sloan called through his open office door.

He knew Edna was just outside, hard at work at her desk. He could imagine the stubborn set of her mouth. ''I'm sure it would,'' she called back, refusing to surrender to his chiding.

He'd settled into an easy routine at the store. An hour every morning spent walking the sales floor with Chloe Durrant. Lunch with any number of business associates at one of Manhattan's top eateries. And the afternoon spent making Edna Crenshaw's life more difficult—at least he figured that was her take on the whole situation.

After his decision to spend more time at the store until the sale had been finalized, Sloan had moved into the co-op apartment his family kept on Sutton Place, just eight blocks from the store. It eliminated the long commute from the farm and gave him more time in the evenings to spend haunting the city's art galleries, looking for new talent for his own.

Satisfying his late-afternoon sweet tooth had also become a regular habit over the past few days. He visited the candy counter between three-thirty and four, but he knew it wasn't just to buy a bag of Belgian truffles and a few Turtles. He'd really hoped he might run into Madeline again. Yet Madeline hadn't reappeared.

He might as well put her out of his mind, the same way he'd been trying to put Chloe Durrant out of his mind. It hadn't been easy. He'd spent a week's worth of mornings with Chloe, listening to all her ideas, watching her lovely, animated expressions as she explained her merchandising strategies. She really was quite innovative . . . and quite alluring.

Miss Crenshaw dropped an inch-thick computer report on his desk with a loud thud, startling him out of his thoughts. "The daily flash reports from the past week," she explained. "You might want to take a look at them."

'Why?" Sloan asked, popping a truffle into his mouth and wiping his hands on his trousers.

Edna smiled inscrutably. "Sales might just be up," she replied.

He stared at her, realizing he'd never in his life seen her smile, especially not at him. "Yeah, right," he mumbled through the mouthful of candy. "I've heard that before. Almost every day from Simpson-Davis."

"This time, it might just be true," Edna said.

He idly flipped through the pages of columns and numbers. "Where does it say that? You know I can't read these
damn things."

Edna shook her head wearily. "They're not that difficult
to decipher. I do it all the time."

"And then you write me a summary that I can understand. Why do you think sales are up?"

"It's hard to tell for sure," she said. "The numbers have
been slightly higher than they were in comparison to last
year's figures. We'll know more when we get a look at the
cumulative figures on the weekly report. The monthly report will give us the most accurate figures."

"When do we get the weekly?" Sloan asked.

Edna arched her brow. "At the end of the week. It will be
on your desk Monday morning."

"Why can't we get it sooner?"

"If we got it any sooner, it wouldn't be a weekly report,
now would it." With that, she turned and walked out of the
office, closing the door firmly behind her.

Sloan stared after her for a long moment, tempted to
throw the report after her. Instead, he grabbed another piece
of candy, popped it in his mouth and began to peruse the
ream of computer paper. He could figure this out on his
own, without Edna's help. After all, he wasn't the village
idiot. He was a college graduate... though an undergradu-
ate degree in Medieval History from Boston College hadn't
done much to enhance his report-reading skills.

He studied the reports for a good long time, trying to find
why Edna suspected what she did. But he'd heard this rosy
optimism before and nothing had come of it.

He was still absorbed in the reports when a soft knock
sounded at his door.

"Since when do you need permission to come in?" he
called out, wondering what Edna was up to now. The door

creaked open, but he didn't look up. "Come to see if I've gone cross-eyed yet?" he asked. "If you come in now and explain these reports, I promise not to fire you."

"It's not Miss Crenshaw." Sloan glanced up to find Chloe poking her head through the partially opened door. "I'm sorry to disturb you," she said, "but Edna wasn't at her desk."

Sloan grinned at the sight of her. Lord, she was beautiful. He'd never known a woman quite like her, all color and light. She could illuminate a room by just stepping through the door. "I guess I'm going to have to buy a stronger chain," he murmured, his gaze drifting along her slender body.

She was dressed in another of her crazy outfits, a long, pencil-thin black skirt that nearly reached her ankles and old-fashioned hobnail boots. Beneath a wildly patterned, fringed shawl she wore a black blouse, sheer at the arms and around the neckline. Her hair, as always, defied description, a riot of curls, like a halo of silvery gold around her face.

Her green eyes went wide and she blinked in surprise. "What?"

"I was joking," Sloan said with a wry smile.

"Oh," she breathed, confusion still etched in her expression. "Well, I wanted to drop off these research reports," she said. "I thought you might like to read them when you have a chance. And I've also put together an outline of my ideas regarding DeWilde's visual merchandising and advertising strategies."

"Why don't you come in and sit down," Sloan suggested.

She hesitated for a moment, then slowly approached his desk.

"Tell me, do you know how to read these daily flash reports?" Sloan asked.

A suspicious look crossed her face, a look that seemed strangely familiar. "Of course. Why?"

"Because I don't," Sloan admitted. "Edna usually summarizes the sales figures for me. I'm not used to all this . . . paper."

She smiled, then circled the desk and bent over his shoulder, bracing one hand beside his. His gaze shifted from the report to her fingers, long and slender with perfectly manicured nails painted a brilliant fuchsia. He fought the urge to touch her, to casually cover her hand with his. Would she pull away, or would she welcome his touch?

"What don't you understand?" she said.

He loved the sound of her voice, craved it like an addictive drug. "Edna says sales have gone up," Sloan told her, pausing after he spoke to draw a deep breath. Her perfume teased at his nose and he leaned a bit closer.

"Here," she said, drawing her finger along a column. "This is the percentage of change over last year, broken down by classification. For instance, here's crystal. Each type is given a different class code—stemware, table accessories, gift items. The more positive numbers you see, the better. You can see that there are almost no negatives, and some of the positives are pretty large, five to ten percent."

He reached out and pointed to another column, letting his thumb brush along the back of her hand. "And what do these figures mean?" he asked, turning to look up at her.

She glanced down at him, her eyes wide, her face just inches from his, her mouth so near he could almost imagine what it might be like to kiss her. He moved closer, a nearly imperceptible distance, and she quickly straightened. "I—I think you might want to wait for the weekly report. It's much more comprehensive and it gives a better indication of the sales trends."

"Maybe," Sloan said, instantly regretting his impulsive behavior.

"I'd better go," she said.

"Stay," he urged. "I'd like to discuss the reports you brought."

He saw her glance surreptitiously at her watch. "I'm sorry. I really have to go. I've got some projects to finish before tomorrow morning and we're putting up a new display in the luggage department. The reports are self-explanatory. If you have any questions, I'd be happy to go over them with you tomorrow morning during our walk-through."

"I'm sorry to keep you," Sloan said. "You probably have someone waiting for you at home."

"Oh, no," she replied. "There's no one waiting for me at home. I just have to pick up something very important before five." She rushed to the door before he could say more, then stopped and turned back to him. "I'm very encouraged by the trend in our sales figures, and I want you to know that I'll do everything in my power to make this store a success. This job is very, very important to me."

He didn't try to stop her. He just watched her leave, fighting back a surge of guilt at her simple, heartfelt statement.

The job was important to her. He groaned inwardly. The job was important to her, and *he* was doing everything in his power to make sure she wouldn't have a job to come to in a few months.

"Damn," Sloan muttered. The sale of the store had seemed so simple on paper, black and white, profit and loss, all so clear cut. But suddenly, the lines had begun to blur. Closing DeWilde's Fifth Avenue would be a boon to his family, but what about Chloe and all the other families that would be affected?

He'd lived in his world for such a long time he'd never really known what it was like to do without, to worry about where the next meal was coming from, whether there was enough to pay the phone bill. Wealth created a comfortable insulation from the day-to-day worries of life.

He leaned back in his chair and rubbed his eyes with the heels of his hands. But it wasn't just Chloe who caused these doubts. It was Madeline.

An image of the little girl flashed through his mind. He'd thought of her so many times over the past couple of days, wondering whether she was all right, whether she was safe at home with a real family or wandering the streets, hungry and alone.

He'd never much thought about children before. He knew they existed and he'd always assumed he'd have a few of his own—someday. And they'd be raised pretty much the way he had been, with everything they could possibly want provided for them. Being raised a DeWilde would give a child every advantage. He'd never considered that some children had nothing.

He tried to push his concerns about her out of his mind. After all, what the hell could he do? He'd given her something to eat. If she had stuck around a little longer, he might have been able to find her a better jacket. But she wasn't his responsibility.

Nor was Chloe Durrant. The sale of DeWilde's Fifth Avenue would take place. He'd just have to separate his interest in her from his business interests. That should be simple enough. Sloan stood, then gathered up Chloe's reports and stuffed them in his briefcase. After all, he'd never had trouble separating business from pleasure before.

But then again, maybe that was because he'd never mixed business with pleasure before.

CHLOE PACED THE LENGTH of the aisle, back and forth through the perfume department, keeping one eye on the revolving door. She glanced at her watch again and tried to quell her impatience. Why couldn't Sloan DeWilde keep regular hours like everyone else? He usually turned up in her workroom anytime between nine and noon, looking for her, ready for their regular walk-through.

"He probably had an exhausting weekend," Chloe muttered to herself. "I'm sure I'll find out with whom before the day is over." The employee grapevine was busier than usual now that a real flesh-and-blood DeWilde had deigned to spend time in the store. Sloan and his social life had been the main topic of water cooler conversation for the past two weeks and Chloe didn't see that changing anytime soon.

She had fought the impulse to eavesdrop on these conversations. After all, what did she care about the company her boss kept? Their own relationship was strictly business. Or at least that's what she had to keep telling herself.

It was hard to deny the attraction she felt for him, the overwhelming flood of warmth that rushed through her whenever they chanced to touch. How many times had he taken her elbow or brushed against her shoulder over the past week? And how many times had she lost all ability to concentrate on the business at hand and, instead, focused her attention on the heat of his touch, the sound of his voice and the incredible golden color of his eyes.

She'd come to look forward to their time together. She'd even begun to spend more time outside her workroom, hoping to run into him on the sales floor. Audrey had even noticed the change in her behavior.

Chloe clutched the monthly sales report to her chest and tapped her foot impatiently. A security guard strolled past, watching her for a moment, then moved on, keeping his attention on the customers. She turned to one of the perfume counters and idly began to rearrange a display of De-Wilde's signature scent, stacking and restacking the navy-and-peach striped boxes until the composition suited her.

"Good morning, Ms. Durrant." His low voice, right next to her ear, sent a shiver skittering down her spine. "Hard at work, I see."

Chloe spun around, her elbow flying out and tumbling her newly arranged display. The boxes scattered across the counter and the tester bottle shattered on the Italian marble floor, splashing over the toe of Sloan's shoe. She glanced frantically between the mess she'd made and Sloan's bemused expression.

"Not exactly my idea of a cordial greeting," he said. "But as usual, your creativity amazes me." Customers stared as they passed by, wondering at the commotion. The cloying scent of perfume surrounded them, and Chloe tried to stifle a cough. Mercifully, a salesclerk rushed over and began to clean up the mess.

They both stepped out of the way, Sloan shaking his shoe and wincing at the overwhelming smell.

"I've been waiting for you," Chloe said. "You're late so I thought I would . . . tidy up."

"I'm the boss," he said. "I'm allowed to be late. So, what was so urgent you had to meet me at the door? And douse me with perfume."

"The monthly sales report," she said, waving the small sheaf of computer paper at him. "I thought you'd want to review it right away."

"I'd love to, but not until I've had a cup of coffee. Would you like a cup of coffee, Ms. Durrant?"

His question took her by surprise. She shrugged, confused by his indifference about the sales report. Everyone in the store from top management down to the newest salesclerk knew the importance of the monthly reports. Next to the quarterly report, it was the most important one of all! "Sure, I'd love a cup of coffee. Why don't we go up to your office and get started?"

"We're not going to my office," he said. "Come on." He grabbed her hand and led her to the front door.

"I can't just leave!" she cried, pulling back.

"Why not?"

"Because I'm working!"

He shook his head. "Do I have to remind you again that I'm the boss? If you leave with me, it's not really leaving. We're just working...off site."

Chloe couldn't help but smile. "You really don't like to work, do you?"

"That's not true," Sloan said in mock defensiveness. "I just don't like to work at the *store*. I have a genetic aversion to retailing."

"But you're a DeWilde," Chloe said. "Retailing's supposed to run in your blood."

"I'm the wrong kind of DeWilde. So I make sure I surround myself with brilliant and creative people who know what they're doing. Like you."

Chloe smiled at the compliment as she stepped into the revolving door. The cool interior of the store was a stark contrast with the stifling air outside. September in New York City could be as murderously hot as July, hot enough to bake a pizza on the sidewalk.

Sloan took her hand and tucked it in the crook of his arm before they headed up Fifth Avenue toward Central Park. The eastern edge of the park, just four blocks away, was visible from the sidewalk, a patch of brilliant green in a world of concrete and steel. As they approached, Chloe watched the horse-drawn hansom cabs leave the head of the line at the Grand Army Plaza, filled with late-summer tourists anxious for a leisurely ride through the park.

The shiny gold statue of General Sherman glinted in the morning sun at the far end of the plaza. Closer to where she stood, the sound of water flowing through the Pulitzer fountain was just barely audible above the roar of the cabs and the buses.

"Where are we going?" she asked.

"Well, you have a choice. We can have a late breakfast at the Plaza or we can grab a coffee and find a park bench."

"The Plaza or a park bench. That's not much of a choice."

"The Plaza it is," he said.

She shook her head. "I vote for the park bench." Chloe plucked at her sunflower yellow silk blouse, pulling it away from her damp skin. "And an iced tea instead of coffee."

They found a vendor at the edge of the park and Sloan purchased two bottles of iced tea and two cheese Danish, then led her to an empty bench just inside the park. The shade of the huge trees provided a welcome relief from the sun and the heat of the street.

"My father used to bring me and my brothers into the city with him during the summer, when we were out of school," Sloan said, twisting the top off her bottle of tea. "He'd give us money and send us out to buy an ice cream. We'd sit right over there on those benches, the three of us, Mason, Russell and me, and we'd watch the horses. We always liked these horses better than the Thoroughbreds on my grandfather's farm."

"Why?" Chloe asked.

"The hats," Sloan said. "These horses wear straw hats with plastic flowers. My grandfather's horses were much too pretentious for that. They also tended to bite."

Sloan took a sip of his iced tea and studied her over the top of the bottle. "So tell me, did you have a pleasant weekend?"

Chloe nodded and placed the report on the bench between them. "Aren't you interested in discussing the sales report?"

"I'd rather hear about what you did this weekend," Sloan said.

"And I'd rather discuss the report," she countered.

"Humor me."

Chloe scraped at the bottle label with her thumbnail. She'd spent the entire weekend with Audrey, but she wasn't about to tell him that. "I did a lot of things. I went shopping and took in the new de Kooning exhibit at the Museum of Modern Art."

"You like de Kooning?" he asked.

She nodded, taking a sip of her drink. "I like all the abstract expressionists."

"What about Rothko?"

"Mmm," she said. "Him, too."

"I have a Rothko at my apartment. I'd like to show it to you sometime. And we've got some interesting pieces at the gallery."

"The gallery?" she asked.

Sloan nodded. "My gallery. I'm part owner of the Talbot Gallery in SoHo. We had an early Rothko there, but it sold a few months ago. Why don't we have dinner tonight, and afterward I can give you a private tour?"

Chloe swallowed hard, trying to force down a bite of the Danish, her mouth suddenly dry. Was he asking her out on a date? She grabbed for her iced tea and took a gulp. The tea went down the wrong way and for a moment she couldn't speak. "No," she finally said. "No, I—I can't."

She groaned inwardly and fixed her gaze on a juggler who had set up shop across the road. This had gone way too far! She never should have agreed to leave the store with him. Outside the doors of DeWilde's, all the unwritten rules were forgotten. They weren't boss and employee anymore, but simply a man and a woman, sharing a discussion about art. Questions about her personal life seemed almost appropriate and an invitation to dinner almost harmless.

They sat in silence for a minute before she spoke again. "I think we should discuss business," she said softly. She drew a long breath and turned to him. "I'm glad you're here."

He chuckled, then slowly reached out across the distance between them. She froze, her heart lurching in her chest, her gaze fixed on his hand. Softly, he brushed his thumb along the corner of her mouth. Good grief, this definitely had gone too far! He drew his hand back and she let out a tightly held breath.

"You had a bit of frosting on the corner of your mouth," he said. He sucked the frosting off the end of his thumb, a gesture so easy, yet so intimate, it caused a tremor to course through her. Then, he leaned back and grinned. "And I'm glad I'm here, too. This is nice."

She felt her cheeks warm. "I mean, I'm glad you've decided to take a greater interest in the store. If DeWilde's is to succeed, we need daily management. We need a focus and clearly defined goals. It's good to finally have someone here who's committed to the long-term success of the store."

"You don't think very highly of me, do you." It wasn't a question, but a statement. He waited for her answer, watching her shrewdly.

"That's not true," Chloe protested. "I guess I just don't understand you."

"What don't you understand?" Sloan asked. "Ask me anything, and I'll try to explain."

She thought about the question for a moment, then frowned. "I guess I don't understand why you've ignored the store for such a long time."

"You enjoy retailing, so it's going to be difficult for you to understand someone who doesn't."

"But you *own* this store," Chloe cried. "How can you not love it?"

"I inherited this store," Sloan said. "That's a very different thing. I didn't have any say in the matter. And technically, I don't own it—the family corporation does."

"I guess unless something comes at a price, it really has no worth, does it," she observed, her voice tinged with sarcasm.

Sloan stared at her, meeting her direct gaze. He slowly shook his head, raking his hand through his hair. "You really *don't* think very highly of me."

"I think you take a lot for granted," she said, her bluntness surprising to her own ears. "But then, that's the prerogative of the wealthy. If I owned DeWilde's, I would do everything I could to see that it was the best it could be."

"And what if you had inherited a...a pickle factory?" Sloan asked. "What if you were forced to work day after day putting pickles into jars, putting jars into boxes and boxes into trucks. Would you look forward to work simply because it was *your* pickle factory?"

She blinked hard and considered his question. "If it were a successful pickle factory," she said. "And DeWilde's will be a success, too. Look—here it is."

Frowning, he glanced down at the numbers on the report she held out to him. "You are determined to talk business, aren't you."

"In the past month, sales rose fifteen percent over last year," she told him. "Fifteen percent!" The announcement was punctuated with a jubilant laugh.

"What?" he gasped.

He was pleased and surprised. Chloe could tell. She sat on the edge of the park bench, her smile wide, her earlier apprehension forgotten. "I know. Isn't it wonderful? This is the first solid feedback we've had that our new visual strategies are paying off."

Sloan shook his head and scoffed. "But this can't be right. Fifteen percent? The computer must have made a mistake."

"Computers don't make mistakes," Chloe said.

"But our sales haven't shown an increase in two years," he countered. "Why now?"

"Because we've finally reversed the trend. And now that we have, I think it's time we took a more aggressive approach. In the London store they're developing in-store designer boutiques for many of the wedding lines. I think we should consider trying the concept."

He was silent for a long moment, then shook his head. "I don't think this is the right time to make major changes." His voice was flat and emotionless. Suddenly he seemed a million miles away, distant and preoccupied. "Simpson-Davis never felt the boutique idea would work here, and I'd have to agree with him."

She frowned. Since when had he listened to Simpson-Davis? "But now is the *perfect* time," Chloe urged. She paused and studied him guardedly. "Why do I get the feeling that you're not happy about this?"

Sloan pushed up off the bench, refusing to meet her gaze. "Don't be silly. Why wouldn't I be happy about a sales increase?" He snatched up his half-eaten Danish and the empty iced tea bottle and tossed it into a nearby trash can.

Chloe stood. "I don't know. You tell me."

"I think it's time to get back to work," he said. "Are you coming?"

He stalked toward the edge of the park and Chloe had no choice but to follow him. He grabbed her elbow as they crossed Fifty-ninth Street, his shoulders stiff, his expression implacable. She watched him surreptitiously, her mind racing with questions.

He couldn't possibly be upset with the sales increase. Real evidence of an increase was the best possible news for DeWilde's. So if he wasn't upset at the turn in business, he must be upset with her. Was he angry with her determination to keep their relationship on a "strictly business" basis?

"I thought you'd be happy," she said.

"I'm happy," he insisted, his voice impatient. "I'm thrilled."

With a soft oath, Chloe stopped in the middle of the sidewalk and allowed him to continue his unrelenting pace toward the store. He didn't even notice she no longer walked beside him, so focused was he on his own thoughts.

She shook her head. Just when she was certain she was beginning to understand Sloan DeWilde, she realized that she really didn't know him at all.

CHAPTER FOUR

"YOU CAN'T JUST WALK in there!" Edna cried. "You don't have an appointment."

Sloan glanced up from the sales reports scattered across his desk to see Miss Crenshaw standing in the doorway of his office, her arms crossed over her chest, her stance rivaling that of a New York Giants middle linebacker. He'd been working all morning to try to figure out how to interpret the columns and rows of numbers. And now, just when he thought he was making progress, an interruption disturbed his concentration.

It didn't take much thought to deduce who was waiting in the outer office. What surprised him was how long it had taken Chloe to personally reply to his memo.

"Let Ms. Durrant in, Edna," he called. "Before she knocks you over. I've been expecting her."

Chloe stepped around Sloan's executive assistant and stalked into his office. "This won't take more than a minute," she said.

"Then you've got exactly a minute," Sloan said, leaning back in his chair and linking his hands behind his head.

Chloe crossed the room and waved a piece of paper under his nose. "What is this?" she demanded, her voice trembling with anger.

Her pale cheeks flamed with color and her green eyes glittered. He found himself wondering if she'd ever looked more lovely. A slow flood of desire warmed his blood as he met her gaze. "A memo?" he asked.

Chloe ground her teeth. "I know it's a memo. What does it mean?"

Sloan took the paper from her hand and scanned the text. "I expected you sooner," he said distractedly. "You really should check your mailbox more often, Ms. Durrant." He handed her the memo. "It means exactly what it says."

"Certainly you can't be serious," Chloe said.

He tossed the memo onto his desk, then relaxed back into his chair again. "About your mailbox or about the memo?"

"The memo!"

"I'm very serious," Sloan replied. "Yesterday you recommended I take aggressive action. In view of our recent increase in sales, that's what I decided to do."

"This is not what I meant!" She snatched up the memo, clutching it in white-knuckled fingers. "'From now on, all merchandising plans and strategies must first be approved by the general manager before implementation,'" she read. She held up her left hand to stop any commentary on his part. "Now, this didn't really concern me until I got to the fine print. This includes all store displays and advertising?" She crumpled the paper into a ball and tossed it on his desk. "Absolutely not."

Sloan pushed forward in his chair, a look of surprise on his face. "Then you're refusing to comply with the memo?"

"When I took this job, Simpson-Davis gave me full creative control. Now you're taking it away from me just when we're starting to see results. How do you expect me to do my job?"

He picked up the wad of paper and flattened it on his desk. "If Miss Crenshaw saw this, she would be very upset. You know, you could be fired for not complying."

Her jaw dropped and her eyes went wide with disbelief. "You'd fire me?" She glared at him. "I should have known. The first positive turn in business in years and suddenly you want to get involved. Things are so much more interesting when there's money to be made."

"They're definitely more interesting, I'll give you that," Sloan said. "I simply want to reacquaint myself with the operation of this store. I felt this was the best way to do it."

"Why? You didn't show much interest when the store was losing money. Why the big change?"

"I *am* the general manager, Ms. Durrant. Do you have some objection to my running this store?" He arched his brow, his question containing the barest hint of a challenge.

She bit her bottom lip as if to stop an angry retort. Slowly, she brought her temper under control, her clenched fists holding all her indignation. He was tempted to jump up and pull her into his arms and kiss the anger out of her, to make her smile at him again the way she had just yesterday, to make her angry green eyes soften with passion.

She took a deep breath. "You're absolutely right," she said, her voice deceptively calm. "You are the general manager and you are my boss. You're aware of how my efforts have helped the store and I'm sure you're as interested in increasing sales as I am."

Guilt surged through him at her words. Yes, his primary concern should be sales, and it was—in a way. He simply wanted sales to move in a different direction than she did. The sale of the store was a simple business decision, yet the whole thing was beginning to make him feel like a first-class jerk. Lying to Chloe was growing increasingly difficult. He couldn't imagine how she'd feel toward him when the sale was announced.

They'd developed a close working relationship at the store, a relationship that engendered trust and honesty—the kind of honesty that justified Chloe's anger over the memo. He should have told her personally, but he knew how she'd react. And he'd come to depend on Chloe's respect.

She was an extraordinary woman, a woman like no other he'd known, brimming with creativity and passion for her work. A free-spirited artist on the outside, she had a steely inner determination and sense of purpose that were contagious to those around her.

Time after time he'd found himself caught up in her excitement, believing in her conviction, anticipating better days ahead right along with her. Until he came crashing back to reality and remembered that they were at cross-purposes.

Still, he couldn't ignore the fact that she believed in him. She solicited his opinions, considered his point of view, then helped him understand her own strategies. Nearly everyone else in the store looked at him as merely a figurehead, but not Chloe.

"You have to trust my instincts," Chloe said. "I know what will make this store great again."

He opened his mouth to respond, but their discussion was interrupted by a knock on the door. Edna Crenshaw stepped inside. Her eyes immediately fixed on the crumpled memo before she glanced condescendingly at Chloe. She'd obviously been listening through the door. With a sniff, she turned to Sloan. "Mr. Simpson-Davis is waiting for his appointment."

"I'll be finished in just a moment," Sloan said, forcing a smile. Edna stepped back out of the office and he turned his attention back to Chloe. "Do you intend to comply with the memo, Ms. Durrant?"

"Do I have a choice?" she said, her green gaze locking on his.

He shook his head, hating what he was about to say. "Not if you want to keep your job."

With a silent curse, she spun and headed for the door.

"Chloe?"

She stopped and slowly turned back to him, a bitter smile curving the corners of her mouth. "Yes, *Mr.* DeWilde?"

"You understand this is business, don't you? This has nothing at all to do with what's going on between you and me . . . our friendship."

Her eyes widened and she swallowed hard. "What could you possibly mean?" she asked, her voice cracking slightly. "There's nothing going on between us."

He leaned forward in his chair, bracing his arms on the desk. "Oh, yes there is. You can't ignore it, Chloe."

"What we have is a business relationship, Mr. DeWilde. There's no room for anything else." She shifted uneasily, placing her hands on her hips. "We're not even friends, and certainly not the kind of friends you want us to be...which really isn't friends at all. I—I'm not even attracted to you," she lied.

He shrugged and grinned. "Not yet. But I'm working on that. I'll expect to see you tomorrow morning for our walk-through. And as soon as you have the opportunity, I'd like to see some new ideas for the Fifth Avenue windows. I think three concepts would be enough to choose from."

She gasped. "*You* plan to choose?"

"That's right."

If there had been a vase or book nearby for her to throw, he was certain it would he heading his way right about now. But Chloe knew her limits, and assaulting her boss was probably beyond what she considered good sense. He was safe—as long as he stayed inside the store.

"Would next week be all right with you?" she asked in an even voice.

"That would be fine, Ms. Durrant," he said, his reply smooth, his grin teasing.

"Fine," she shot back. She opened the door and walked out, ignoring Edna's curious stare as she passed.

Edna was neither shy nor tardy about expressing her opinion on the matter. "You should fire her immediately," she advised.

"Fire Ms. Durrant?" Sloan asked. He chuckled and shook his head. "But, Miss Crenshaw, she's the most interesting part of this job. Except, of course, for these sales reports."

THE NOONDAY SKY was threatening a downpour when Chloe stepped through the front door of the Cabot Gallery. The cool, peaceful interior was a welcome relief from the noise and confusion on the street. She took a deep, soothing breath and glanced around at the ultramodern gallery.

She'd spent many of her lunch hours frequenting the string of galleries lining Fifty-seventh Street between Fifth and Sixth avenues. With Audrey and all her after-school activities, Chloe had little time to feed her hunger for beautiful art, so she took what time she could in the middle of her workday.

Most of the gallery managers recognized her and left her to her own thoughts as she strolled through the precisely arranged maze of partitions and track lighting, sipping at a sweating bottle of iced tea.

Today, she headed right for a sculpture she'd discovered just last week, a small postmodern bronze of a Madonna and child. She knew the piece was well out of her price range, but that didn't stop her from admiring the artist's vision of motherhood. From the moment she'd first seen it, the beautifully wrought image seemed to speak to her of all the love and devotion she had for her own child.

After her argument with Sloan early that morning, she needed something to calm her nerves, and the sculpture did just that. It made her remember what was really important in her life—not her job and all her troubles with Sloan DeWilde, but Audrey, her daughter, the center of her life.

But as she stared at the sculpture, her mind kept wandering back to the events of that morning, to her confrontation with Sloan. The man was stubborn and arrogant and controlling and— She sighed. And he was her boss. Nothing, not even her low opinion of him, would change that very important fact.

What was she really worried about? He wasn't planning to do anything to jeopardize the success she'd achieved, so she shouldn't be upset. They both had the same goals for the store, didn't they?

And they did make a good team. They'd spent nearly every morning together for the past two weeks, strolling the aisles of DeWilde's, Chloe outlining her plans, Sloan nodding and listening to her every word. If Sloan DeWilde had had an agenda of his own, she'd probably feel differently, but as far as she could tell, he had absolutely no capacity for retailing.

The one thing he had a capacity for was testing her resolve. He seemed determined to break through the veneer of professionalism she'd fought to maintain, charming her at every turn, drawing her into something more intimate.

Maybe a better woman could respond to him without losing control. But her experience with men like Sloan—and men in general—was somewhat limited. She had to admit that he was the sexiest man she'd ever met. But for him, she suspected that the chase was more important than the ultimate capture.

Chloe squeezed her eyes shut, then opened them, determined to put Sloan DeWilde out of her thoughts. But that was easier said than done.

"Do you like it?" a familiar voice asked.

She slowly turned to find Sloan standing behind her. An apologetic smile touched the corners of his mouth and she sighed, feeling her anger melt under his magnetic appeal. How could she stay mad at him? It was impossible.

"What are you doing here?" she asked.

He glanced around the nearly empty gallery. "Scoping out the competition," he said in a loud whisper.

"The competition?"

"I like to keep an eye on what's selling uptown. Though the Madison Avenue and Fifty-seventh Street galleries might be *the* place to shop for overpriced art, SoHo is where all the good stuff is happening."

"Mmm," Chloe said, turning back to the sculpture. "I'll keep that in mind before I spend my paycheck here."

Sloan bent over her shoulder, so close that she could smell his spicy cologne, and squinted at the price on the sculpture. "Do I pay you enough to afford this?"

"No," Chloe said. "Not even close."

They stood in silence for a long time before Sloan moved to stand next to her. He shot her a charming grin. "So, do you come here often?"

Chloe smiled. "That's a pretty tired pickup line, isn't it? Does it usually work for you?"

Sloan grabbed her elbow and turned her toward him. "See what you've done to me? You've got me spouting clichés. I'm usually much better at this."

"I know," Chloe teased. "Your reputation precedes you."

"So, if I don't get points for originality, do I get points for location?"

"No," Chloe said.

"Tell me, Ms. Durrant, what *will* work?" Sloan asked, a wicked glint in his eye.

"Nothing," she said. "It doesn't make any difference if there's something going on between us. You're my boss and that's as far as it goes."

"Then you're finally admitting there is something between us?" Sloan said.

Chloe drew a deep breath. "There is a certain level of attraction. But that doesn't mean we have to act on it. We're both adults. We can simply ignore it in order to preserve our professional relationship."

"Yes, we are both adults," he agreed. "And as adults we should be able to separate business from pleasure, don't you think?"

"No, I don't think," Chloe said, turning back to the sculpture.

Just how much longer could she resist him? A simple smile from him was enough to set her heart pounding and when he touched her she could barely breathe. The attraction between them was almost electric, so strong that she could feel it in the air between them, like lightning in a summer storm.

If only their circumstances were different, if only he weren't her boss or she weren't his employee. They'd be free to pursue their attraction. But then, how long would that last? Sloan was not the type to stay with one woman for long, and she wasn't interested in anything but a committed relationship. So the whole thing was a moot point in the end.

He grabbed her hand and slipped it through the crook of his elbow. She wanted to snatch her hand away but couldn't bring herself to do it.

"I'm glad to see you're not angry at me anymore," he said softly, covering her fingers with his other hand.

Chloe shrugged. "You're the boss. It would be silly of me to think that we'll agree on everything."

A long silence grew between them as they studied the sculpture. "It's very nice," he commented offhandedly.

"Yes, it is," Chloe replied, her voice soft. "Every time I come in here, I'm afraid it will be gone. So I feel like I have to commit it to memory before someone buys it."

"What do you like about this particular work?"

She shrugged. "I can't really put it into words. I just like looking at it. Mother and child is a classic subject, but this sculpture is special. It makes me feel . . . content."

"So you like expressionistic art. And you like this sculpture."

She nodded. This was more like it, she mused. A benign conversation about art between co-workers with no sexy subtext. She could handle this. Maybe she and Sloan could get past this attraction they felt for each other.

"I have an invitation for a gallery opening in the Village tonight," he continued smoothly. "It's a showing of found-object sculpture. Would you like to come along? We could grab some dinner on our way downtown and then we—"

"I can't," Chloe interrupted, refusing to look at him. So much for giving him a break. She should have known Sloan DeWilde wouldn't settle for polite conversation. He wanted something more from her and he wasn't about to give up until he got what he wanted. Trouble was, she knew exactly what he was after.

"Why not?" he asked.

She turned and moved on to a small plaster rendering of a horse, a piece that provided a brief respite from his tenacious pursuit. Brief, but not total. He followed her a moment later, placing himself between her and the sculpture.

"Come on, Chloe. It's just dinner and a gallery opening. It's no big deal."

She stepped around him and circled the sculpture. "I know you're used to getting exactly what you want, especially from women. From what I've heard around the store, you've never suffered for willing female companions. Why not ask one of them?"

"Because I don't want to have dinner with one of them, whoever they are. I want to have dinner with you. Do they really talk about my social life at the store?"

"Yes, they do," she said. "And no, you don't," she added. "You want me to *agree* to have dinner with you."

He crossed his arms over his chest. "Well, that would do for a start. But the eating part is what I'm really after."

"And after I agree to have dinner with you, you won't care if we have dinner at all. Because all you really wanted in the first place was for me to say yes."

He scowled at her and shook his head as if her explanation had somehow addled his brain. "Am I supposed to understand what you're saying, or is this another one of those convoluted conversations that only women understand? I just want to have dinner with you, it's as simple as that. Food, maybe some wine, and after that, a gallery opening. That's all I'm asking."

"My point is that you're used to getting what you want and you don't stop until you get it. But I know your type. Once you have what you want, you won't want it anymore. So, if it will make you happy, I'll agree to have dinner with you."

Sloan raised a brow. "So you're saying yes?" He laughed disbelievingly. "Really?"

"Yes," she said. "I'm saying yes."

He paused for a moment, as if uncertain of his next words. "Then...I'll stop by your workroom at five and we'll go?"

"No," she said.

Sloan swore softly.

"I agreed to go, but that doesn't mean I'm *going* to go," she explained. "I'm merely satisfying your need for a conquest. You've won, I've said yes, so now you should be satisfied and we can go on as if nothing has changed between us."

With another muttered oath, Sloan grabbed her arms and yanked her toward him. His lips came down over hers, and she squeaked in protest. But his kiss worked a gentle magic on her senses, and moments later, she felt her breath leave her body and her resolve take flight.

He kissed her long and deep, moving his mouth over hers, until she was certain every nerve in her body had packed up and moved lock, stock and barrel to her lips. Unbidden, her arms wrapped around his neck and she felt her body melt against his like *gelato* on a hot New York afternoon.

Time seemed to stand still and the kiss went on forever. Then he pulled away and stared down into her wide, unblinking eyes. "I would have asked to kiss you, but I was more interested in the kissing part than the saying-yes part."

"Do you always get what you want?" she murmured, trying to put her thoughts in order but failing miserably. All she could think about was the feel of his mouth against hers. She licked her bottom lip, the taste of him still lingering there, and his gaze drifted down to her mouth. She felt her face flush, her cheeks warming with embarrassment.

He reached out and cupped her cheek in his palm, his brow arching sardonically. "I wanted a pet iguana once when I was a kid and I didn't get it."

"I meant with women, not lizards," she said, pulling her arms from around his neck. She let her fingers slip through his silky dark hair along the way, then clasped her fingers in front of her, stilling the impulse to skim her palms along his chest, as well. It had been a long time since she'd touched a

man. She'd nearly forgotten how unsettling the whole experience could be.

A devilish grin curled his firm mouth. "I don't always get
what I want." He paused and reconsidered his answer.

"You don't?" she asked, her voice breathy.

"Well, maybe...yeah, now that I think of it, I guess I do.
But it's not my fault that women never say no to me."

"I did," Chloe countered.

He shrugged. "I'm still trying to figure out where I went
wrong on that one. You and the iguana. My only failures."

She waited for him to ask her about dinner again, but instead he glanced down at his watch and shook his head. "I
have to go. I'm expecting a call at the office."

"Wh—what about dinner?" she asked.

"You said yes," Sloan replied. "I guess I'm going to have
to be satisfied with that much for now. But I'll warn you, it
took six months before I accepted defeat on the iguana."

He bent over and brushed a quick kiss on her cheek, then
turned and walked to the door. She watched him as he left,
then slowly sank down onto an upholstered bench along the
wall, her knees wobbling all the way.

What had happened to all her resolve? Good grief, the
man was her boss! They'd just shared the most intimate
moment she'd had with a man in...well, in a lot longer than
she cared to remember. And worse, she'd enjoyed it.

It would be so easy to fall into a relationship with Sloan.
He was charming, handsome—and incredibly wealthy. And
she hadn't *been* with a man for ages. Given the thin selection over the past eleven years, Sloan DeWilde stood out as
a celibate woman's dream come true.

But Chloe had responsibilities, the largest of which waited
for her every afternoon in the sixth-floor ladies' lounge. No
matter who Chloe brought home, at this point in her life
Audrey would see him as a potential father, someone to re-

place the father she'd never known. Chloe couldn't do that to her, couldn't risk Audrey's heart as well as her own. Besides, she knew exactly the kind of man Sloan DeWilde was, and he certainly wasn't a "family" man. If he'd had any desire for home and family, he would have married long ago.

So what was she left with? She could have a discreet affair with him and satisfy her carnal curiosity. But an affair would probably end badly, which could mean the loss of her job. Or she could pretend that there was nothing between them and go on as before, maintaining a cordial but distant relationship with him, keeping her job *and* the status quo.

The choice was obvious—she had to choose the job over him, reason over emotion. Chloe pinched her eyes shut and berated herself roundly. So, if the choice was that obvious, why was her pulse still pounding and her mind racing to find a way to have both? She groaned.

Maybe one little dinner wouldn't be such a bad idea after all. What harm could it do now? Besides, if there was even a chance that he might kiss her like that again, she couldn't help but say yes.

THE SALES FLOOR WAS as busy as Sloan had ever seen it. He slowly strolled through the jewelry department, noting the return of the stuffed tiger to the top of the polished mahogany diamond case. Chloe had somehow sensed that it would please him to see the jungle cat there again and she'd been right.

He hadn't seen Chloe in two days. She was in the store, but she'd managed to avoid him entirely, canceling their early morning walk-throughs with a feeble excuse about departmental meetings. He'd taken to haunting the sales floors twice a day in hopes that he might run into her. But she obviously knew every hiding place in the store by heart.

He leaned against a marble pillar near fine jewelry and watched as a young man shopped for a diamond ring. When the man moved along the display case, Sloan caught sight of a young girl dressed in a tattered denim jacket and a black beret. Her arms rested on the edge of a locked case that held a jeweled pin of New York's skyline, a signature piece from the DeWilde family collection. She stared up at the stuffed tiger.

With a smile, he approached and tapped her on the shoulder. "Hi there, Madeline."

She turned and looked up at him. "Hi, Jack." Her gaze went immediately back to the stuffed tiger. "That tiger blinked at me."

Sloan smiled. "Did it?"

She nodded emphatically. "I swear, it's true."

"I believe you," he said.

With a sigh, she pushed away from the case and wandered along the length of it, drawing her finger across the glass and leaving a long smudge. The salesclerk gave her a sour look, then grabbed a bottle of glass cleaner and set to work in Madeline's wake.

"I haven't seen you around lately," Sloan said.

She shrugged. "I haven't seen you around, either. Whatcha been doing?"

"Not much. How about you?"

"My life is a total bore," she said.

"Are you hungry?" Sloan asked.

Madeline sighed dramatically and rolled her eyes. "Starved. Can we get some candy? I have some money."

"I was thinking of something better," Sloan said. "How about a triple fudge sundae at Rumpelmayer's? My treat."

Madeline frowned, then crinkled her nose, then finally sighed again. "I guess that would be okay," she said. She looked down at a hot pink watch on her wrist, then made a quick survey of the sales floor before she shrugged and headed for the main entrance.

Sloan had been to Rumpelmayer's a number of times as a kid, after he and his brothers had spent a Saturday afternoon skating at the ice rink in Central Park while his father worked at the store. The restaurant served the city's best hot chocolate and old-fashioned egg creams, and the decor boasted a huge collection of stuffed animals that could charm any child.

As he and Madeline crossed Fifth Avenue, he took her small hand in his. She continued to hold on to him after they'd stepped back onto the sidewalk and made their way past the Plaza. He felt strangely protective of her yet was surprised at how familiar she seemed with the street.

She walked through the crush of pedestrians like a native New Yorker, a purposeful stride, eyes straight ahead, dodging and passing, yet always keeping the same quick pace.

Without dropping her hand, he pushed open the door of the ice cream parlor and they both stepped inside. Madeline's eyes lit up at all the stuffed animals that lined the walls. He tugged her along as the waitress showed them to a table. She slipped into her chair, her attention still focused on the animals.

"This place is so cool," she said.

"Have you been here before?" Sloan asked.

"Yeah, lots of times." She stared down at the menu. "My mom brings me here."

"I thought you said your mother died in a bus crash."

Madeline blushed and smiled winsomely, looking up at him through thick lashes. "I was just goofing on you. Can I have anything I want?"

"Sure," Sloan said. "But only if you answer a question."

She gave him a leery look. "What question?"

"Does your mom have a job, Madeline?"

"Yeah," Madeline said. "She's got a job. Can I really have a triple fudge sundae?"

"Sure. And do you live in a nice place?"

"It's kinda small, but it's okay. Will they put nuts on it? I love nuts."

The waitress appeared at the table and Madeline studied the menu, her nose crinkled in concentration. When she'd finally decided, she ordered the biggest chocolate sundae on the menu, complete with brownies, ice cream, fudge sauce and whipped cream—and double nuts. Sloan ordered a cup of coffee.

"Madeline, does your mom know you hang around the store after school?"

"Sure. She doesn't care. She's working, so I can pretty much go where I want. I'm almost twelve, so I don't need a baby-sitter."

"I see," Sloan said, considering her startling statement for a long moment. Good Lord, how could a mother allow her child to run wild on the streets of New York? Didn't the woman realize the danger, the trouble a child could encounter? Sure, Madeline seemed streetwise, but even *he* was watchful when strolling the sidewalks.

The waitress reappeared with their order. He watched the little girl as she methodically devoured the ice cream. Beneath the ragged-looking clothes, she was a beautiful child. He could tell she spent a lot of time outdoors, for her skin was brown and a sprinkling of freckles dotted her nose and cheeks. She had huge blue eyes ringed with dark lashes, nearly black like her hair. And her mouth seemed perpetually curved in a mischievous smile.

He'd never seen a child eat as much as she did, and he wondered how long it had been since she'd had a decent meal. When she finished, she wiped her chocolate-stained mouth with a wadded paper napkin, then groaned. "I'm stuffed."

"I'm glad," Sloan said. "You must have been hungry."

She glanced around the restaurant, her eyes coming to rest on a huge clock. "Uh-huh." She pulled back her tattered sleeve and stared at her own watch. "Is that clock right?"

Sloan glanced at his watch. "It's a little fast. Do you have to be somewhere soon?"

"Nah. I just like to know what time it is."

The waitress brought the check and Madeline began to dig through her pockets for money. Sloan snatched up the check. "It's my treat," he said.

She smiled, her eyes lighting up with childish delight. "Thanks, Jack." She slipped out of the booth and scampered toward the door, only stopping to look at a huge lavender elephant for a moment.

Sloan quickly tossed a few bills on the table, then caught up with her just as she was pushing the door open. "Anytime you're hungry," he offered, "you just stop by the store and we'll get something to eat. I'm there most afternoons."

"Me, too," Madeline said, falling into step beside him on the sidewalk.

She slipped her hand inside his as if it were the most natural thing in the world, and he felt his heart tug with affection. She really was quite a charmer. He had no doubt that if he were twenty-five years younger, he'd probably fall head over heels in love with her.

"DeWilde's is the best place to hang out," she continued. "All those jewels are so cool. The guy who owns that store must be a gazillionaire. I mean, who would have so much money that they could buy all those diamonds and rubies and emeralds? I saw a bracelet once that cost ten thousand dollars! I wasn't supposed to see the price, 'cause they always keep the tags turned over, but I saw this one and I couldn't believe it! Why do you suppose they keep the tags turned over?"

Sloan glanced down at her. "I don't know. I guess because they probably don't want people to know how much the jewelry costs?"

"Yeah, I s'pose that's it. It's better to get the person to like the jewels before you hit 'em with the price. Someday I want to have a store of my own, just like DeWilde's. Only I'd have cooler clothes in it, and nicer salesladies. And I'd give away candy to all the kids. Wouldn't you like to own a store like DeWilde's?"

The overdose of ice cream had obviously loosened Madeline's tongue. She chattered on and on, mostly about the store and all the interesting things she'd seen. She seemed to know the store better than he did. Sloan listened carefully for any more clues about her family, but she revealed nothing. Either she had nothing to say, or she cleverly avoided the subject. He suspected the latter was probably the case.

"Trying to guess what people want to buy, that's the hard part. But I think I'd be really good at it. I've been in lots and lots of stores and I can always tell what's going to sell."

By the time they reached the front entrance of De-Wilde's, Sloan was certain that he'd get her to tell him about her mother and where she lived if he asked the right way. She let go of his hand to step into the revolving door, then met him on the other side, weaving her fingers back through his.

As they walked through the accessory department, he caught sight of Chloe talking to one of the sales associates. He smiled down at Madeline. "I'll be right back," he said. "There's someone I need to talk to over there. Stay right here, okay?"

Madeline nodded, then occupied herself with examining a silk scarf, hand-painted with the image of a lion. Sloan shot a warning look at the saleswoman who quickly approached, and she immediately backed away. Satisfied that Madeline would still be there when he got back, he headed down the aisle toward Chloe.

"Ms. Durrant," he called.

Chloe turned, a look of surprise in her green eyes. "Mr. DeWilde," she replied, an uneasy expression crossing her perfect features.

Though he hadn't seen her for a few days, he was still surprised at how her presence affected him. He could barely stop from staring, from drinking in her beauty like a man with an unquenchable thirst.

Sloan took her elbow and steered her away from the interested ears of the sales associate, leaving his fingers on her arm until she pulled away. "If I didn't know better, I'd think you were avoiding me," he murmured, bending close and inhaling the enticing scent of her perfume.

"Why would I avoid you?"

"You tell me."

She drew a shaky breath as two spots of color rose in her cheeks. "About the other day, at the gallery. About what happened between you and me..."

Sloan smiled, recalling the touch of her mouth on his, the soft pliancy of her body in his arms. "I don't recall that anything happened," he lied.

She blinked in surprise and gasped. "What? What do you mean nothing happened? Of course something happened." She lowered her voice. "You *kissed* me!"

He cleared his throat and raised a brow. "Ms. Durrant, whatever I did—or you did—outside the store has nothing at all to do with what goes on *inside* the store. I've always said that it's important to—"

"Separate business from pleasure," she finished. "I know."

"And I'm sure, with a little effort, you'll be able to do the same."

She stared at him, openmouthed. "Then, everything is all right? Everything is back to normal."

"Everything is just fine with me." Everything was better than fine, now that they were talking again.

"Good," she said, shooting him a quick smile. "I'm glad we got that cleared up." She glanced down at her watch. "Well then, I have to go."

"So do I," he said. "I'll see you tomorrow morning?"

"Yes," she said. "Tomorrow morning."

"Have a nice evening, Ms. Durrant."

"I will. Thank you."

He watched as she slipped her portfolio under one arm, then quickly walked to the front entrance, the heels of her shoes tapping on the marble floor. She glanced back at him once, her gaze lingering for a long instant, before signing out with the security guard and stepping into the revolving door. And then she was gone and he felt as if the sun had suddenly disappeared behind a cloud.

He was tempted to follow her out the front door and press his dinner invitation one more time. But he had another lady waiting for him, a little lady much more enigmatic and mysterious than Chloe Durrant.

He smiled to himself, then glanced around the busy sales floor for Madeline. Back at the accessory counter, he found the silk scarf tossed on the counter in an elegant heap.

Sloan motioned to the salesclerk behind the counter and she hurried over with an enquiring smile. "Where did the little girl go?" he asked. "The one who was looking at this scarf?"

"I'm afraid she's left the store, Mr. DeWilde. She hurried out while you were speaking with Ms. Durrant."

Sloan cursed silently, then stalked over to the security guard keeping watch over the entrance. "Did you see a little girl leave the store? She has dark hair and she was wearing a denim jacket and a black beret. She's about this tall." He held his hand up just below his elbow.

"Yes, sir, Mr. DeWilde. I saw her. She walked out a few minutes ago." The guard pushed open one of the side doors and Sloan stepped back onto the street. But the five o'clock rush had begun and the sidewalks were clogged with pedestrians. Even if Madeline were tall enough to see, he couldn't have found her in the mob of people.

Raking his fingers through his hair, Sloan turned and strode back inside the store. Next time, he would not let Madeline get away without finding out exactly what her situation was. If she and her mother needed help, he'd give it to them. After all, there had to be some benefit to being rich.

And next time the opportunity presented itself, he'd follow Chloe and convince her that a little pleasure was exactly what their business relationship needed. For after all, there had to be some benefit to being her boss.

CHAPTER FIVE

A SHARP RAP ON SLOAN'S office door startled him out of an idle contemplation of his left shoe and Chloe Durrant's incredible beauty. His mind had been focused on an image of her as she had glanced back at him before stepping through the doors of DeWilde's an hour ago.

"Come in!" he called, not taking his eyes off his shoe or his thoughts off Chloe.

As he considered that last look, replayed over and over in his mind, he wondered just where he stood with her. The kiss they'd shared at the gallery hadn't been all one-sided. She had participated in the experience as enthusiastically as he had.

But something was holding her back. At first he was certain it was his position as her boss. But now he was beginning to think there was something more, something he had seen in her rush to leave the store just an hour ago.

"That desk is not a footstool." Sloan glanced up to find Miss Crenshaw standing in the doorway, a tight-lipped scowl on her face. Sloan shot her a blinding smile in response.

This battle of wits was getting to be more fun than he'd ever anticipated. Now he knew why his father had thought so highly of Miss Crenshaw. The woman had pluck. "I thought I'd put it to some good use," he teased. "Since I don't do much else on it."

"Impertinence is very inappropriate in a boy of your advanced years."

"I'll take that into consideration. And while I'm mulling it over, I'd like you to type a memo."

"Another memo?" Edna asked.

"Yes," Sloan said. "To the candy department. From now on, children visiting the store will be given a free piece of candy. Anything they choose."

Edna scowled. "May I ask how you came upon such an unusual idea?"

"No, you may not. But I think it's a stroke of retailing brilliance, don't you? Just make sure it's done, Miss Crenshaw. Now, was there something else you wanted, or did you just come in here to insult me?"

"There is a Mr. Nicholas Santos here to see you."

Sloan leaned back in his chair and linked his hands behind his head. "Does he have an appointment?"

"No, he does not," Miss Crenshaw replied in a haughty tone. "We went over your schedule this morning and, if you remember, it was completely open."

"Then tell him I don't have time to see him. Besides, it's nearly six. The store closes in just a few minutes."

She arched a dubious brow. "Shall I tell him you're busy stringing your paper clips together? Or are you occupied with bouncing that ball of rubber bands off the ceiling again?"

Sloan laughed. "Right now I'm too busy dodging that rapier-sharp tongue of yours. I'll have you know that any other boss would have had you fired long ago for such unabashed insubordination."

She sniffed. "If you want *my* advice, you'd best see Mr. Santos right now. He doesn't look like someone who likes to be kept waiting. He claims he's been sent by your cousin Jeffrey. You may remember Jeffrey. He's the CEO of DeWilde's . . . and the man you answer to."

A knot of tension twisted in Sloan's gut and he sucked in a sharp breath. What the hell was cousin Jeffrey about now? Had he learned of Sloan's covert maneuvering with the board? Sloan groaned inwardly. If so, his well-laid plans were probably being undermined at this very moment. Jeffrey was a formidable businessman and would stop at nothing to preserve the integrity of the family business.

Sloan dragged his feet off his desk and sat up in his chair. "All right," he said tightly, "just this once I will defer to your judgment."

He had wondered how long he'd be able to keep his plan to sell DeWilde's and dump his family's stock a secret. And he'd also speculated as to who would be the first to jump in and stake a claim once the plan was announced. Since Jeffrey and Grace had split, he'd figured that Jeffrey would be first, wanting a larger voting block for himself to protect the interests of the store against Grace's plan to open a San Francisco operation. But Sloan had hoped that Grace might enter the fight as well, driving the price of the stock up even further.

Grace and Jeffrey had seemed the perfect couple, their marriage rock steady and their devotion to DeWilde's equaling their devotion to each other. The pair had worked side by side from the London headquarters, Grace adding her own special mixture of American marketing know-how, common sense and people skills to DeWilde's traditional business atmosphere.

Now Grace had returned to her hometown of San Francisco, determined to open her own retailing venture. But Jeffrey was determined to undermine her plans, stripping his wife of her rights to the estimable family name and attempting to veto any connection she might make between her new store and the DeWilde retailing empire.

Never had DeWilde's been in such a state of flux. With Grace holding ten percent of the stock, everyone on the board had been waiting for her to sell, including Sloan. The sale of her shares would no doubt depress the price of DeWilde stock and hinder the ability of the corporation to raise capital. But Sloan had convinced the nonfamily board members that selling DeWilde's piece of Manhattan Fifth Avenue real estate would keep the stock value strong and his own selling price high.

Maybe it was best to get the whole thing out in the open, anyway. Most of the board members standing behind the sale of the Fifth Avenue store had urged this from the start, well aware that Grace's departure would probably threaten the corporate profits. But Sloan had learned to be wary of Jeffrey DeWilde and had chosen to wait on his announcement, hoping that the element of surprise would hinder the effectiveness of Jeffrey's response. No doubt his cousin would try to block the sale, hoping to keep the New York store as a weapon to use against Grace and her new store. And the first volley in the battle was waiting in the outer office.

Sloan glanced up as Edna ushered his visitor through the door. The tall stranger crossed the office in a few long strides and Sloan tried to recall whether he'd ever met the man before. Though he wasn't fully familiar with his cousin's staff, he was certain he hadn't. He would have remembered the slight limp and the powerful build ... the dark, subtly dangerous and street-smart look of the guy. Sloan stood and held out his hand. "I'm Sloan DeWilde. Edna tells me that you've been sent by my cousin."

He clasped Sloan's hand firmly and shook it just once. "Nick Santos. Thanks for seeing me."

Sloan detected a slight lilt in his voice, not quite an accent but enough to confirm the man's Spanish or Portuguese parentage. Though his words were polite, there was nothing in his tone that indicated real gratitude. Sloan pointed to a chair in front of his desk and Santos sat down.

"Can I get you a cup of coffee or a beverage?" Miss Crenshaw asked from the door.

Santos twisted in his chair and shook his head. "No, thanks. I'm fine."

"You could get *me* a beverage, Miss Crenshaw," Sloan said, sinking into his own chair. "Coffee, black."

She snorted in disgust, then turned and walked from the office, slamming the door behind her. Santos looked back at Sloan and frowned. "Problems?"

Sloan picked up a pen from his desk and tapped it distractedly against the intricate inlaid surface. "Miss Crenshaw has a rather low opinion of me, but I'm hoping to change that. Until then, what can I do for you?"

"I've been retained by your cousin, Jeffrey DeWilde, on a matter of family business."

Sloan tossed the pen down and leaned forward, bracing his forearms on the desk. He smiled tightly. So Jeffrey *had* uncovered the plan and was ready to negotiate. "And what family business is so important that it's become *your* business, Mr. Santos?"

The man's expression hardened and he returned Sloan's stare with a cold gaze. "Are you familiar with the DeWilde family jewels?"

Sloan stopped short and frowned, startled by the unexpected question. He slowly leaned back in his chair, careful not to reveal the full extent of his surprise. "Of course. Who in the family isn't?"

Santos reached into the breast pocket of his suit jacket and withdrew a small notepad. "In 1948, your father's brother Dirk disappeared without a trace," he said, distractedly flipping through the pages. "You may not be aware that at the same time Dirk dropped out of sight, so did six pieces from the DeWilde collection. The missing pieces were quickly replaced with paste replicas and the theft was covered up."

"Are you telling me some of the famous DeWilde family jewels are fakes?" Sloan chuckled, shaking his head. "Why am I surprised? The DeWildes have always been overly concerned with appearances."

Santos looked up from his notes. "Recently, one of the stolen pieces, a tiara set with pavé diamonds and pearls, turned up."

"The Empress Eugénie tiara?" Sloan asked.

Santos nodded.

"What does this have to do with me?"

"The piece turned up right here in New York, Mr. DeWilde. An antique dealer called Jeffrey when he recognized the distinctive design. Jeffrey hired me to track down the lead. I'm a private investigator."

Sloan breathed a silent sigh of relief. So his plan hadn't been compromised. Jeffrey was simply working damage control on an old family scandal. "But why come to me? I wasn't even born when Dirk disappeared. Hell, I wasn't even aware of the theft or the substitution."

"But your mother and father were both around and they both knew about the theft. I've tried to speak with your mother several times, Mr. DeWilde. The first time, she slammed the door in my face. The last time she set her dogs on me."

Sloan chuckled. "I'm not surprised. My mother has little to say on the subject of the DeWilde family."

"And why is that?" Santos asked.

Sloan shrugged. "It's no secret. The bad blood goes back pretty far. My father was serving in the RAF as a pilot when he fell in love with my mother. She was an American hospital volunteer, following her two older brothers into the war effort. A headstrong eighteen-year-old who helped nurse my father back to health after his plane was shot down over the English countryside. She was ten years younger than he was, but they shared a true love of adventure...and of each other."

"But the family didn't approve?"

"The DeWilde family, and Uncle Charles in particular, considered Maura Kelly a rowdy, unsophisticated Yank. Even though she came from a very wealthy Connecticut family and possessed a considerable fortune of her own, the fact that she encouraged my father's love of flying and shared in his aversion to the family business did nothing to endear her to the Royals."

Santos scribbled something on his pad, talking as he wrote. "So both your father and mother held a grudge of sorts against the family."

"I suppose you could call it that." Sloan stared at him through narrowed eyes. "What's your point, Mr. Santos?"

"At the time, the family suspected that Dirk took the jewels. Maybe they ignored another suspect in their haste to cover up the scandal of the theft?"

"Who?"

He looked up. "Your father." The detective's voice was cold, emotionless. He stared at Sloan, waiting for his reaction.

Sloan grinned. "Not a chance. My father was a proud and honorable man. He would sooner have died than stolen anything from the DeWilde family. He didn't want much to do with the family money in the first place."

"Then you're certain your father had nothing to do with the theft?"

Sloan studied the man shrewdly. A tense silence grew between them. The guy had plenty of nerve, that much was

certain. But Sloan also sensed a high level of professionalism. Santos knew exactly what he was doing, and a lie could
just as easily be detected as the truth. "Absolutely nothing," he finally replied.

Santos didn't seem surprised. "I'd like to hear your
mother's story," he said.

"I can't make her talk to you. No one makes Maura Kelly
DeWilde do anything she doesn't want to. It's a trait she's
handed down to all her children, I might add." Sloan saw
the detective's expression tighten at his backhanded warning.

"Listen," Santos said, "my gut tells me your father
probably had nothing to do with the theft. And my gut is
never wrong. Besides, you wouldn't be stupid enough to try
to fence the jewelry in your own backyard."

"Should I be flattered by the compliment?" Sloan asked.

Santos ignored the sarcasm. "I need to speak with your
mother, Mr. DeWilde. I'm not going to give up until she
talks to me. She might know something that could be help-
ful, something that your father may have told her, some clue
that's been ignored all these years."

Sloan watched him for a long moment. This was not the
kind of man who respected the subtle art of negotiation. He
didn't ask, he didn't cajole, he demanded. He looked as if
he'd grown up on the streets, settling disputes with his fists
while trying hard to maintain the sizable chip on his shoulder. But, hell, Sloan had nothing to lose.

If the scandal of the jewelry theft and the subsequent
cover-up leaked to the press, there was no predicting what
it might do to the price of DeWilde stock. And right now,
he had a vested interest in keeping that stock as bullish as
possible.

Sloan folded his hands in front of him. "I'll help—under one condition."

"I don't like conditions," Santos said, an edge to his voice.

"You haven't heard the condition yet," Sloan countered.

After a long moment, Santos nodded his assent, the movement barely perceptible. It was the first concession the man had made since he entered the room. Sloan held back a satisfied grin. "I'd like you to investigate a small matter here at the store. It shouldn't take you long and I'll cover your daily rate, whatever it is."

"Don't you have a security manager?"

"I don't want our security personnel involved in this. This takes a . . . more discriminating investigator."

"Discriminating?" Santos repeated. A smile touched the corners of his mouth. "Should I assume this matter involves a woman?"

Sloan shook his head. "No, it's not that simple. There's a child—a little girl—I've seen in the store, usually around four in the afternoon. She's got long dark hair and wears an old denim jacket and a black beret. She's maybe eleven or twelve years old. I think she might be a runaway living on the street. I want you to find out who she is and where she belongs. And if she's shoplifting, I want you to tell me, but I don't want you to stop her. You'll need to be careful, because if she knows you're watching her, she might bolt."

"Sounds simple enough. When do I get to see your mother?"

"I'll talk to her this weekend. I'm sure I'll be able to set up something for next week."

Santos stood and tossed his card on Sloan's desk. "My hotel number's on the back. If I find anything out about the girl, I'll let you know. Oh, and there is one other thing you might be interested in knowing."

"What is that?" Sloan asked.

"Your merchandising manager, Robert Simpson-Davis, has been stealing from the store. I can't say how long it's been going on, but if he's not stopped soon, my guess is we're talking enough to make a felony theft charge stick."

Sloan scowled. "How do you know this?"

"I'm a damn good investigator," Santos said with a cocky grin. "After a week on surveillance, a guy's bound to pick up a few surprises along the way. No lead is too insignificant to follow. By the way, I've got photos. I'll send them over tomorrow morning."

With that, he turned and walked out the door, leaving Sloan speechless—and vaguely aware that his every move over the past week had been observed and carefully noted in a written report to Jeffrey. He swore softly and rubbed his forehead with his fingertips.

"What did Mr. Santos want?"

Sloan let his hands drop to his desk. Edna held a steaming mug of coffee in front of him. "Did you bring that in here just to tease me or is that a bribe?" he asked. She placed the mug in front of him and Sloan couldn't help but smile. He nodded his head knowingly. "You want to know what went on in here and you're willing to pay for it by fetching coffee. Miss Crenshaw, you never fail to amaze me."

"If Mr. Santos's visit impacts the store in any way, I believe I have a right to know what he was here for."

Sloan rose from his chair. "Whatever we have to discuss, we'll discuss over dinner. I've got a gallery opening in SoHo I've got to get to and I'm famished. We can grab a bite on the way downtown. Have you ever been to a gallery opening, Miss Crenshaw?" He snatched his jacket from where it was draped across his credenza, then turned back to find a shocked expression on Miss Crenshaw's face.

"We can't have dinner," Edna said.

Sloan frowned. "Why not?"

"Well, it wouldn't be proper. We're business associates, Mr. DeWilde, and our business should be done within the confines of this store."

Sloan shook his head. He was definitely losing his touch. If he couldn't even get a dinner date with Edna Crenshaw, how the hell could he expect to woo Chloe Durrant into an after-work assignation? He drew in a deep breath and let it out slowly. "You're right, Miss Crenshaw, it wouldn't be proper. You'll just have to wait until tomorrow morning to hear about my meeting. Right now, all I care about is dinner." With that, Sloan stalked out of his office.

The crush of pedestrians enveloped him as soon as he stepped out onto the sidewalk. He made for the curb to hail a cab, then stepped back. Suddenly he didn't feel like another solitary dinner out. He'd walk the eight blocks to the apartment and send out for Chinese. Later, if he felt like it, he'd drive down to the gallery opening.

As he turned down Fifty-fourth and headed toward Sutton Place, he unbuttoned his cuffs and rolled them up, then loosened his silk tie. Shedding his businesslike look was easy, but ridding himself of the problems he'd left behind at the store would be much more difficult.

Sometimes, being the boss wasn't all it was cracked up to be. Firing Simpson-Davis would not be pleasant, but it had to be done. He slowed his pace for a moment, considering his options. As one alternative coalesced in his mind, a grin curled the corners of his mouth.

Maybe there was a way to turn this odious task to his advantage. Once Simpson-Davis was out of the picture, a myriad of opportunities and possibilities arose. Sloan tossed his jacket over his shoulder and lengthened his stride, whistling a soft tune as he walked.

There *was* a way to get exactly what he wanted, and first thing tomorrow morning, he'd make it happen.

"YOU'RE LATE," Gina said. "What's your excuse this time?"

Chloe dropped her portfolio on her worktable and sank onto a stool, brushing a strand of damp hair from her eyes. This morning she'd allowed her hair to go natural and it now fell in kinky waves around her face, still damp from her two-minute shower. "Don't even ask," she said.

"Then let me guess," Gina said. "Lost shoe or field trip permission slip?"

"Cookies for a bake sale. Luckily the corner store had some of that cookie dough in a tube. I offered to send money instead of cookies, but Audrey wouldn't hear of it. If I don't send cookies, her classmates will think we don't have a housekeeper, which is almost as bad as not having a summer house in the Hamptons."

"Miss Crenshaw has called three times. Mr. DeWilde wants to see you immediately."

"Immediately?" Chloe asked.

"That's what the Stepford secretary said. Immediately, if not sooner."

"He probably wants to check on my progress with the designs for the Fifth Avenue windows. I worked up some sketches last night. One great design and two real stinkers. He thinks he's choosing, but he's got another guess coming. I've already made the choice for him." Chloe grabbed her sketch pad from her portfolio and tucked it under her arm. "I'll let you know how it goes."

After a quick stop in the ladies' room to pull her hair back in a tight chignon and apply the rest of her makeup, Chloe hurried up to Sloan's ninth-floor office. Edna Crenshaw was at her desk when Chloe arrived. "Mr. DeWilde has been waiting for you," she said, without looking away from her computer monitor. "You may go right in."

As she quietly pushed open the door, she paused for a moment. He was bent over a thick computer report, his jacket tossed over the back of a guest chair, his tie loosened and his sleeves rolled up.

She felt her heart skip a beat as the memory of their kiss flashed in her mind, his warm mouth on hers, the taste of him on her tongue, the spicy scent of his cologne filling her senses.

She'd never been kissed like that before, so unexpected, yet so arousing, a kiss filled with the promise of even greater passion—and untold danger. In her younger days, she might have surrendered to such intense desire. But she was older now, a woman with responsibilities, a woman who had made her mistakes and learned from them. She would not allow Sloan DeWilde to be another mistake.

Still, that didn't stop her from secretly fantasizing about him. How could she help herself? He seemed to test her resolve at every turn. And now, without a single word or a single glance, she found herself wanting him to leap over his desk and yank her into his arms and kiss her until her toes curled.

"I think I've got it, Edna," he murmured, his gaze still fixed on the report. "I think I've finally figured out these damn reports. The second column refers to the increase over previous—"

"I'm not Edna," Chloe interrupted.

Sloan looked up and a quick smile broke across his face. Her heart skipped a beat, then resumed at a faster pace. "I can see that." His brow shot up as he took in her hot pink sleeveless sheath and matching sixties earrings. "I never quite know who's going to greet me in the morning."

"I was in the mood for pink," Chloe said, smoothing back her hair distractedly.

He nodded. "I like it. It's very... bright. Very fashionable. Did you buy it here?"

She shook her head. "Our merchandise is a bit too..." She paused, trying to find the right word.

"Boring?" he asked.

"Conservative," she corrected him. "I like bright colors, unusual designs. We cater toward a more traditional customer."

He stared at her for a long moment and she met his gaze, losing her concentration somewhere in the depths of his hazel eyes. "And you certainly aren't the traditional customer," he murmured, his voice warm and tantalizing.

Chloe drew in a sharp breath, then laid her sketch pad on his desk. "I assume you want to see the new designs for the front windows. I've worked on some rough sketches last night and I—"

"We'll get to that later," he said as he stood and circled his desk. He took her elbow in his hand and drew her toward the door. "Come with me, Ms. Durrant. I have something to show you." He led her through the reception area and into the spacious office next to his.

"What are we doing? Do we have a meeting with Simpson-Davis?" she asked, glancing around the merchandising manager's office.

"What do you think of this office?" he asked in return, ignoring her question.

She glanced around. "It's nice enough. It's a bit dark with all this wood—very masculine. Men seem to like things dark and foreboding. I think it's hormonal. It gives them a sense of power."

"Look around," he urged.

"What are we doing in here?" she asked again.

At that moment, Edna appeared in the doorway. "Mr. DeWilde, your brother Mason is on the line. He claims he needs to speak with you immediately. Something about a—" she sniffed "—horse?"

"Wait here," Sloan said, giving Chloe's elbow a gentle squeeze. "I'll be right back." He strode from the room, but Edna stayed behind, eyeing Chloe suspiciously.

"Do you have a meeting with Mr. Simpson-Davis?" she asked.

"I don't know," Chloe replied.

Edna arched a brow. "You don't know?"

Chloe shook her head. With that, Edna deserted her post at the door and went back to her work, leaving Chloe to her own devices. Slowly, she wandered around the office, studying the oil paintings of hunting scenes on the walls. As she passed a heavy cherrywood credenza, her gaze fell on a small sculpture.

With a quiet cry, she reached out and touched it, running her hand along the cool bronze.

"I think it looks good in here, don't you?" Sloan asked softly from the doorway.

Chloe spun around. "You bought it? But why?"

"Because I thought it belonged here," he said, strolling toward her.

"In Simpson-Davis's office?" Chloe shook her head. "He doesn't seem like the Madonna-and-child type."

Sloan shrugged. "No, he doesn't. But then, this isn't his office anymore, it's yours."

She laughed lightly at his teasing. "My office? But this office is for the merchandising manager."

Sloan grinned and sauntered across the room. "Like I said, it's your office, Ms. Durrant."

"But that can't be," Chloe protested. "That would mean that I'm—"

He looked directly into her eyes, so intimately she almost felt as if he were touching her. "That's right. And it must be so, since I just informed Miss Crenshaw and she's typing the memo as we speak. Now, if you'll excuse me, I have some work to do."

He bent and brushed a chaste kiss across her cheek. "Congratulations, Ms. Durrant." He headed for the door, then turned back to her. "We have a late meeting tomorrow evening after closing with a contractor to discuss your idea for boutiques in the bridal department. And I'd also like to hear your ideas about what we might do in crystal and china. Make whatever arrangements are required to work Saturday and tell Miss Crenshaw what you'd like for dinner. We'll order in. And while you're at it, order in some new furniture. This stuff doesn't quite look right on you. It's not . . . romantic enough."

She stood in the middle of the office and stared at the empty doorway for a long time, rendered completely speechless by Sloan and his startling news. *She* was the new merchandising manager? *She* was now second in command at DeWilde's Fifth Avenue?

Chloe had always dreamed about a promotion like this, but she had thought it would take years before she'd even be considered qualified. Sure, she knew the fashion side of the business better than anyone, but the administrative duties were well beyond her extensive experience.

Slowly, she made her way around the massive cherry desk to the equally massive chair. She lowered herself into the tufted burgundy leather and placed her palms flat on the desk, then took a long, deep breath and closed her eyes.

"I can do this job," she murmured. "I *can* do this job."

She waited a few moments before opening her eyes, certain that she'd end up back in her workroom and it would all have been a dream. But everything was as it had been.

She hadn't dreamed the whole incident. She was sitting in the executive suite at DeWilde's Fifth Avenue. With a delighted giggle, she reached for the phone and punched in Gina's extension. Her friend picked up the line after only one ring.

"Hi, it's me," Chloe said. "I'm in Simpson-Davis's office. Get up here, right now. And hurry!"

A few minutes later, Gina appeared in the doorway. "What's wrong?" she asked, searching the room before stepping inside. "Did he see the typo in the Sunday ad? I just knew he wouldn't let it go by without a mention." She made a quick search of the office. "Where's Mr. Priss?"

"I don't know," Chloe said. "I'm not sure I want to. For all I know, he's stuffed in a closet somewhere."

"What is going on?" Gina demanded. "And why are you sitting at his desk?"

Chloe leaned back in the chair and kicked her feet up on the desk. "I think I'm the new merchandising manager."

"What?" Gina shouted.

"It's true. This is *my* office now."

"Get out!" Gina cried. "You're kidding, aren't you? You *have* to be kidding." She stared at Chloe then slowly shook her head. "You're not kidding."

Chloe shrugged. "I didn't believe it myself. But Sloan— I mean, Mr. DeWilde—just told me. Edna Crenshaw is typing the memo as we speak."

"Then you did it!" Gina cried. "You followed my advice."

"What advice?"

"The flirting advice. Remember?"

Chloe frowned. "No! I didn't follow your advice."

"Then how did you get this job?"

"I'm not sure. But it had nothing to do with flirting." Even as she said the words, she wondered if Gina might just be right. Why *had* Sloan promoted her so suddenly? And what had happened to the former merchandising manager of DeWilde's Fifth Avenue?

"You're saying nothing is going on between you and the big boss?"

"No!" Chloe felt her cheeks warm under Gina's shrewd perusal. "Absolutely not. That would be highly improper."

"Tell me you haven't once considered what Sloan De-Wilde might be like outside the office," Gina challenged.

Chloe composed a suitably bland expression on her face. "Never," she lied. "Our relationship is strictly business...which is why I need to ask you a favor. Could you take Audrey to the park tomorrow instead of next weekend?"

Gina raised a brow speculatively.

"Sloan—I mean, Mr. DeWilde—needs me to work tomorrow. We have some things we have to discuss."

"Working on a Saturday?" Gina asked. "Alone? That's how it starts."

"I don't need a lecture," Chloe replied.

Gina grinned, then headed for the door. "Sure, I'll take care of Audrey," she said. She stopped and turned back to Chloe. "Under one condition."

Chloe leaned forward, bracing her elbows on the desk and watching her best friend through suspicious eyes. "All right, what is it?"

"Admit that you're just a tiny bit attracted to Sloan DeWilde and that he might just be a tiny bit attracted to you."

Chloe groaned, then wadded a piece of paper and threw it at Gina. "Get out of here before I sic Miss Crenshaw on you."

As Chloe sat alone, staring at the empty doorway, nagging doubts began to creep into her thoughts. Why *had* Sloan offered her this job? Was she truly the most qualified, or was there another reason? Could he possibly expect something in return?

Whatever his motives, before tomorrow was over, she'd know exactly what this promotion meant—for her and Sloan DeWilde.

THE STORE WAS WONDERFULLY peaceful, the racks and displays shrouded in shadow, lit only by an exit sign or the light filtering from the now still escalator. The sound of their footsteps on the parquet floor that ringed the bridal department echoed in the darkness, and the silhouettes of the mannequins created an almost eerie atmosphere.

Sloan waited as the contractor, accompanied by a security guard, made his way to the elevators. Their afternoon meeting had lasted well past closing. The doors opened and then closed after the pair stepped inside, and he realized he and Chloe were alone.

"So, have you adjusted to the fact that you're now DeWilde's new merchandising manager?" he asked.

"I'm still a bit overwhelmed," Chloe replied.

"Don't be. Miss Crenshaw will work with you for several hours each morning," Sloan told her as they strolled aimlessly down the aisle. "She can outline all the administrative tasks, answer all your questions. And don't let her intimidate you. She knows this store better than anyone and she won't let you forget it."

"Miss Crenshaw doesn't care for me," Chloe said. "She never has."

"What Miss Crenshaw thinks of you makes no difference at all. Besides, once you've learned the ropes, you'll need to hire your own assistant. Simpson-Davis's assistant asked for a transfer to the sales floor after his boss was fired.''

"Why *did* I get this job?" Chloe asked, a hesitant catch in her voice.

He glanced over at her to find her face luminous, cast in the soft glow of a light coming from somewhere behind him. She wore a black skirt and a short-sleeved fuchsia sweater that hugged the curves of her breasts. Her wavy hair, pulled back in a haphazard knot, formed soft silvery tendrils around her face. She looked so lovely, like an angel, and he was tempted to reach out and touch her, to see if she was real or just an illusion.

"Because you're the most qualified," he said, his voice nearly dying in his throat. "And I needed someone I could trust."

"Simpson-Davis was qualified," she countered.

"He was also stealing from the store. It's a bit hard to trust a thief, don't you think?"

At first she looked surprised, and then she smiled. "Then it didn't have anything to do with—" she groped for the right word "—us?"

He grinned. "Us? I thought there was no us."

"You know what I mean. This...obsession you have with me and . . . fine dining. I thought you might have fired him because—well, just so you could . . ."

Sloan laughed out loud, the sound echoing the length and breadth of the bridal department. "My dear Ms. Durrant. Though having dinner with you would be a joy, I wouldn't go so far as to fire a competent employee to make it happen. I simply want to get to know you a little better. And if that involves dinner, then so be it."

"Is that why you promoted me?" she asked. "To get to know me better?"

He couldn't tell her why he really promoted her. In fact, he wasn't quite sure anymore if that was the reason. At first, the promotion had made perfect sense. Promote Chloe and keep her occupied with administrative tasks. But, consciously or subconsciously, he was certain she was the right person for the job. That she be rewarded for her talents was only right.

The more he watched her work, the more he wondered whether closing the store was such a good idea. If anyone could turn DeWilde's around, she could. But he had no way out. He was committed to this course of action, swept along with the plans he'd set in motion months ago. And she was just as committed to making a success of the store.

His family was anxious to divest themselves of their last connection to the DeWildes. He'd made a promise to them and he couldn't very well break it now. This was business, and what he hoped to have with Chloe had nothing at all to do with business.

"I promoted you because you're the best person for the job. That's it. There's nothing more. If you'd like me to interview other candidates, I'd be happy to do that, just to satisfy you."

She sighed. "No," Chloe said. "It's just that if you did have ulterior motives, I was prepared to turn the promotion down."

"Oh, believe me, I still have ulterior motives where you're concerned," he teased. "They just don't have anything to do with your promotion."

"I wish you wouldn't say things like that," Chloe said, stopping in the midst of a bridal accessories display. "You make it very difficult for me."

Sloan reached out and clasped her hands in his, massaging her delicate fingers between his. "I can't change the circumstances under which we met, Chloe. I'm not sure that

I'd want to. I'm the boss here and there's nothing I can do about that. But now you're the boss, too.''

"Are you saying we're . . . equal?''

"As equal as we can get. We're residing on the same latitude on the flow chart, but since I own five percent of the stock, that does put me a few degrees to the north.''

"But you're the one who promoted me. And you can fire me just as easily.''

Sloan slid his hands up along her bare arms, enjoying the feel of her warm skin beneath his fingertips. She shivered and stepped away from him, standing just beyond his reach. He sighed. "Chloe, business is business. But if it will change your mind about us, I'd be happy to fire you.''

Her green eyes went wide. "I don't want you to fire me,'' she said. "I want this job.''

"Good. Because now that you're merchandising manager, I can't fire you. Jeffrey DeWilde has to approve your promotion, and once he does, he's the only one who can fire you.''

"But you fired Simpson-Davis,'' she said.

Sloan shook his head. For someone who had just been promoted to her dream job, she sure was challenging that promotion. Could she truly believe that she didn't deserve the position? He'd always thought Chloe to be one of the most confident professionals he'd ever met. "That was for just cause and I was acting as a member of the DeWilde board,'' he explained.

"I see,'' she said.

"Hey, I could always fire me,'' he teased. "I never liked working at this store, anyway. I'm incompetent, I'm insubordinate and I'm irresponsible.''

A reluctant smile curled the corners of her mouth. "Maybe that would be best,'' she murmured. "It would solve all our problems.''

Sloan took a step toward her, staring down into her eyes. "I have a better way to solve our problems." Slowly, he bent and brushed his lips along hers, lingering for a moment before pulling back.

"Please don't," she said breathlessly, avoiding his gaze.

He kissed her again, this time with more conviction. At first she didn't react, but then he felt her soften in his arms and her lips parted slightly. He pressed her gently into his body as his tongue rimmed her mouth, softly probing, tasting, savoring. "Why not?" he asked. "There's nothing standing in our way."

Slipping his hands around her tiny waist, Sloan slowly backed her against a Queen Anne table filled with beaded white pocketbooks. With a sweep of his hand, he cleared a spot, the pocketbooks tumbling to the floor around his feet. Then he gently lifted her up and placed her in front of him. Her short skirt rode high on her thighs and he stepped between her legs, deepening his kiss. His mouth never left hers while his hands fumbled to free her hair.

"You can't deny this any longer, Chloe," he murmured against her lips as hairpins dropped to the floor. "We don't have to. We're two adults. We can handle this."

"I don't know," Chloe said. "Every instinct tells me this is a mistake. We shouldn't do this."

He furrowed his fingers through her hair, working at the hairpins, tugging softly until she was forced to look up at him. "Why? Give me one good reason."

"I—I don't . . ." She drew a shaky breath.

"You don't have a reason. Chloe, give me a chance. Let me show you that this can work. Forget the damn store. Forget who I am. All we have to worry about is you and me. No one else."

She bit her bottom lip as her gaze locked with his, a war of emotions taking place deep in her green eyes. Just when he thought she would acquiesce, she shook her head resolutely.

"I have to go," she said, sliding off the table. She pressed a beaded pocketbook into his hand, then stepped around him.

Sloan swore softly but didn't turn around, didn't attempt to convince her to stay. Damn it, if this was truly what she wanted, then he'd give up trying to change her mind. He was tired of her reticence. They'd work together and that would be all.

He tossed the beaded bag back onto the table, then walked away from the mess. In the end, it was probably for the best. Chloe Durrant was standing squarely in the way of his plans, plans he had a nasty habit of forgetting when she was around.

CHAPTER SIX

SLOAN TURNED HIS BLACK BMW off the road into the long, winding drive of Kelly Farms. A white-washed fence lined both sides of the drive, and a cast-iron green shamrock was tacked to the top of each post, a pattern repeated on the Kelly Farms racing silks.

Through a bower of oak leaves, he watched a pair of Thoroughbreds canter across the paddock, tails high, manes whipping in the wind. He smiled to himself. Sheba's Prize now belonged to Kelly Farms, and the mare was already enjoying the company of the stable's prized stallion, Paragon.

He pulled the car to a stop in front of the rambling white clapboard house. A wide porch ran along the facade and green shutters decorated the windows, giving the huge house a cozy, welcoming look. Baskets of his mother's well-tended flowers hung at intervals along the length of the porch, and the afternoon breeze wafted the scent through the humid air.

Though his family kept the small co-op apartment in the city, Sloan and his siblings spent most of their time on the Connecticut farm. It was here the family had retreated after Henry's death, and this was where they called home, with the family matriarch, Maura, still presiding over nightly dinners.

To one side of the house, the low horse barns and dirt training track were visible beyond a sweeping lawn. Sloan shut off the ignition and stepped from the car. He stopped for a moment and rested his arms on the edge of the car door, watching one of the trainers take a promising three-year-old through his paces on the dirt track.

Before long, he would be able to take an equal part in the running of the farm. The thought should have caused a surge of anticipation, but lately all he felt at the prospect of finally selling DeWilde's was an odd sense of dread.

He slammed the car door and jogged up the front steps. Before he could open the door, it swung wide in front of him and Sylvie, the family's cook and housekeeper, greeted him with a pleased smile. "Welcome home, Mr. Sloan. Your mother is the library with your brother Mason."

"Thanks, Sylvie." Sloan handed her his suit jacket, then unknotted his tie and unbuttoned his cuffs as he walked toward the back of the house. Compared to the heat and bustle of Manhattan in September, the house was like a soothing balm to the senses.

He found his mother and Mason huddled over the desk in the library, a room that also served as the farm's office. Maura Kelly DeWilde, perched on the arm of Mason's chair, looked up as Sloan entered the room. Her still-lovely face broke into a smile. "Darling! It's about time you came home! You usually never stay in the city this long."

She tipped her cheek up and Sloan bent over and kissed her. It never ceased to amaze him how beautiful she was. Her face was smooth and unwrinkled, which made her look much younger than her seventy years. She wore her silvery hair in a classic chignon that accentuated her high cheekbones. A daily ride and a healthy diet kept her figure trim and her energy boundless.

Sloan circled the desk and flopped down into one of the tufted leather wing chairs that flanked the bay window. "So, Mase, I saw Sheba's Prize in the paddock on my way in. She looks great, don't you think?"

"She's lovely, darling," Maura said, her blue eyes sparkling with humor. "Isn't she, Mason? Tell your brother he made a fine choice." Even now, after all these years, she was still mediating disputes between her many and very stubborn offspring. There was always a heated discussion going on between siblings in some corner of the house, usually with Maura standing squarely in the middle.

"Sloan made a fine choice," Mason muttered reluctantly.

Sloan grinned and crossed his legs in front of him. "Why, thank you, partner. I did, didn't I."

Mason's jaw tightened and Maura patted him affectionately on the cheek. "Don't make that face, darling. You look like your father's side of the family, all grumpy and constipated."

Sloan laughed out loud, winking at his mother as Mason shook his head wearily.

"So, little brother," he said, "what's new at DeWilde's Fifth Avenue? Sales still plummeting, I presume?"

"Everything's going pretty much as planned," Sloan lied. "No problems."

Maura smoothed her hair distractedly, a wistful expression crossing her face. "I must say, I'm not sorry to see that store go. Henry never wanted any part of it, nor did I."

Sloan nodded and a long silence descended over the room. Taking a deep breath, he leaned forward in his chair and braced his elbows on his knees. "Mason, we need to talk after dinner. I want your input on a proposal for a severance package before I head back to the city. If we're going public at the October board meeting, I want to have all the details of the sale ironed out."

Mason's brow furrowed. "A severance package? What are you talking about?"

"If the store closes, there are going to be plenty of people out of work. We should compensate them in some way."

Mason's scowl deepened. "Since when do you give a fig about that store or the people that work there? We can't afford a severance package, Sloan. Besides, with all the stores in Manhattan, there are plenty of jobs for salesclerks out there. And those who don't get work can collect unemployment until they find a job."

"Some of these people have worked for DeWilde's for years," Sloan countered. "We can't just cut them loose. And unemployment won't come close to what they make at the store."

"I can't believe what I'm hearing!" Mason cried, rubbing his forehead. "Where is this coming from? You're the last person I'd expect to stand up for the little people."

Sloan shifted in his chair. Mason was right. A month ago he wouldn't have given a second thought about the future of his employees. But for some reason that had changed. "Damn it, Mase, we have some responsibility here! We can't always reduce every business transaction to profit and loss. We're going to be putting a lot of people out of work, a lot of loyal, hard-working employees—with families and bills to pay."

"My heart bleeds," Mason said sardonically. "Especially for my little brother who's gone completely soft in the head."

"Maybe I have. And maybe I'm beginning to realize that there are a lot of people out there who have a helluva lot less than we do. You sit here on this horse farm all day, nice and safe in your insulated little world, surrounded by your rich friends, while there are kids out there living from hand to mouth, maybe even sleeping on the streets. How long has it been since you've walked the streets in New York?"

Mason scoffed and shook his head condescendingly. "What do kids living on the streets of New York City have to do with DeWilde's?"

Sloan cursed beneath his breath. How the hell was he supposed to explain this? How was he supposed to tell Mason about Madeline and the brutal self-examination she had caused him to undergo over the past few weeks. Or about Chloe and her unswerving devotion to her job. "Nothing. I'm just saying we need to think beyond our own interests on this one."

"Even if it costs the family a million or two?"

"The family can afford it."

Mason laughed harshly. "When were you elected head of this family? As I recall, we all have a vote on family business."

"The store is my responsibility, Mason, and I'll handle the sale any way I see fit. If that means ensuring the future of our employees, then so be it."

Mason got out of his chair and began to pace the room. "Mother, talk some sense into him."

Maura studied them both for a long minute, an indomitable air of calm about her. "I think he's right," she said quietly. "What did you have planned, Sloan?"

Knowing he had won over his most important ally, Sloan felt himself relax once more. "Any employee within five years of retirement will receive a full pension immediately. Those within ten years will receive a lump sum plus full pension upon retirement age. All the others will receive severance commensurate with seniority, plus free outplacement counseling. It should cost just over a million."

"A million?" Mason shouted. "A million? Do you know what a million could do to improve the farm?"

"Horses before people?" Sloan asked, a sharp edge to his voice. "I'm sure we'd win that one on moral *and* ethical grounds."

Mason looked at Maura. "And you expect me to give *him* equal say in running the farm? You can see where this is going, can't you? Before we know it, we'll be rescuing horses from the glue factory and providing them with a comfortable retirement."

Maura slowly stood, then moved behind the desk chair. "Sit down, Mason," she ordered.

"But, Mother, I—"

"Sit down, Mason," she repeated in a voice just slightly louder but with an expression that brooked no disobedience from her son.

With a sulky look, Mason returned to his place behind the desk. Maura crossed the room to stand before Sloan. She placed her palm on his cheek and smiled down at him. "Your father would have been proud," she murmured, softly enough so that only he heard. "And I am proud."

Sloan grabbed her hand and kissed it. "Thank you, Mother."

Maura turned back to Mason. "I warn you now, I will not mediate any disputes that arise between you two regarding the farm. If you can't work together after Sloan sells DeWilde's, then I'll turn the farm over to one of your siblings."

"Who?" Mason demanded. "Russell and Linda don't have time."

An ingenious smile curled her lips. "There's always Suzanne or Carolyn," she suggested. "Even Cameron might do a good job. Heaven knows, I have plenty of children to choose from." She gave Sloan a sideways glance and a subtle arch of her brow. "I'll expect you both for dinner. You'd better work this out now, because I certainly won't allow it at the table.'' With those words, she swept from the room, leaving a strained silence in her wake.

''Do you want to tell me what this is really about?'' Mason said. ''Or can I just assume you've lost your mind?''

Sloan ran his fingers through his hair and sighed. ''Do you ever wonder what we'd be doing today if we hadn't been born into the family we have?''

''Never,'' Mason said.

''Well, I've wondered. I met a kid a few weeks ago. She was wandering through the store in a grubby-looking jacket, trying to scrape together enough money to buy a piece of candy. She never knew her father, couldn't tell me where she lived, wouldn't talk about her mother. For all I know, she could be living under a bench in Central Park.''

''You don't know that,'' Mason said.

''No, I don't. But the thing is, it could be true. Just as easily as it couldn't be. And that made me start to realize the safety net that all our family money provided for us. We never had a care in the world when we were growing up. We didn't have to worry where the next meal was coming from, or whether we'd have enough money for shoes and clothes.''

''What do you want to do, provide a pension plan for street people, as well?''

''Minus a regular paycheck, the children of our employees could be in the same situation as that little girl. And as long as we have the money, I'm not going to let that happen. We can afford this, Mason. And we're going to do it.''

His mind flashed an image of Chloe. He didn't look forward to facing her once the sale of the store was announced. But if he did the right and honorable thing, she might be able to go on with her career, none the worse for taking the job at DeWilde's.

Hell, he shouldn't care what she thought of him, but he did. Over the past few weeks he'd developed quite an admiration for Chloe and her talents. They'd become friends, colleagues, and he sought her respect. He needed it, even more than he needed her touch, wanted her body.

The women in his past were just that, women. Not friends, not peers, simply companions meant to pass the time—or maybe objects of desire meant to stir his passion.

But Chloe was something more, a woman beyond all that. He felt a loss when she left him after their time together, not a sense of relief, as he had with so many others. He'd always considered himself a solitary man…until he met Chloe Durrant. Now he found himself wanting to spend every waking hour with her, watching her work, listening to her laugh, learning more about her.

He glanced up to find Mason staring at him. "Just don't forget where your loyalties lie, little brother," he said, his words slightly threatening.

"I'll try not to," Sloan replied, rising from his chair. "Now, if you'll excuse me, I have a matter to discuss with Mother."

As Sloan left the library, he heard his brother curse softly. Mason would stew for a while, but Sloan did have the last word on the store. And what he needed right now was a nice, tidy way to assuage his guilt. He would simply make sure that Chloe—and all the rest—were adequately compensated. Job or no job, it all came down to money, didn't it?

But somehow he suspected that, money or none, Chloe wouldn't be any too pleased when she found out the store would be closing.

He found his mother in the conservatory, a lovely, semi-circular room filled with plants and flowers from the terracotta floor to the glass ceiling. She stood behind a rough-hewn table and arranged roses cut from her garden in a crystal vase.

"Has Mason calmed down at all, or can we expect an argument at dinner?" she asked.

"I don't plan on doing any more arguing," Sloan said, picking up a rose and sniffing it. "But there is something I need to discuss with you in private."

She put her work aside and turned her full attention on him. "This sounds serious."

"I had a visit from a private detective that Jeffrey hired. It seems that one of the stolen pieces from the DeWilde collection showed up in the city."

She looked away. "Then you know about the theft?"

Sloan nodded. "He's tried to speak to you several times, but he tells me you haven't been very cooperative. Do you know anything that might help him?"

"They think your father is a suspect, don't they," she murmured.

"Should they?"

His mother snatched up a rose and began to snip off the thorns, a long silence growing between them. "No, of course not," she said at last. "Your father had nothing to do with the theft." She sighed before going on. "There is one thing your father witnessed that I always thought might have had something to do with the missing jewels, though. It involved the fiancé of your aunt Marie-Claire, your father's younger sister. She was engaged to a handsome and quite wealthy young man named Armand de Villeneuve before the war broke out in Europe. Your father told me that there was bad blood between Dirk and this man, for what reasons I'm not sure. But right before Dirk disappeared, Armand showed up in New York. There was a terrible confrontation and many threats were made. In a rage, Villeneuve even smashed one of the display cases for the jewelry. Your father found it hard to believe that his brother Dirk had anything to do with the theft. He always suspected Villeneuve was responsible.''

''Why didn't you tell this to the family?''

''After the theft, they didn't want to speak of it. Charles was convinced that Dirk was responsible, and he thought any investigation into Villeneuve's motives might end up in the press, making the family vulnerable. But two of the stolen pieces had been promised to Marie-Claire on the day of her wedding to Jean-Luc du Plessis, the man she married shortly after she and Armand ended their engagement. Armand may have stolen them to spite her, and taken a few more pieces for good measure.''

''Mother, I want you to talk to Santos. He's not going to go away until he knows everything you do. I want my father's name cleared of this suspicion.''

Maura smiled. ''I suppose I could do that for my favorite son.''

Chuckling, Sloan bent to kiss her on the cheek. ''I bet you say that to all your sons.''

She patted him on the cheek and turned her attention back to her flower arrangement. ''Tell me, is everything going well at the store?''

Sloan nodded. ''Sure. Why do you ask?''

''You seem bothered by something. Would you like to talk about it?''

''No,'' he said. ''It's nothing I can't handle on my own.''

As Sloan watched his mother arrange the roses in the crystal vase, he was tempted to confide everything—his growing confusion over the sale of the store, his growing infatuation with Chloe Durrant, and his growing concern for the mysterious child, Madeline.

In the end, he kept it all to himself. After all, he was the general manager of DeWilde's Fifth Avenue. If he couldn't handle these problems, who would?

"LOOK AT THIS! This has gone too far. My lovely beaded bags tossed about as if they were at some trashy tag sale."

Chloe was standing in the middle of the bridal accessories department. Mrs. Llewellyn, the department manager, stood next to her, an angry scowl on her aristocratic face. Like so many of the sales managers and clerks at De-Wilde's, Mrs. Llewellyn had worked at the store for years, aging right along with the store's clientele. And she considered bridal accessories her own personal domain.

Chloe glanced down at the subject of Mrs. Llewellyn's concern and felt a blush heat her cheeks. Around a lovely Queen Anne table, white beaded handbags lay scattered on the floor, tumbled down from Mrs. Llewellyn's precisely arranged display.

"It's that security guard, Walter," the sales manager said. "He's having a liaison with the cleaning lady, Bernice. It's not a big secret, the whole store knows about it. One of the other guards caught them kissing in the beauty salon one night."

"A liaison?" Chloe asked hesitantly.

Mrs. Llewellyn held up a fistful of hairpins. "I found these on the floor among the bags. For all we know they could have had an—" she lowered her voice "—assignation, right here on this very table. Disgusting. It has to stop. I will not have my displays torn apart by—by uncontrolled passion."

Uncontrolled passion. At least Mrs. Llewellyn had that right, though she had the participants wrong. What she and Sloan had shared on this table had been plaguing her mind for too long.

How had things gotten so out of hand? She'd spent the entire day Sunday worrying over their indiscretion in the bridal department, wondering just how she'd be able to face him on Monday. She knew it would be impossible to forget the brief flare of passion that had ignited between them, the touch of his hands on her skin, the feel of his tongue invading her mouth.

But then, to be reminded of it all by Mrs. Llewellyn. Well, it was an embarrassment, sheer and utter mortification. Something she never wanted to go through again. She didn't need this kind of stress in her life.

"What would you like me to do?" Chloe asked, trying to sound detached and in control.

Satisfied that she was going to get a swift and proper response to her complaint, Mrs. Llewellyn considered the point for a moment. "I think you should have a talk with the parties involved. Tell them that they should keep their feelings under control when in the store. DeWilde's is an institution in this city, known for good taste, not cheap and tawdry lust."

Chloe swallowed hard and forced an understanding smile. "You're absolutely right, Mrs. Llewellyn." She plucked the hairpins from the department manager's hand. "I'll just take these," she murmured. "As evidence."

Chloe headed directly for the executive suite, taking the stairs rather than risking the chance of meeting any of the employees in the elevator. Though everyone was sure Walter and Bernice were the culprits, she knew the truth. She and Sloan had been carried away by their own "uncontrolled passion." And it was about time to rein that passion in.

The ninth-floor executive suite was silent as she hurried into the outer office. "Is he in?" she asked, not waiting for Miss Crenshaw to answer. Chloe knocked on Sloan's door then flung it open, again not waiting for an answer.

Sloan sat at his desk, her sketches for the new window design spread out in front of him, his expression intent yet slightly confused. "Edna," he murmured. "Please have Ms. Durrant step into my office, would you?"

Chloe frowned. She was getting a little tired of being mistaken for Edna Crenshaw. How much time did those two spend together? Soon the DeWilde rumor mill would have a new duo to gossip about around the water cooler—Edna and Sloan. "Ms. Durrant is already here," she said, closing the door behind her.

Sloan glanced up in surprise. "Whoa. I knew Miss Crenshaw was good at her job, but I didn't realize she was psychic, as well. I was just thinking about you and here you are."

"We have to talk," Chloe said. "This has gotten way out of hand."

Sloan looked down at the sketches. "I do have some questions, but I think I've made the best choice."

"I'm not talking about the designs," Chloe said in frustration. "I'm talking about—" she lowered her voice "—Bernice and Walter."

His gaze snapped up to hers and he stared at her, then shook his head. "Who are Bernice and Walter?"

"They're us!" Chloe cried. "You and me."

Sloan leaned back in his chair and studied her openly. "I know *you* know what you mean, but maybe you could explain it to me."

"Look at these," she said, approaching his desk. She tossed the hairpins on his desk, where they scattered across her pencil drawings. "Mrs. Llewellyn found these on the floor of the bridal department this morning, along with all her precious beaded bags. Couldn't you have picked up after you—I mean, we—" Chloe sighed, trying to collect her scattered thoughts, but she couldn't seem to bring herself to say more.

"I take it these are your hairpins?" Sloan asked.

"Of course they are. You're the one who pulled them out of my hair. Or don't you remember?"

Sloan grinned. "I remember a lot of things about you, Ms. Durrant, but your brand of hairpins isn't one of them. Now, your hair, that's something I—"

"We cannot continue like this," Chloe interrupted. "I'm even more certain of it now than ever before. If we don't stop things right here, the whole store is going to know. They'll all be talking about us instead of Bernice and Walter."

He stood up and circled the desk, Chloe watching him. He moved with such unabashed masculine grace that she couldn't help but admire him. Slowly, he approached, each step causing her to take one of her own backward, until she bumped up against the edge of his desk. She braced her hands behind her.

"Let them talk," he said.

"That's easy for you to say. Your reputation is already a mess. They've been talking about you and your women for years. But I still have a reputation left to protect at De-Wilde's. I won't compromise my position here with idle gossip. The employees would lose all respect for me."

"What exactly would you like me to do?" he asked softly.

Her heart pounded in her chest and her pulse drummed through her veins. Clenching her fingers around the edge of the desk, she tried to quell the urge to reach out and touch him.

"I want you to leave me alone," she said, the words spoken with sheer determination.

"That's going to be hard, considering we have to work so closely together," he replied.

"You know what I mean. I'm not talking about work. I'm talking about this. What you're doing to me now."

Sloan glanced around the office, his gaze resting meaningfully on the drawings behind her. "We *are* working. We're discussing your new window designs, aren't we?"

"This is not about work!" Chloe cried. "This is about . . . well, certainly not work!"

"What is it you want from me, Chloe?" he murmured, standing so close she could feel his heat warm her skin. She fixed her gaze on his chest, examining the paisley design on his silk tie and stubbornly refusing to look at him. He shifted and she watched as his shirt tautened over the muscles of his chest.

"Would you like me to kiss you?" he asked, his voice rich and seductive.

Jerking her head up, she met his teasing eyes, a flood of heat rushing into her cheeks.

"If you'd like me to kiss you, I will," he continued, reaching out to lightly trace a line along her jaw. "All you have to do is ask."

"I don't want you to kiss me," Chloe said. "Never again. I don't want you to even touch me."

"Hmm. Are you sure? Remember, I'm not your boss anymore."

Chloe stepped to the side, breaking away from the powerful magnetism of his body. "I think we'd better get to work," she said.

A long silence grew between them. She risked another glance at him, only to find him watching her, an enigmatic expression on his handsome features. "All right," he replied with a shrug. "If that's what you want. We'll simply forget what happened between us."

"It'll be easy," Chloe said reassuringly, more in an attempt to convince herself. "We just won't allow ourselves to get . . . personal. Everything will be strictly business."

He smiled seductively. "Believe me, Ms. Durrant, nothing about you is easy. But if you ever want me to kiss you like that again, all you have to do is ask. I'll be happy to oblige."

Chloe drew a shaky breath and stepped behind his desk. "I'm sure that won't happen. Now, back to business. Which design do you like?" she asked, hoping desperately that a change of subject would calm her frazzled nerves.

"I've made my choice, but I'll just take one more look to be sure," he said.

Slowly he walked along the length of the desk behind her, staring at the three window designs, so close she could feel the gentle brush of his breath on her exposed neck. As he moved from side to side, she watched him surreptitiously, stealing a look every now and then.

She found her attention drawn to his mouth as he hooked his thumb under his chin and tapped his lips with his index finger, concentrating on the choice before him. Distractedly, she reached up and touched her own lips, wondering why they suddenly tingled.

How was she supposed to forget all that had happened between them when she couldn't stop thinking about it? Sloan DeWilde held a strange power over her, a fascination that she couldn't deny. He had a way of making her feel as if she were the most desirable woman on the face of the earth, as if he, too, spent every waking hour thinking about her.

She hadn't felt like this for so long, not since Julien had torn her confidence to shreds. She'd never been able to please Julien, in or out of bed. But Sloan seemed pleased with just a simple touch, a brief kiss, a longing glance. He challenged her to forget her inhibitions, to put her doubts aside and explore what lay between them.

How could she *not* think that things between them would be good? Very good. In fact, knowing Sloan, he'd probably make sure they were absolutely fantastic. The complaint box on his bedpost was in all likelihood filled with cobwebs. He'd be a wonderful, sensitive, passionate lover. He would—

Chloe squeezed her eyes shut for an instant, attempting to put such crazy thoughts out of her mind. Forgetting what had happened between them would be much easier if she didn't keep thinking about it!

She glanced over at Sloan. Obviously, he had no problems putting *her* out of his mind. As he stood beside her, studying the designs, he acted as if they had shared nothing more than a professional relationship.

Chloe pulled her fingers from her lips and clasped her hands behind her back. But wasn't that exactly what she wanted, what she'd been asking of him for days? He was only respecting her wishes.

She should be happy she'd finally gotten through to him. She bit her bottom lip. Then why did she feel so bereft? Why did she have to force herself to stop fantasizing about him?

"I like this one," he said, reaching out to point to the sketch in the center.

"Good," she said absently, turning to look at him. Her gaze drifted from his dark hair curling over the back of his starched collar to his firm jaw. "That's good."

He picked up the design and held it out in front of him. "I must say, I'm impressed with your work."

She looked down at the sketch, then drew in a sharp breath, startling herself out of her daydream. "You like *that* one?"

He gave her a sideways glance. "That's what I said. This is the one. When will you change the windows?"

She snatched the paper out of his hand. "But—but you can't like this one," she stammered. It was possibly the most unimaginative design she'd ever done. She'd shown more creativity coloring within the lines in first grade. And Chloe Durrant hated coloring inside the lines! "This design is terrible, cliché. Boring."

Sloan arched his brow. "I don't understand."

"I'm just not happy with it," she replied, backpedaling. "Not anymore. Choose another one."

He reached out and took the drawing on the right. "All right. This one."

Chloe stifled a groan of frustration. Was he doing this on purpose? She knew he possessed very little talent for retailing, but the man owned an art gallery. He should be able to distinguish between good design and the work of a purposeful hack.

"I don't like that one, either."

"Well, I like it," Sloan countered. "But I like the first one better. How long will it take to change the windows, Ms. Durrant? Can we have it done over the weekend?"

"But how can you like this one? White handbags and shoes lined up in rows like little soldiers, embroidered handkerchiefs folded neatly over a rod and little boxes of perfume in a large window! It would take binoculars to see them."

"If this concept is so bad, why did you present it to me?" Sloan asked.

Chloe shifted uneasily, then looked away. She couldn't tell him the truth, that she had fixed the contest. That she'd expected he might have some taste. "It's just not my favorite."

"Well, it's mine," he said.

She turned to him. "I should be making these choices. I'm the director of visual merchandising and advertising."

"You're the merchandising manager," Sloan countered. "And I've been meaning to talk to you about that."

Chloe grabbed the sketch out of his hands. "Here it comes."

"Here what comes?" Sloan asked.

"You know exactly what! You're going to fire me! I knew this was coming. This is exactly why I was against anything but a professional relationship between us. I refuse to kiss you anymore and you fire me. I knew what happened between us would affect my job here. I never should have let you kiss me. I should have—"

Sloan reached out and placed his fingers over her mouth. "I'm not planning to fire you, Chloe. Hell, I just hired you. I simply thought we should discuss hiring a new display person. And a new assistant for you, for that matter. You've been working very hard. Too hard." He smiled crookedly. "I think the strain is starting to show."

"I'll hire an assistant," Chloe mumbled from beneath his finger. "Soon. But I'm perfectly able to design the visuals, as well."

He shook his head. "But it's no longer your responsibility. I want you to begin a search for your replacement immediately. You should be more concerned with all the administrative tasks you have."

"I can do both jobs," she argued.

"I have other things I want you to focus on."

She shot him a wary look.

"You're going to have plenty to do working with the buyers," he told her. "We've discussed your ideas for changing our merchandising strategy, and I think you should be concentrating on those goals."

"But the buyers have already placed their spring orders and there's very little left on their open-to-buy. The most I can do right now is work with what they've ordered and wait until next fall's merchandise starts showing."

"Ms. Durrant, take my advice. Hire a new director of visual merchandising."

"Is that an order?" she asked.

"It's a recommendation. You're going to have to meet with Jeffrey DeWilde and I want you to be sure you know every nook and cranny of this store, including all the duties of the merchandising manager. That is, if you want to keep this job. You won't have time to do the visuals and get everything else under control."

Chloe crossed her arms over her chest, reluctant to acknowledge that he was probably right. "I suppose I can turn over the visuals to Gina Calafano. She's worked in display before and she and I have the same taste."

"That would be fine, just as long as someone else is doing the work." He handed her his choice of window designs. "Have Ms. Calafano get to work on the new windows immediately. I want them up as soon as possible."

With that, he walked to his office door and pulled it open. "Thank you, Ms. Durrant," he said, his voice coolly efficient and purposefully distant.

Rendered speechless by his strange behavior, Chloe slowly walked to the doorway. She gave him one last look before she stepped through. The door nearly hit her on the backside as it swung shut behind her.

Edna held up a pink message slip as Chloe numbly walked past the desk. "Miss Calafano called. The ad proofs are ready. She'd like you to stop by the art department as soon as you have the opportunity."

Chloe plucked the message out of Edna's hand and continued right out of the executive suite. "Am I losing my mind?" she murmured as she walked down the silent hallway to the elevator. "I'm making a complete fool of myself over this man. I need a good shrink." She punched the down button on the elevator. "Or maybe I need a cold shower," she said as she stepped through the doors. She hesitated, then pushed the fourth-floor button. "But first I need chocolate. Large quantities of chocolate."

The candy counter was busy when she arrived, and she stood in line, watching as the clerk passed boxes and bags of handmade chocolates over the display cases in exchange for DeWilde's navy blue credit card.

"Good morning, Ms. Durrant," the salesclerk said, once the customers had all been cared for.

Chloe glanced at the woman's gold nametag and smiled. "Good morning, Agnes. I'd like five of the pecan Turtles with the dark chocolate. And some of those cashew clusters. And throw in a few of those Amaretto truffles."

The clerk nodded curtly, then pulled out an ornate silver tray from the case.

"So," Chloe said. "How have sales been going in candy?"

Agnes snorted and shook her head disgustedly. "They'd be going fine if it weren't for Mr. DeWilde," she muttered. "Our markdowns have been way out of line."

"Mr. DeWilde?"

"He sent down a memo ordering us to give free candy to children. Anything they choose. Yesterday, I gave away nearly $100 worth of the finest Belgian chocolates. Truffles! To children! They'd be happy with bubble gum and we're giving away hand-dipped masterpieces of chocolate confection."

"I don't understand," Chloe said. "This was Mr. De-Wilde's request? *Sloan* DeWilde?"

"That's what the memo said. Free candy to any child that comes into the store."

Chloe frowned. "I suppose it's a good idea. We do want to appeal to a younger customer, a customer with a family possibly." But she found it hard to believe that Sloan had made this connection on his own. He tossed most reports on target demographics aside with the comment that they contained too many columns and rows of numbers. "I just didn't know Mr. DeWilde liked children."

Agnes stuck out her lower lip as she contemplated the comment. "Well, I suppose he does," she said. "I've seen him about the store with a young girl and he treats her very fondly. She must be a niece or the child of a friend. He's quite good with her. Always buying her special treats."

Chloe took the bag of chocolates from Agnes's outstretched hand and signed her employee charge slip. "I guess Mr. DeWilde is just full of surprises."

"That man is full of more than surprises," Agnes replied.

As Chloe rode the escalator down one floor to Gina's office, she distractedly munched on a Turtle and considered what she'd been told. Sloan was the last man in the world she'd expect to harbor an affection for small children.

But then, maybe she didn't know the real Sloan DeWilde at all. And maybe she'd just squandered her last opportunity to find out who he really was.

CHAPTER SEVEN

AUDREY PLACED HER HANDS on either side of her face and peered into the candy case. Her warm breath clouded the glass as she perused her choices. "I'll have a piece of the fairy food," she said. "Not too big." She pointed to a spot on the silver tray. "I want that one, the one that looks like Nevada."

The salesclerk plucked the proper piece out with silver tongs and dropped it in a pretty DeWilde's bag, then handed it to Audrey.

"How much?" Audrey asked, digging in her pocket for the remains of her lunch money.

The clerk shook her head and forced a gracious smile. "It's free," she muttered.

"Really?" Audrey asked, looking down at the bag, then back up at the salesclerk. "Cool! Can I have a Turtle, too?"

The clerk raised a haughty brow. "Only one piece per child," she said. "That's all we're allowed to give."

With a shrug, Audrey turned and headed toward the escalators. As she walked, she kept one eye out for the security guard who usually prowled the fourth floor. The old guy moved kind of slow, so she didn't consider him much of a threat, but he did have a gun and holster. And he wouldn't have a gun and holster unless he had used it once or twice.

But it wasn't the uniformed guard who caught her attention as she stepped off the escalator onto the third floor. Another man, tall and dark and a bit menacing in appearance, had been following her since she left the sixth-floor ladies' lounge. He wore a tie and a light-colored suit, so at first she didn't pay much notice. But then she'd caught him staring at her from behind the pillar in the candy department and decided to see just what he was doing there.

As soon as she hit the third floor, she hurried around to the up escalator, hoping to lose him by doubling back. But when she looked down from between the third and fourth floor, there he was, one flight below her and closing in fast.

Pushing past a large lady with three shopping bags, Audrey hurried up the final steps, glancing back every few seconds. She reached the fourth floor, then set off at a run, veering sharply to her left into the luggage department. It was always quiet here, and the salesclerk usually filled in across the aisle in stationery. She stepped behind a huge stuffed gorilla that carried a set of designer luggage and scrunched down, pulling her knees to her chest.

She waited there, her heart racing. Geez, she should have stayed in the lounge and done her math like her mother had ordered. She would have, if she hadn't been so hungry. How was she supposed to know some goon would catch her? He was probably a cop or maybe the FBI, but either way, she couldn't risk being seen.

After counting to one hundred twice, she peeked over the top of a suitcase to find the aisle clear. She was just about to make a dash for the escalator when she saw Jack slowly strolling toward the candy counter. He stopped and stared at a display of briefcases, and she took off toward him.

"Boy, am I glad to see you," Audrey said, coming up behind him and grabbing his hand.

At first he was startled, but then he smiled down at her. Audrey blinked hard. Wow, she'd never noticed before, but when he smiled he looked just like her old Ken doll—except he had better clothes.

"Hey there, Madeline, I'm glad to see you again. What's up?"

"Some guy was after me," she said. "He's been following me around the store. I've been hiding out behind those suitcases practically forever."

Jack frowned. "Did he try to hurt you?"

"Nah," Audrey replied, glancing around. "He was tailing me but I lost him. Come on," she said, tugging on his hand.

Jack chuckled. "Where are you taking me?"

She dragged him toward a door at the back of the luggage department and pulled him inside. The dimly lit storeroom was piled from floor to ceiling with dusty boxes. She wove through the maze, crawling up and over boxes along the way, until she reached the back of the room, where a glass block window high on the wall provided a stream of light.

"Where are we?" Jack asked.

"I want to show you something," Audrey said. "It's back here."

The filtered sunlight fell on an old carousel horse, painted in faded reds and yellows and flaking golds. Audrey hopped up on the horse's back. "I found this yesterday. What do you think it's doing here?" She wrapped her arms around the horse's neck and stared up at him. "Do you think it came off a real carousel? It looks just like the ones in Central Park."

Jack shook his head. "Aren't you afraid someone's going to catch you back here?"

"Nah. The clerks only come back here if they need something, which is hardly ever, since sales in this department have been a little slow. And I know all the best hiding places. Nobody can find me in this place if I don't want to be found."

He watched her for a long moment. "So, how are things going?"

Audrey smiled. "Okay. I found a dollar on the sidewalk yesterday. And I got a free piece of candy." She paused. "Oh, yeah, I think my mom's flipped over some major dweeb. She hasn't brought him home yet, so I figure he must be pretty bad."

"Your mother dates?" Jack asked. "Men?"

Audrey sighed. "If that's what you call 'em. She doesn't do it very often—once every couple years. And it never lasts very long and most of the guys are pretty pitiful. At least they never sleep over." Audrey thought back a year to her mother's last "boyfriend," the stockbroker who drove the fancy sports car—the car with only two seats, one for him and one for her mom. She could tell *that* relationship was going nowhere from the start. "She hasn't said anything about this one yet, but I can tell something's going on with her. She's spending too much time on her hair and makeup in the morning. It won't be long before I'm looking at some dope across the dinner table and he's talking to me like I'm an alien being."

"Maybe you're mistaken," he said.

"Not a chance. Do you go out with lots of women?"

Of course, he probably had lots of dates. All the really neat guys did, especially if they looked like Ken.

Jack considered her question for a while before answering. "A few," he finally said.

She bit her bottom lip. "Do you ever sleep at their houses?"

He shook his head. "Never."

Audrey studied him discretely. This looked hopeful. After all, Jack was a nice guy. He bought her candy and took her out for ice cream. He was handsome, too. And from the way he dressed, he definitely knew how to shop. "How many seats do you have in your car?" she asked.

He frowned. "Four?"

Audrey sat up straight and wrapped her hands around the saddle horn. "I think *you* should go out with my mom."

Jack chuckled. "Sweetheart, I'm not sure you should be making dates for your mom. You don't even know me. I could be a real jerk when it comes to women."

She shook her head. "I know you're not a jerk."

Jack stared down at his shoes. "Well, maybe I am."

"You'd be a lot better than the guy she's mooning over now. She won't even let me meet him, so he's got to be really bad. Can't you just try? My mom is really pretty."

Jack reached out and covered her hands with his. "I've sort of got a lady friend right now," he said.

Audrey felt a flood of disappointment wash over her. "Is she nice?"

"Yeah, she's really nice."

"Are you going to marry her?"

"We haven't really talked about that yet," Jack said.

Audrey stretched out along the horse's neck, linking her hands over his nose. "My mom and dad weren't married."

"They weren't?" Jack asked.

"Nope. It's no big deal, but my mom doesn't like to talk about it. I kinda figured it out on my own since my mom's mom and dad have the same name as me. I never met my dad, but I think I might want to visit him sometime. My mom says he lives in France."

"France," Jack repeated. "That's a long way from here."

Audrey had looked at France on her globe every night for the past week. She'd almost asked her mom about going there but just couldn't work up the courage. Not because she was afraid to go to France, but because she suspected that her father didn't really want to see her. If he did, he would have asked her to visit a long time ago...but he hadn't.

It wasn't as if she really needed a father. Especially a father who didn't need her. She and Claude did all right by themselves. And having a father around would only make for one more person telling her what to do. All she really wanted to know was the truth about him and her mom. Once she found that out, she figured she would have to find another father, anyway.

She sighed. "Maybe I'll go and maybe I won't. I haven't decided yet."

A long silence grew between them. Jack patted her hand. "You know, I think I would like to meet your mom. I'd like to talk to her."

Audrey looked up at him, her suspicions on alert. She frowned. "Yeah, maybe. I'll have to think about it for a while."

"No, really," Jack insisted. "I would like to meet her."

Audrey slid off the carousel horse and headed back through the luggage storeroom. "I gotta go now," she said.

"Hey, wait," Jack called, following her.

"I gotta go!" Audrey picked up her pace, weaving through the maze of boxes until she reached the door. She could hear him fumbling around behind her, cursing under his breath as he ran into dead ends. By the time he emerged, she'd found a hiding spot behind a stack of steamer trunks. She watched as he scanned the department looking for her, then slipped back behind the display when he turned her way.

If her mom found out she'd been wandering around the store, she'd put an end to all her afternoon adventures. And Jack would probably tell her how they met. After all, Jack was an adult and adults tended to stick together when kids disobeyed orders.

Besides, he wasn't really interested in dating her mom. Maybe she'd just have to take a look at the new dweeb and see if her mother's taste had improved over the past year. Heck, he might not be *that* bad. He might even like kids.

SLOAN WATCHED from a distance as Chloe fussed with the position of a mannequin's arm before she stepped back to study the entire display. She stood in the middle of the ladies' designer cruisewear department, a clipboard clutched in her hand, her attention focused on adjusting the trio of mannequins to her precise specifications.

He wasn't quite sure what to think about her concept for the display. The appearance of King Kong in the luggage department had caused such a stir that he couldn't even begin to predict what a benign trio of mannequins with television heads would do for DeWilde's conservative clientele. But he had to admit the display was clever. Already the first monitor was flickering with images of the South Seas—turquoise waters and pristine beaches and swaying palm trees.

The more outlandish her displays, the more customers seemed to be drawn to them . . . and the more he found himself drawn to her. By now he'd realized that if he ever hoped for his plan to succeed, he'd have to find another way of stifling Chloe's creativity. There had to be some way to keep her busy outside of the display department.

He glanced over at her and watched as she attempted to untangle a mess of cables. This morning, she was dressed in a baggy, short-sleeved chartreuse sweater and a purple suede miniskirt, her clothes a brilliant flash of color against the conservative taupes and maroons of the display. The miniskirt revealed her long, slender legs and tiny feet, clad in purple tights and purple shoes. A wildly patterned scarf was wrapped through her pale, curly hair—her own hair today.

Sloan slowly strolled over to her side and gazed up at the display. "You're lucky I didn't catch you dressing that mannequin, Ms. Durrant. I'd have been forced to believe that you haven't found a new display manager yet."

Chloe turned, eyes wide with surprise. She took a step around the back of the display, neatly avoiding any possible contact. "These old mannequins are so hard to work with," she complained. "It takes a day just to find enough intact limbs to put a body together. We had a mannequin in cruisewear that was missing two fingers and her left foot. It looked as if she'd had a run-in with a shark."

"Why don't you buy new mannequins?" Sloan asked, stepping back to her side.

Chloe turned and frowned at him. "Probably because we don't have the budget for new mannequins."

Sloan forced back a flood of desire as two spots of color rose in her cheeks. He could tell she was working herself into another one of her "keep-your-distance" speeches. For such a prickly woman, how the hell did she manage to look so damned sexy! "You're in charge of the merchandising budget," he challenged. "Find the money. But before that, find a new display manager."

She shook her head. "Why do you care if I continue to do both jobs?" she asked, turning back to the display. "We could save my salary and buy new mannequins."

"Hire a new display manager, Ms. Durrant," he repeated.

Chloe glared at him. "I will. Soon."

Sloan smiled, satisfied that he'd made his point. "By the way," he said, "I just got a call from Jeffrey DeWilde's London office. He's stopping in New York on his way to some business meeting in Toronto. We're having dinner with him at the Rainbow Room tonight. Formal dress." Sloan smiled cynically. "I do believe Jeffrey came out of the womb dressed in a tux."

"The Rainbow Room?" Chloe asked, her green eyes wide. "Tonight?"

Sloan nodded. "I hope you're ready."

An uneasy look crossed her face. "Can you excuse me for a moment? I just remembered I have to call Gina—about one of the displays. I'll just be a minute." Chloe rushed over to one of the register tables and picked up the phone, while Sloan idly straightened a rack of silk blazers. After a few hastily whispered instructions, a relieved smile broke across her expression and she hung up the phone.

"Jeffrey can be a tough old nut when he wants to be," Sloan said when she rejoined him. "He's got to approve your appointment, so if I were you, I'd be prepared to answer a lot of questions."

She winced. "What do you think he'll ask me? No, no, tell me what he's like first. He's British, isn't he?"

"They all are," Sloan muttered. "We call them the Royals." He started down the aisle and she fell into step beside him, shooting questions at him with each step. Every so often, her arm would brush up against his as she listened intently to his responses. He fought the urge to reach out and draw her against his body, effectively replacing one torment with another. He remembered the feel of her fingers in his, so delicate with skin as soft as rose petals.

Touching her had become an almost daily obsession with him. On their morning walk-throughs, rather than markdowns and inventory, he found himself thinking about the feel of her hair between his fingers, the touch of his fingers on her cheek, the heat of her body against his and the taste of her lips. But he'd had to hold himself back, knowing that any move on his part would be met with total and uncompromising resistance.

He allowed Chloe to move a few steps in front of him, half listening to her side of the conversation and admiring her from behind as she walked. She possessed an innate grace, her every movement stirring a strange desire within him. Sloan stopped and closed his eyes, tipping his head back and stifling a groan. Lord, he *was* obsessed. But what was it about Chloe Durrant that fascinated him so?

He suspected it was the fact that she showed absolutely no susceptibility to his charms. Lately, when they were together, she seemed to operate under some unwritten rule that prohibited anything more than a friendly association with her co-worker. She'd managed to forget the intimacies they'd shared without much trouble at all. He'd never met a woman so immune to his overtures.

"I don't have a thing to wear," she cried, realizing he was no longer beside her. He deliberately bumped into her from behind, then grasped her shoulders, allowing his hands to drift down her upper arms. She turned quickly and stepped away from him, giving him a warning look.

"Ms. Durrant, you're standing in the middle of a department store," Sloan said. "I wouldn't consider that a major problem. If I were you, I'd head to designer eveningwear and find a dress. Jeffrey likes to see his executives wearing DeWilde's merchandise."

She glanced down at her chartreuse and purple outfit, then back up at him. "He won't like me," she said, starting down the empty aisle toward the escalator.

"He hates me, too," Sloan replied with a grin. "So you'll be in good company."

"Jeffrey DeWilde hates you?" Chloe asked, turning back to him. "You never told me this."

"The two branches of the family don't get along very well. We've had a long-standing difference of opinion. He's never cared for the way I run this store."

Chloe gripped the handrail of the escalator. "Well, if he hates you, he'll hate me by default."

"He'll like you," Sloan replied. "Just tell him about all your plans for the store. He likes anyone who likes De-Wilde's."

"You didn't like me when you first met me. In fact, you hated me."

Sloan chuckled. "Who told you that?"

"I could tell. I knew we weren't going to get along."

"But you were wrong, weren't you," Sloan said, reaching out to grasp her fingers in his as she stepped off the escalator. He tucked her hand in the crook of his elbow, and this time she didn't pull away. "We get along just fine. We have a very good working relationship."

"I'm glad you're going to be there," Chloe said softly. "I mean, at the Rainbow Room, when I meet Jeffrey De-Wilde. I'm probably going to be a little nervous so it will be nice to have someone there I know. I want to make a good impression. What do you think I should wear?"

"I'll help you choose something," Sloan said. "I have excellent taste in women's clothing."

She shot him a sideways glance and laughed. "Why am I not surprised?"

"Gee, maybe retailing does run in my blood," he said in mock mortification. "Just don't let Jeffrey know. I wouldn't want to raise his low opinion of me."

The fifth floor was silent when Chloe and Sloan walked to the luxurious salon. A rainbow of gowns, beaded and sequined, taffeta and chiffon, glittered under track lighting. The sales floor lights were turned on an hour before the store opened to allow sales managers and clerks to rack new merchandise. But the eveningwear salon was empty of store personnel.

Sloan went right to the rack, made a good guess at her size and methodically flipped through the hangers. He stopped when he found exactly what he was looking for, a dress he knew would set off her eyes and her incredible hair. "Try this one," he said, holding the dress out to her.

"I can't try this on," Chloe objected.

"Why not?"

"Well, there's no salesclerk here," she said. "We can't just barge in and—"

"I'm the general manager and you're the merchandising manager. This is our store, Ms. Durrant. We can do whatever we want. Now take the dress and try it on."

Reluctantly, Chloe held out the dress, her gaze taking in the sequined, floor-length sheath the color of emeralds. To his relief, she didn't look at the back, which was, in a word, nonexistent. Sloan sat down on a couch and watched the closed door of the fitting room. He imagined her slowly undressing, only a few feet away, and he was tempted to step into the fitting room and help her with a zipper—or two.

In his mind, they were no longer in the store but in a luxurious suite at the Plaza, or maybe in his apartment. He imagined her in the bathroom, slipping into something more comfortable, while he waited, stretched out on the bed. And when the door opened, she would come to him, dressed in a gown that was so sheer it left little to the imagination, a gown that would soon lie puddled on the floor around her feet.

The fantasy slowly shifted and she was dressed in white, a wedding dress made of yards and yards of silk taffeta. He worked at the tiny buttons along her back, kissing each inch of skin he exposed, with each touch, realizing how lucky he was to have found her, to have found a woman to spend his life wi—

Sloan sucked in a sharp breath and yanked himself out of his daydream. What the hell was he thinking? Marriage? To Chloe? He'd never even considered the possibility in the past, so why now? How had Chloe Durrant managed to do what so many other women never could?

It was lust, pure and simple. He was confusing his desire for her with something else. Something like love, for instance. He didn't love Chloe. He didn't! Did he?

"Are you still out there?" she called.

He cleared his throat and shifted in his chair. "Yes, I'm still here," he called back. "Was I right? Come out and show me."

"I don't know. It's very... daring."

"Let me be the judge of that, Ms. Durrant."

A moment later, Chloe stepped out of the dressing room into the large open area of the salon, her bare feet sinking into the plush carpeting as she walked. The gown fit as if it were made for her, hugging every curve of her luscious body.

She turned around in front of him. The dress plunged to the base of her spine, ending well below the small of her back and the skirt was slit to mid-thigh, revealing a long length of bare leg with every step. Her skin seemed to glow and he ached to touch her, the urge so strong he felt a tightening between his thighs.

"Wow," Sloan said. "I was right."

A smile curled her lips. "Yes, you were. And I think my first duty as merchandising manager should be to name you eveningwear buyer. You have uncanny instincts, Mr. DeWilde. I love it." She paused. "Unfortunately, I can't afford it. This gown would cost me a month's salary at least."

"You don't have to buy it," Sloan said. "You can borrow it. I'll make all the arrangements and have it sent up to your office."

"But I couldn't," she protested. "What if I—"

He held up his hand. "Ms. Durrant, you forget yourself. You're representing DeWilde's now. Of course you'll wear our merchandise. You wouldn't be seen in anything else."

"Well, if you insist," she said. "I do want to create a good impression."

"You'll create a whole lot more than a good impression in that dress," he said. He stood and immediately buttoned his suit jacket, hiding his uncontrolled reaction to her. If he were smart, he'd make his exit before desire got the better of him and he pulled her into the fitting room for a romantic interlude. He'd have plenty of time to admire Chloe Durrant in that dress. For now, he had other plans to make.

"Our dinner reservation is for eight. I'll pick you up at your apartment at seven-thirty. Where do you live?"

An uneasy look crossed her face, a look that he suddenly realized he'd seen more than once. He bit back a curse. Just what, or who, was she hiding at home? At first he'd thought it was simply her natural reticence, but now he realized that whenever he mentioned her home life she seemed to go silent.

"Actually, I was thinking that I'd stay at the store," she said. "I'm going to try to get an appointment at the salon and let them do my hair. I'll take a cab and meet you there."

Sloan studied her for a long moment. "Be out in front of the store at precisely eight o'clock," he said, then quickly held up his hand to stop a further excuse on her part. "And don't bother arguing with me, Ms. Durrant. Just do as I ask."

He turned on his heel and walked out of the salon, a satisfied smile curving his lips. Jeffrey DeWilde and his sort may have just accomplished what Sloan had been working on for weeks.

Hell, maybe the Royals were good for something after all.

THE STORE WAS DARK as Chloe made her way to the front entrance. A security guard stood watch over the door. He smiled at her as she approached, as if he had been expecting her. Chloe smiled to herself. Sloan had taken care of everything.

As he promised, the dress had been delivered to her office by a salesclerk at four o'clock. Chloe had pulled it out of the DeWilde's garment bag and hung it on the back of her door, admiring it from her desk. Shoes in a selection of sizes, an assortment of evening bags and expensive hosiery had followed on the half hour, adding to her anticipation.

At five o'clock, she had met Audrey in front of the store and given her careful instructions before she sent her home with Gina, promising her uncharacteristically sullen daughter that she'd wake her up when she got home.

At precisely five-thirty, a delivery boy had arrived with a white paper box. Chloe had peeked inside, realizing that Sloan had also been kind enough to send a plate of sliced fruit and cheese to tide her over until dinner.

Ten minutes later, Miss Crenshaw had knocked at her door and walked in with a huge vase of white roses. The card simply read, "Good luck tonight" and was signed with a flamboyant "S."

On Thursday nights, the store closed at six, but Chloe had managed to convince the salon's best hairdresser to stay a few minutes later to fix her hair. To her surprise, when she had arrived at the salon, a staff of three had been waiting to do hair, makeup and nails.

Now, as she stepped through the front door of the store, she felt like a princess going to a fairy-tale ball. Was this what it was like in Sloan DeWilde's world—to have every whim catered to, to dress in expensive clothes and eat at the best restaurants, to dine with the CEO of a chain of world-famous bridal stores? How different his world was from hers...everything so easy, yet so exhilarating.

"Miss Durrant?"

Chloe looked up to find a silver-haired man in a chauffeur's uniform standing in front of her. The sidewalk was busy, but pedestrians steered a wide path around the hulk of a man.

"I'm Lew. I'll be your driver tonight." With that, he stepped aside, clearing a path for her, and motioned to a waiting limousine.

She half expected Sloan to be inside, but all that she found was an open bottle of champagne chilling on ice and a single crystal flute. With a giggle, Chloe poured herself a half glass of bubbly and settled back into the soft leather seats for the six-block trip to Rockefeller Center.

In the waning light of the evening, Rockefeller Center was lit up like a jewel in the midst of midtown Manhattan. Lew helped her out of the limo at the entrance to the G.E. Building with the explanation that Mr. Sloan would be waiting for her "upstairs."

As she walked up to the building, she stared at the 70-story facade, a masterpiece of modern architecture, so elegant yet so simple. The entrance was decorated with striking Art Deco mosaics and she paused to admire them before seeking out the elevator to the Rainbow Room.

Chloe shared the ride up to the sixty-fifth floor with an elevator full of tourists dressed in their Sunday best. Both the women and men sent admiring glances her way and she felt her confidence grow. She looked beautiful and she felt beautiful and it was all thanks to Sloan DeWilde. She'd meet his cousin Jeffrey and she would knock him dead with her beauty and her brains.

When the elevator doors opened and she stepped out, a young man in an old-fashioned porter's uniform approached her and asked if he might help her find her way. He accompanied her to the entrance of the Rainbow Room, and seconds later, a maître d' was leading her through the dining area to a quiet table near the huge windows. The city glittered below, broken only by the lush green expanse of Central Park, barely visible in the twilight.

Sloan stood and pulled out her chair for her. He was dressed in a tux and looked devastatingly handsome, the finely tailored jacket lying perfectly over his wide shoulders. "You look lovely," he murmured into her ear as she sat down.

"Thank you," she said, trying to control a sudden attack of nerves. "I take it Jeffrey hasn't arrived?"

Sloan shook his head and sat down in the chair next to her. "I can't imagine where he is. Jeffrey's never late. 'Tardiness is terribly bad form, old chap.' Maybe he ran into traffic. Or possibly his plane was delayed. But I'm sure I can entertain you until he arrives." He graced her with a dazzling smile, then called a waiter over to order her a drink.

A kir royale was prepared right at the table, and Chloe sipped her drink as she took in her posh surroundings. "I've never been here before."

"A shame," Sloan said. "You belong in a place like this." He slowly slid a navy velvet jewelry box across the table toward her. "I thought you might like these."

She reached out and touched the DeWilde's box, then drew her hand away.

"It's not a gift, just a loan," he said. "Go ahead. Open it."

With a tentative smile, she picked up the box and flipped the lid open to find a stunning pair of emerald earrings, each deep green stone surrounded by tiny diamonds that cascaded down and dangled to catch the light.

"The DeWilde's do have a way with jewelry," he said, watching her clip on the earrings. "That's how the dynasty started, with my great-grandfather, Maximilien. He trained with a diamond merchant in Amsterdam, then he and my great-grandmother, Anne Marie, started their own business in Amsterdam."

"I can't imagine what these cost," Chloe said. "I'm almost afraid to wear them."

"There's not a jewel in that store that could make you more beautiful than you already are. They're just baubles, Ms. Durrant, meant to be enjoyed like a pretty flower or a lovely sunset."

"Thank you for the roses," Chloe said. "I was so surprised when Miss Crenshaw brought them in. I think she was a bit surprised, too. I suspect she peeked at the card."

"So, are you ready?" Sloan asked. "Have you studied your DeWilde family history?"

Chloe blinked in astonishment. "Was I supposed to? You didn't tell me this."

He relaxed back into his chair and grinned at her. "It's all very easy. Max the First and Anne Marie had two children. Max the Second made his living fixing watches, and his sister, Marie, made her living designing jewelry. Max married Genevieve and they had the disappearing Dirk, the controlling Charles, my father, the heroic Henry, and Auntie Marie-Claire. And Charles begat Jeffrey. Jeffrey married Grace and they run the show. At least they did until Grace left the family fold to return to her own family in San Francisco. She and Jeffrey are separated."

"She's American?" Chloe asked.

"True blue."

"But I thought the DeWildes had a problem with Americans."

"Times change. And hell, Grace was good for business so her nationality could be overlooked."

"Tell me more," Chloe said.

Sloan wove a tapestry of stories, filling Chloe in on the colorful history of his father's family and the jewelry dynasty they built. She listened to his deep voice, not really paying attention to all the intricate family relationships but reveling in the warm sound of his words washing over her. When he finally finished, she glanced down at her watch, shocked to find that a whole hour had passed.

"I don't understand where Jeffrey could be," she said, craning her neck to watch the entrance.

"Neither do I," Sloan replied, as if he really didn't care.

She studied his satisfied smile, then glanced around the room again. As she looked back at him, she caught an odd expression on his face. Realization slowly dawned and a flood of temper rose inside her.

Jeffrey hadn't arrived because he never planned to come! "I can't believe this," she breathed.

"What?" Sloan asked.

"You! You set this all up. There never was a meeting with Jeffrey."

"What are you talking about?" Sloan said. "Of course there's a meeting with Jeffrey."

"You lied to me." Chloe snatched her linen napkin off her lap and tossed it onto the table. "You are despicable." She pushed her chair back and stood up. "I can't believe you'd do this," she whispered harshly. "This is so low. This is lower than low. You're nothing but a—"

"Miss Durrant?"

"What!" she snapped, spinning around to face a surprised maître d'.

"I'm sorry to intrude, but there's a phone call for you. A Mr. Jeffrey DeWilde?"

Chloe looked at Sloan suspiciously, then at the phone, then at Sloan again. "Is this some kind of trick?"

He shrugged. "You tell me. You're the one who has all the answers."

She snatched the phone from the maître d's hand. "Hello?"

"Miss Durrant? This is Jeffrey DeWilde." His clipped British accent was quite clear, even through the bad phone connection. "I'm sorry, but I'm afraid I'll have to excuse myself from dinner tonight. I'm still in the air. We got fogged in at Heathrow and I'll have all I can do to make my connecting flight to Toronto. Pressing business matters and all. I'm sure Sloan will be happy to entertain you. Please enjoy your evening and accept my sincere apologies. I will certainly meet you on my next trip to the States."

Chloe opened her mouth to speak, then frowned at Sloan.

"Miss Durrant? Are you still there?"

She swallowed hard. "Yes, Mr. DeWilde, I am. And I'm sorry we won't have an opportunity to meet."

"Please give my regards to Sloan, and have a lovely evening. And, Miss Durrant?"

"Yes?"

"We are quite happy to have you working for De-Wilde's. I do hope you know that."

"Thank you, sir," Chloe said.

The line went dead and she numbly handed the phone back to the maître d', then took her seat. "That was Jeffrey," she said.

Sloan grinned. "I gathered that. Had to beg off?"

Chloe braced her elbows on the table and covered her face with her hands. "I'm sorry."

Sloan reached across the table and pried her fingers from her face, one by one. "I don't blame you. I'm just surprised I didn't think of using Jeffrey as a ruse myself. It's so...me."

Chloe couldn't help but giggle. "I guess I'm just a little tense. Maybe it would be best if I went home."

"Absolutely not," Sloan said. "DeWilde's is picking up the tab, so I think we should have dinner as planned." Without waiting for her agreement, he motioned the waiter over and ordered a bottle of champagne.

They dined on Caesar's salad, then grilled swordfish in a red wine sauce and roast lamb, eating slowly as they chatted about inconsequential things—work, art, music, his family. Her champagne glass was always full, the delicate bubbles relaxing her until she couldn't remember why she'd ever refused to have dinner with him in the first place.

Sloan was a brilliant conversationalist, teasing her, making her laugh, asking her opinion on every subject they discussed and listening raptly to everything she said. She felt special, as if she and Sloan had connected somehow, gotten past their titles and job descriptions to the human beings underneath. Gone was her reticence and her resolve, replaced by a burning desire to know this man, to share something more with him than what they'd had up to now.

As they finished dessert, a chocolate basket filled with white chocolate mousse and a raspberry sauce, he reached across the table and placed his hand over hers. "I'm glad you decided to stay," he said, slowly drawing his fingers along the back of her hand.

"I am, too," Chloe replied.

Sloan wove his fingers through hers, then stood. "Dance with me," he said. "Just one dance."

Without a second thought, she joined him on the dance floor, stepping into his arms as the small combo played a Gershwin tune. He pulled her close against him, his fingers spread wide across her bare back, warm and firm on her skin.

One dance turned into two, then three, and soon after, she lost count. They didn't say a word, just moved in rhythm to the music, their bodies in sync. She floated between reality and all the fantasies that had captured her imagination since she'd met Sloan, the soft music weaving a spell around them. This seemed so right, to be here with him, in his arms.

Chloe nuzzled his neck and inhaled deeply, the scent of his cologne swimming in her head along with the champagne bubbles. His hand slowly slid up her back until he furrowed his fingers through the hair at the nape of her neck. He pulled her head back and lowered his mouth to hers, kissing her softly.

They kissed for a long time in the middle of the dance floor, sixty-five stories above the city. Yet even with all the people moving around them, and below them on the street, Chloe felt as if they were alone, two lovers who had finally found each other after years of searching.

Sloan's hands moved over her body as they danced, touching her where he could, learning every curve through the fabric of her dress. If they truly had been alone, she knew her dress would have been discarded long ago, allowing him to touch her where she longed to be touched.

But she was glad they were here, among people, for she wasn't sure she was ready to let Sloan love her, to open herself to him and all the possibilities he represented. She wanted to believe they might have a future together, yet common sense told her that theirs would be nothing more than a passing passion.

"I should really go," Chloe said, tipping her head back to look up at him.

"Stay," Sloan urged her, drawing her closer, his voice soft against her ear.

"We have to work tomorrow," she reasoned. "It's getting late."

"Forget work. I could hold you all night, just like this."

"Sloan, please," she protested.

"Say my name again," he demanded, staring down into her eyes.

"Sloan," she murmured.

He kissed her once more, long and deep, until her knees felt as if they might give way beneath her.

"I'll let you go... for now, Chloe," he finally said, his expression intense. "But one of these days soon, you aren't going to want to leave. You're going to face what's happening between us and realize it's something you can't control simply by ignoring it."

Then he gently turned her around and gave her a shove, sending her on her way back to the table. She glanced back to find him watching her from the middle of the dance floor, his arms crossed over his chest and an appreciative smile on his face. As she collected her purse and made her way to the door, she was aware he still watched her, and in that, she took an odd satisfaction.

She knew there would come a time when she could no longer walk away from him, when desire would overrule common sense and passion would outweigh the lessons of the past.

But instead of dreading such a prospect, she felt a surge of pure, shameless anticipation.

After all, it was just a matter of time.

CHAPTER EIGHT

"OUR MARKDOWNS in silver and gifts have increased the turn in that department to a respectable level," Chloe said. "I'd suggest we—" She swallowed hard. "I'd suggest we hold at this point with further price cuts and see what sales look like on Monday's flash report." Her eyes were fixed not on her notes but on Sloan's thumb, which was slowly stroking the inside of her wrist.

Chloe's office was silent except for the sound of Edna Crenshaw tapping on her computer keyboard in the outer office, the incessant rhythm audible even through the thick mahogany door. She closed her eyes and focused on the businesslike sound, trying to summon just a tiny shred of her resolve.

But Sloan seemed intent on destroying her concentration. From the moment he had sat down next to her at the conference table in her office, he'd found excuse after excuse to touch her. After only fifteen minutes, he'd forgotten he needed an excuse and touched her whenever the whim struck him—which now seemed to be continually. At this rate, she'd get through her report sometime next month.

"Very good," Sloan murmured distractedly, his fingers drifting along the sensitive skin of her inner arm.

She knew he wasn't listening to her. In fact, he probably hadn't heard a single word she had said, so transfixed was he by her limb. "Stop that," she said in a soft plea.

He lifted her arm and pressed his lips against her pulse point. "Stop what?" he asked, gazing deeply into her eyes.

A delicious shiver skittered down her spine. She forced back a sigh of pleasure. If she'd really wanted him to stop, she would have pulled her arm out of his grasp. But right now, her arm had a mind of its own, and that mind wanted more of Sloan's sweet teasing.

Since their evening together at the Rainbow Room, all bets were off. Over the past week, Sloan had begun a full-scale offensive that including taking advantage of every opportunity he had to touch her. And she wasn't able to muster any type of resistance.

Chloe cleared her throat. "I think we should move on."

"Mmm," Sloan said, leaning close to nuzzle her neck. "Let's move on." His mouth was warm on her throat, his breath heating her skin until she had no choice but to tip her head back and allow him to have his way.

"We shouldn't be doing this," she said, her words holding only a hint of conviction. They'd been doing this—and much more—for hours now, and neither one of them had been able to stop. "What if Miss Crenshaw walks in?"

"Miss Crenshaw is nothing if not discreet," Sloan said, his mouth moving slowly, inexorably toward her lips.

His kiss was deep and mind-numbing, dissolving Chloe's defenses so thoroughly she couldn't remember why she'd wanted him to stop. His tongue teased at hers, and with a tiny sigh, she wrapped her arms around his neck and gave in to his gentle seduction.

Sloan slowly stood, pulling her up with him, molding her body against his. She placed her hands flat against his muscular chest but couldn't bring herself to push him away. Beneath her fingertips and through the crisp, starched fabric of his shirt, she felt his heart beating strong and steady, such a contrast to her wildly rapid pulse.

His kiss became more demanding as they stumbled back against the wall. Drawing her thigh up along his, he shifted his hips against hers, the hard ridge of his desire evident through the fine fabric of his trousers. She moved slightly and he groaned, deep in his throat, responding to her inadvertent caress.

How could she resist this? When she was with Sloan, in his arms, she felt desirable, alluring, a sensual being who lived only for their next encounter. She was no longer Audrey's mother, or even DeWilde's merchandising manager. She was the object of Sloan's desire, and in that, she found a certain sense of who she really was as a woman.

Ever since Audrey had been born, she'd held men at arm's length. She'd buried her own needs, focusing all her attention on her responsibilities as a mother. For a very long time she'd believed that she would never feel unbridled passion for a man again, or complete trust. She'd never find a man who would love her beyond reason, beyond all else in the world.

But that rationalization had crumbled in the face of Sloan's determined pursuit. Day after day she fought him, but he'd gradually chipped away at her defenses, first with a touch, then a chaste kiss, and then much more. And now she realized that she wanted him as surely as he wanted her—completely, without reservations.

"Go on with your report, Ms. Durrant," he whispered in her ear. "I'm listening."

His hands slipped beneath her short-cropped sweater, skimming along her ribs until his palms cupped her breasts. He teased at her nipples with his thumbs, drawing them into hard peaks through the silky fabric of her bra. Chloe opened her mouth, but no words came out. Only a soft moan and his name, breathless with urgency.

"Mmm. I love it when you talk business to me," Sloan said, nipping at her earlobe.

Through a haze of passion, she heard her intercom buzzer sound, but she ignored it in favor of Sloan's whispered words. But the summons became more insistent until Sloan drew back and groaned.

"Answer it," he muttered.

Chloe slipped out from beneath his hands and hurried over to the phone. She drew a deep breath before punching the intercom button. "Yes, Miss Crenshaw?"

"Would you inform Mr. DeWilde that he has a visitor?" The intercom clicked off at Miss Crenshaw's end, inviting no reply. If Sloan's assistant knew what was going on in the office, she obviously had no reservations about interrupting it.

Chloe heard Sloan curse beneath his breath. "I'll tell him," she replied softly to herself. She turned and faced Sloan. "You have to go."

He raked his fingers through his hair, his jaw tense. "This has got to stop," he said, his frustration reflected in his hazel eyes.

"That's what I've been saying all along," Chloe replied.

"Damn it, that's not what I mean," he snapped. "We need more than a few minutes here and there, Chloe. We need time together, without any distractions."

"Time?"

"Alone, without phones, without Miss Crenshaw standing guard at the door and sales reports waiting to be analyzed. We need to get away from this store."

"What are you suggesting?"

"I don't know. You tell me. I've asked you every night for a week to have dinner with me, to spend more time together outside the store, and you always have an excuse. I've been a patient man, but either you want this or you don't, Chloe. It's time for *you* to make a decision here.''

"I—I want this," Chloe murmured. "I do. It's just not as simple as you think.''

"It *is* simple," Sloan said. "We're both adults here. Spend the weekend with me. We'll find out just what's going on between us, whether what we have will survive outside the rarefied atmosphere of this store."

"What if it doesn't?" Chloe asked. "What if all this . . . this passion you feel is simply because I'm forbidden fruit?''

Sloan leaned back against the wall and shook his head. "Don't you know how I feel about you, Chloe?''

She looked away and shrugged. "I know what you think you feel, but that isn't necessarily what you really feel.''

Sloan groaned and thumped his clenched fists against the paneled wall. "This isn't going to be another one of those strange forays into feminine logic, is it?''

"I'm just saying that we don't know each other very well and—''

"I know everything I need to know about you, Chloe. I know how much I've come to care for you. I know how much you mean to me. Sweetheart, you've changed my life, for the better.''

"I have?''

"Look at me. I'm working twelve-hour days at a job I used to despise. I live for the weekly flash reports. Hell, I've even figured out how to turn on my computer.'' He crossed the office and placed his hands on her shoulders. "I think about you all the time.''

Chloe felt a flood of affection rush through her. "I think about you, too.''

"Then what's standing in our way?" Sloan asked. "Tell me so I can fix it.''

"There are some things you don't know about me."

Sloan placed his finger on her lips, stopping her words. "I don't care," he said. "I don't care if there's another man, I don't care about your past. None of that makes any difference. It won't change the way I feel about you, Chloe, unless *you* let it. Just you and me, that's all that matters."

If only it were just the two of them. She wouldn't hesitate to accept his invitation. But she had to think about Audrey, as well. How could she let things go any further without telling him about her daughter? It wasn't fair to him, keeping such an important part of her life a secret.

She'd just never expected things to get so serious so quickly. She had thought Sloan would lose interest after a time and move on to someone more willing. But the more she pushed him away, the more determined he became.

And now, after all this time, she wondered whether telling him about her daughter might drive him out of her life for good. It could all be so simple. She could tell him now and end everything in a matter of minutes.

Or she could wait.

After all, how could she predict the future? How could she know what might happen between them tomorrow, or next week, or next month, for that matter? What they shared might just be a passing fling, a momentary passion between co-workers.

But she wouldn't really know—until she took a chance.

"All right," Chloe said. "I think we should spend the weekend together."

Sloan bent his head and brushed a kiss along her lips. "I think we should start with the Plaza. I want you to meet me there after work. I'll arrange everything."

"I'll have to go home and pick up some things," Chloe said.

Sloan grinned. "No, you won't. I'll take care of whatever you need. You just be there."

"Where?"

"In the lobby," he said. "Five o'clock sharp. Now that you've agreed, I don't want to waste a single minute."

"All right," Chloe replied. "Five o'clock."

With that, he kissed her forehead, then turned and strode out the door. She stood frozen in place for a long time, her mind whirling with the consequences of what she'd done.

"All right," she murmured. "This is what you wanted. You'll finally find out just what this attraction to Sloan is all about. You can handle this." She groped for a chair and slowly sat down. "I mean, it's not as if you've never been with a man before. Audrey's proof of that. It's just been twelve years."

Chloe groaned and buried her face in her hands. Good grief, what was she doing? Every cell in her brain told her this was a mistake, yet this was what she wanted. She wanted to feel like an attractive, alluring woman again. She wanted to experience what went on in the bedroom at least once more before she left this world. And she wanted Sloan DeWilde in the worst way.

What was wrong with taking advantage of the moment, of following her impulses? So maybe they'd make love. That didn't mean they had to make a lifelong commitment to each other. Plenty of women had...flings. And if she wanted a fling, she should have one. After all, she certainly deserved one.

And if it didn't work out, that was fine, too. She'd already proved she didn't need a man in her life to be happy. She could easily go on without him. And working with him couldn't be any harder than it was now. In fact, it would probably be much easier.

Chloe slouched down in the chair and rubbed her temples with her fingertips. So she would go to the Plaza and spend the weekend with Sloan DeWilde. It was probably fate that Audrey was spending the weekend with one of her friends. If she hadn't been, Chloe would definitely have refused Sloan's invitation. But this way she would find out just how deep the feelings were that ran between them.

And then she'd decide whether to tell him about her daughter.

SLOAN STRODE OUT into the reception area, intending to start on his plans for his weekend with Chloe. He wasn't ready for what was waiting for him there. His brother sat on the corner of Edna's desk, chatting with her amiably. Mason DeWilde looked up as Sloan pulled Chloe's office door closed.

"Hello, little brother," he said.

"Mase! What are you doing here?"

Mason stood, straightening his tie and watching Sloan with an astute gaze. "I thought I'd check up on you. See how things were going at the family store. So how *are* things going, Sloan?"

"Great," Sloan told him. "Terrific, in fact."

"That's exactly what Miss Crenshaw was telling me," he said. "Imagine my surprise to learn that sales have actually been rising here at DeWilde's Fifth Avenue. That hasn't happened in—what?—years. Is there a rush on weddings I don't know about?"

Sloan crossed the reception area and grabbed his brother's arm. "Why don't we have some lunch and we'll discuss it," he said, steering Mason toward the elevators and away from Edna's boasting.

"I had lunch already," Mason said. "I just want to know what's going on, little brother."

"We'll talk business," Sloan said through clenched teeth. "But not here."

Sloan knew he was in trouble. All their plans were in danger of falling apart and he hadn't done a whole lot about it. He'd deliberately kept Mason in the dark, hoping he'd be able to turn things around before it was too late.

But what was he supposed to do? He was caught in the middle of something he couldn't control, feeling a desire he'd never felt before, a responsibility to a woman he cared about more than all his plans. Chloe had changed his life. This store had become her dream as much as it had once been his nightmare. And now he'd begun to see the store through her eyes, as an exciting and vital business, a place of strong traditions and endless possibilities.

He and his brother didn't say another word to each other until they'd taken the elevator down to the first floor and stepped out on the street in front of DeWilde's.

Mason didn't wait more than an instant before he launched an all-out attack. "What the hell is going on, Sloan? I thought you told me you had things under control. Crenshaw says sales have been on the rise since early last month!"

Sloan kept his gaze straight ahead as they walked. "Everything is under control," he said. "How about lunch at the University Club?"

"I don't want lunch! And it doesn't sound like you've got a handle on this anymore. How could you let this happen?"

"I didn't let it happen," Sloan replied with a calm shrug. "Someone else made it happen."

"Who?" Mason demanded.

"Chloe Durrant," Sloan said. An image of her flashed in his mind and he couldn't help but smile.

"Who the hell is Chloe Durrant?"

He'd been asking himself the same question now for more than a month and he still wasn't quite sure. She was the woman who had managed to captivate his mind and stir his desire. She was honest and open, yet the most mysterious woman he'd ever known. Chloe Durrant was a study in contradictions, a puzzle he was determined to unravel. "She was DeWilde's director of visual merchandising and display," Sloan told him.

"Was," Mason repeated. "Then I assume you got rid of her before she did any more damage. You fired her, right?"

Sloan considered his answer for a long moment, then decided it would be best to tell Mason the truth. "Actually, I fired Simpson-Davis. He was caught stealing from the store. Then I promoted Ms. Durrant to his position."

Mason stopped in the middle of the sidewalk and gaped at Sloan. "Tell me you're kidding."

Sloan shook his head. "I thought that would be the best way to control the rise in sales. Get her off the front line and into administration. I was wrong."

"Damn it, Sloan, we're running out of time. You can't afford to be wrong. The board meeting's next week."

"I know," Sloan said.

"So what are you going to do about it?"

"First, I'm going to have some lunch." He started across Fifth Avenue, not really caring where he was going. If he had his way, he'd make a dash for the nearest subway stop and try to lose Mason in the crowd. "How about the University Club?" he asked again, glancing up at the pink marble exterior of the venerable old institution that sat across the street from DeWilde's. Both Dirk and his father had been members, and it was the one DeWilde tradition that Sloan found worthwhile. The interior was as lavish as the exterior, the food quite good, and the atmosphere quiet and conservative. Maybe not the right place for the argument that loomed between him and his brother.

"I don't want any lunch," Mason insisted. "I want an explanation."

"You're right," Sloan said, continuing down Fifty-fourth. "I'm more in the mood for something different. How about Scandinavian?"

"All right," Mason said in frustration.

One of Sloan's favorite restaurants was located in a town house that once was home to Nelson Rockefeller. They were given a table in the main dining room, an eight-story atrium complete with waterfall and birch trees. Sloan ordered the smorgasbord appetizer plate and a double vodka martini, then turned his attention to his brother.

"Maybe this isn't the right time to make a move," he said. "Maybe we should wait until this sales trend shows a strong reversal."

"We've got everything in place," his brother replied in a low voice. "We've got the votes we need on the board. You can't back out now, brother."

"I'm not backing out. I'm just saying we might need more time."

"I've made plans for that money, Sloan. We're ready to make the next move in our breeding program. We can't put everything on hold now."

"This is my decision, Mason. If I say wait, we wait."

"Your decision?" Mason cried, the color rising in his face.

To Sloan's relief, the waiter reappeared with the appetizer, and they sat through an explanation of the different selections. When the young man left, he picked up a fork and held a morsel out to Mason. "Eel?" he offered. "It's quite good."

Mason sniffed disdainfully, ever the adventuresome diner. The man wouldn't set foot in a restaurant that didn't serve a plain grilled chicken breast and a dry lettuce salad. Pickled herring, reindeer pâté, and eel were far beyond his limited tastes. "You really should try to expand your culinary horizons, Mase," Sloan said.

"What the hell is going on with you?" Mason demanded. "A few months ago you were determined to sell the store. I can't believe you've changed your mind."

"I think it's best to keep an open mind," Sloan said. "You never know what life has in store for you. You have to live for the moment."

"What happened to that moment when you decided it was time to dump DeWilde's?"

"It passed."

Mason ground his teeth. "Listen, little brother, I've got a lot riding on this. Millions, to be precise. If you're not going to come through for me, I'm going to have to go over your head."

Sloan took a slow sip of his martini and regarded his brother with deceptive calm. "I wouldn't do that if I were you, Mason," he said. "I don't think you want to tangle with me on this one. I've got a personal stake in this."

"Damn right you do! The family is counting on you," Mason reminded him. "You can't back out!"

Sloan placed the crystal tumbler on the table. "Let me repeat myself just once more. This is my decision, Mason. I decide when and if we sell the store. I hold the vote on the board."

"That can easily be undone. Mother assigns that vote and she can just as easily assign it to me. She's as anxious to rid the family of DeWilde's as you used to be."

Sloan sighed and shook his head. "I've said all I need to about this matter, Mason. If you want to fight me for control, go right ahead. Talk to Mother. Convince her to give you the vote.''

Flushed with anger, Mason pushed back his chair and stood. "This is not over, Sloan. If you're not going to make it happen, I will."

"Take your best shot," Sloan said. "I'll be ready."

Sloan watched his brother weave through the tables in the atrium, then walk out the door. When he was certain he was alone, Sloan released a tightly held breath, then took a long sip of his drink.

Mason wouldn't let this drop, that much was clear. His intransigence was legendary in the family. Once Mason set himself on a course, there was nothing short of an atom bomb that would shake his determination. It was Mason, not Sloan, who had convinced the nonfamily board members to side with the Kelly contingent and sell DeWilde's. Mason held most of the cards.

Sloan rubbed his temple, trying to fight off the knot of tension growing in his head. He could take the easy way out and let Mason engineer the sale. At least he'd be expurgated from guilt by participation. Chloe would never know of his involvement and he could simply blame it on the board.

But was that what he really wanted? Could he just stand by and watch the store be sold out from under him . . . and Chloe?

Sales had turned around, but not that dramatically. Not enough to rule out a year-end loss and strengthen his case. And did he want to fight this battle year after year, Mason and his family on one side, him on the other? The prospect was bound to divide the family and make life miserable for him.

He could always tell Chloe the truth. After all, this was a business decision, pure and simple, based on profit and loss.

He couldn't be blamed for looking out for his family's interests.

But what about Chloe's interests? In more ways than one, she came first in his mind...and in his heart. To his surprise, he didn't give a damn about the horse farm anymore. Mason could have it, free and clear. What he wanted was right here, in the city, inside DeWilde's Fifth Avenue... inside the office next to his.

Sloan groaned inwardly. What the hell was he doing? How could he plan his future around a woman he barely knew? Sure, they might have plans to spend the weekend together, but what about next weekend and the weekend after that? Was he prepared to fight the future sale of DeWilde's based on what he shared with Chloe now? If so, he was taking an awfully big risk.

But then, Sloan DeWilde had never been one to shy away from a good fight.

CHLOE STARED ACROSS her workroom at the clock tacked up on the wall. Five minutes. That's all the time she had. Five minutes until she'd have to walk out of the store, stroll the four blocks to the Plaza and throw caution to the wind.

It wasn't as if she were scared. There wasn't another man she'd rather be seduced by than Sloan DeWilde. But she'd had a long dry spell between seductions and she wasn't even sure she'd remember how to react.

"Hey, there," Gina said, poking her head in the door. "What are you doing down here?"

"Hiding," Chloe replied, wrapping her arms around herself to quell a sudden shiver.

"I was just heading out. I wondered if you and Audrey had plans for tonight. I thought we could pick up a pizza and rent a video."

"Audrey's spending the weekend at a friend's house," Chloe said.

"How about you and me, then? We could go out for a few drinks, then have some dinner and take in a movie."

"I can't."

"Do you have to work late again?" Gina asked.

"Not really."

Gina gave Chloe a long-suffering look. "Then what?"

"I'm going to spend the weekend with..." Chloe drew a deep breath. "With a man," she said, letting the words out in one great rush.

Gina's jaw dropped open and her eyes grew wide. She hurried across the room and sat down next to Chloe. "You mean a *real* man?"

Chloe sighed and rolled her eyes. "No, I mean one of those blow-up dolls they sell in the shops in Times Square. Of course I mean a real man."

"Who? You don't know any real men. I mean, not well enough to spend the weekend with."

Chloe reached out and grabbed a green marker from the rack on the table. "Yes, I do," she said softly, twisting the cap on and off.

"Who?" Gina insisted, studying Chloe with a penetrating gaze. Chloe looked away uneasily, pulled out a piece of drawing paper and scribbled his name across it.

"Sloan DeWilde?" Gina cried.

Chloe nodded as she felt her face flush. She crumpled up the paper and threw it into the trash.

"How could you?"

"I haven't. At least, not yet," Chloe said defensively. "That's kind of what this weekend is for."

Gina frowned. "Everyone in the store's been talking about you two, but *I* didn't believe any of it. I said, no, if there was something going on, my *best* friend would have told me."

Chloe winced. "*Everyone's* talking? What are they saying?"

"They're worried about you," Gina said. "Sloan De-Wilde is a notorious lady-killer. Carmen in perfume says he's been known to have two dates in one evening. Louise in floral says he's their biggest customer. And just six months ago, he was supposedly engaged. They know how easily he charms women and they're afraid you're going to be his next victim."

"You know how the rumor mill works around here," Chloe said. "All innuendo and exaggeration. How do you know any of that is true?"

"How do you know it isn't?" Gina asked.

"I guess I don't," she said. "But I think I know Sloan DeWilde better than anyone in this store, except maybe for Edna Crenshaw. I'd know if I were just another one of his conquests." Though she said the words easily enough, she couldn't help but acknowledge the niggling doubt she felt. "I'm a big girl. I think I can handle myself."

"But can *you* handle Sloan DeWilde?" Gina asked.

"I don't know," Chloe said. "I guess I'm about to find out."

"What about Audrey?"

"I'll tell her about him ... sometime soon. But not until I'm absolutely certain of my feelings ... and more important, his. And I guess I really won't know how he feels until I tell him about Audrey."

"He doesn't know you have a daughter?" Gina asked, slapping her hand to her forehead.

"I'm going to tell him tonight, before this goes any further. It could either be a very long weekend or a very short discussion, depending upon how he reacts."

"What time are you meeting him?" Gina asked.

"I'm supposed to be at the Plaza in two minutes," Chloe told her.

"Then I'll make a dinner reservation at Porta Bella for six," Gina said, slipping off the stool. "Just in case things don't work out. And I'll rent *Casablanca*. You'll probably feel like a good cry." She dragged Chloe up from the stool and led her to the door of her workroom. "Smile, sweetie. Either way, you'll have plenty to tell me when we see each other."

"I'm not sure I want to do this," Chloe said.

"You'll be fine," Gina reassured her. "It's like riding a bike."

"I haven't ridden a bike since I was thirteen," Chloe cried.

Gina patted her on the shoulder. "I wouldn't worry. From what I've heard, Sloan's been doing enough bicycling for the both of you."

Chloe didn't remember walking through the store or out the front door, nor did she remember crossing Fifth Avenue. The next thing she knew, she was standing in front of the majestic facade of the Plaza. Flags from different nations snapped in the breeze above the entrance in honor of VIP guests, while taxis and limos vied for parking spaces in front of the hotel.

The Plaza overlooked the south end of Central Park and was only a short walk from the store, yet in all the years she'd lived in New York, she had never once stepped inside. But now, as the uniformed doorman held open the door, she was almost afraid to enter.

Why should she be afraid? After all, she was a grown woman. And grown women spent weekends alone with grown men all the time. Those who were lucky enough to find a *wealthy* grown man spent their weekends at the Plaza.

The elegant lobby bustled with guests and she looked around for Sloan. She felt almost relieved when she didn't find him and sank down onto an upholstered sofa. At least she'd have a few minutes to work out exactly what she'd say.

"Sloan," she murmured to herself. "I have something to tell you. I have a—I have a—"

"Miss Durrant?"

She glanced up to find a distinguished-looking concierge standing in front of her. "Are you Miss Chloe Durrant?" he asked, his voice deep and very French.

Chloe fumbled to her feet. "Yes, I'm Chloe Durrant."

He smiled smoothly and held out a room key. "Monsieur DeWilde is waiting for you upstairs. Suite 1540."

Chloe stared at the key, her eyes wide.

"If you would like, I will show you the way," he offered.

She hesitantly reached out and took the key from his fingers, then searched through her purse for a tip. "No, thank you," she said, pressing a five-dollar bill into his hand. "I can find my own way."

He pushed the money back into her hand. "There is no need, *mademoiselle*. Monsieur DeWilde has taken care of everything." He turned on his heel and walked back to his post, an elegant marble stand on one side of the lobby.

"I'm sure he has," she muttered. Clutching the key in her fist, she sat back down on the sofa. So he'd rented a suite. A logical move. What better way to be alone than in a quiet hotel suite? And at the Plaza, no less.

Still, the thought of joining him upstairs was disconcerting at best. Especially when she knew exactly what he had planned for her. "This is too much pressure," she said to herself. "I can't take the pressure."

She took a deep breath, then stood up and headed toward the elevators. But halfway there, she made a quick turn and headed back to the safety of the sofa. She just needed a few more minutes to gather her thoughts.

She glanced over at the concierge and he gave her a friendly nod, then went back to his work.

A few minutes later, she made her second attempt at the elevators. She got as far as pushing the up button before she turned back. This time she didn't stop at the sofa but made it all the way out to the sidewalk.

"Taxi?" a uniformed footman asked.

"Yes," Chloe replied. She frowned. "I mean, no. No taxi." She turned back to the door. "Wait," she cried, spinning back around. "I think I would like a taxi."

The footman hailed a cab and she pressed a tip into his hand as he helped her inside. She stared straight ahead, her mind whirling in confusion. Was she doing the right thing by just leaving? Maybe she should have called Sloan and at least told him she'd decided to go home.

"Where to, lady?" the cab driver asked.

"The Village," Chloe said. "Take Sixth, it's faster. But you'll have to detour near Herald Square. Drop me on the corner of Bleecker and MacDougal."

The driver made it all the way to the end of the block before she asked him to pull over and let her out. She gave him double the fare and a large tip. During the walk back to the Plaza, she realized she'd go broke if she didn't make a decision soon.

The concierge didn't seem to be surprised when she stepped up to his desk and handed him the key. "Would you please inform Mr. DeWilde that I won't be joining him this evening?" Chloe asked, handing him the key.

"If that's what you'd like," he said.

Chloe bit her bottom lip. "It's not exactly what I'd like, but I think it would be best."

"As you wish," he replied, the picture of discretion.

"Actually, I'd really like to tell him myself," Chloe explained, "but...well, I just don't know what to say. You see, I have to tell him something that I really don't want to tell him and I just can't bring myself to tell him . . . what I have to tell him."

"I understand," he said sympathetically.

"Maybe I should write him a note? Do you think a note might be better—" she squinted to read the name on his pin "— Georges?"

"A note would be very nice, *mademoiselle*," he said. "Would you like paper and a pen?"

"Yes," Chloe replied. "I think that would be best."

Georges withdrew a sheet of hotel stationery with an ornate gold *P* at the top. Then he handed her an expensive fountain pen. "Please," he said, indicating a small writer's desk near his stand. "Have a seat."

Chloe smiled and sat down, then stared at the blank sheet of paper. "I—I'm not sure what to say. I feel so bad about this, but I just can't bring myself to go up there. It's not that I don't want to, because I do. I just have something I have to tell him and I don't think he's going to take it very well."

"I see," Georges said from his post. "This is quite a dilemma."

"Maybe I should tell him in the letter. Then if he's angry he'll have a chance to cool off before we see each other again." Chloe scribbled a few lines on the stationery then signed her name. She folded the letter in thirds and handed it to Georges. He slipped it inside a vellum envelope.

"I will have this delivered up to Monsieur DeWilde's suite."

Chloe forced a smile. "Thank you, Georges. I'd appreciate that."

The concierge nodded curtly. "It has been my pleasure." Chloe reached for her purse again, but he held out his hand. "No need."

With that, she turned and started toward the door. But halfway across the lobby, she stopped. How could she sink so low as to spring this news in a hastily written letter? Sloan didn't deserve this. He didn't deserve her.

Georges was still waiting at the desk when she returned. He held out the letter and she took it from his fingers with a grateful smile. "Maybe I will tell him in person," she said. "When I'm ready."

"That would be best," Georges agreed.

Chloe slowly walked through the lobby and out the Fifth Avenue door. This would not happen between them, not tonight, and maybe not ever. For in all honesty, she wasn't ready to make love to Sloan DeWilde. Every instinct told her an affair with him would only end in pain.

She had protected herself from the hurt so long that, as she rode home in the cab, a numb indifference settled over her. On Monday, she would set things right. She would tell Sloan that they would no longer be personally involved. And if he refused to keep his distance, she would threaten to resign.

She only hoped that her threat worked for her, instead of against her.

CHAPTER NINE

CHLOE STOOD IN THE MIDDLE of the display window and surveyed the scene around her. Mannequins, silent and still in the boudoir setting, watched her with blank stares as she slowly plucked pieces of lingerie from the antique chests and tables scattered about the scene. The soft track lighting illuminated the figures as well as the large iron canopy bed, which was draped with sheer netting.

Chloe sighed and ran her free hand through her hair. If she worked hard, she'd be able to dismantle all six display windows by the end of the evening. On Monday, she and her staff would begin to assemble the new windows, replacing her peep show with the boring design that Sloan had chosen.

She had never worked on the weekends, preferring to spend every free minute with Audrey. But this weekend she couldn't face another minute cooped up in her apartment alone, her mind replaying the events of Friday night over and over again until she thought she might go crazy.

She snatched up a lacy black bra hanging from an open drawer and stared down at it, fingering the fabric distractedly. If only she had been sure about her actions, she could have put the whole incident behind her as an exercise in common sense.

But in her heart, she knew she'd taken the coward's way out. Sooner or later, she'd have to face Sloan with the truth...or forget whatever feelings they shared for each other. And she'd have to admit that she wanted him just as much as he wanted her.

A sharp rap on the glass startled her out of her contemplation, and Chloe turned to find a face staring at her through the peephole. With an impatient curse, she grabbed a roll of masking tape from her supply bin and covered the peephole, effectively shutting out the curious eyes of the pedestrians outside. She wanted to be alone, with her thoughts and her work.

She turned away from the window, wondering how long he had waited for her before leaving the Plaza. An image flashed in her mind of an elegant hotel suite and champagne on ice, fresh flowers and candlelight, and Sloan lying across a king-size bed, anticipating her arrival. The whole night probably would have been wonderfully romantic—and wonderfully passionate—and wonderfully—

"I thought I might find you here."

Chloe froze at the sound of his voice, not sure whether her mind was playing tricks on her or whether she was simply fantasizing his presence. Slowly, she turned to find Sloan standing at the small doorway into the display window. He stepped inside and pulled the door shut behind him, but didn't move any closer.

She swallowed hard as she realized that he was blocking her only exit. She'd have no choice now but to explain herself. "How did you know I was in here?" she asked, forcing her voice to work even though her heart had stopped dead.

"The guard told me you were in the store," he replied.

A shiver skittered down her spine, and she clasped her arms in front of her as if to protect herself from the shattering effect his appearance had on her senses. He looked as if he hadn't slept all night. His thick, dark hair was mussed, combed with nothing more than his fingers, and he wore a faded pair of jeans and a bright white polo shirt. His casual dress was so at odds with the businesslike man she knew that she had a hard time thinking of him as the general manager of DeWilde's.

She dragged her gaze away and stared down at the lingerie she had wadded into a ball in her white-knuckled hands. "I suppose you're wondering why I didn't come to you last night."

"No," Sloan said.

She jerked her head up and met his gaze. "You aren't?"

He shook his head and shrugged. "I told you once before that I wasn't going to force you into a decision, Chloe. When the time is right, all you have to do is tell me. I've waited this long, I can wait a little longer."

She took a long, deep breath. "It's not that I didn't want to," she said. "Because I did."

"Then what's standing between us?" His jaw tensed. "Is there someone else, Chloe?"

"Someone else?"

"Another man?" he asked, an edge to his voice.

She sighed. "Oh, no. You're the only man . . . I mean, there's no one else. No other man."

She watched as relief flooded his expression, all the while knowing that she hadn't been completely truthful. *Tell him,* her mind urged. *Now, before you lose your nerve.* There *was* someone else, and that someone was her daughter. But the words wouldn't come.

"Chloe, you've got to give me a clue here. I feel like I'm flying blind."

"I'm sorry," she said. "I know I've been a little—undecided. But you have to admit, this is not an easy thing. I just don't want to make any mistakes we'll regret later on."

Sloan slowly crossed the room. He stared into her eyes for a long moment, then bent and brushed his lips over hers, keeping his hands to himself, his mouth making the only contact with her body. "Is this a mistake?"

"I don't know," she replied.

He placed her hand on his chest and held it there. "Feel what's in my heart, Chloe. And then look into your own. How can you think we're a mistake?"

She gazed up at him with wide eyes. She knew the answer as well as he did, and she shook her head. "It's not a mistake," she admitted.

"Then it's time for you to make a decision, Chloe. Either we go ahead with this, or we stop. Tell me to leave," Sloan ordered. "Or tell me to stay. But know that if you tell me to stay, there won't be any going back. I won't let you run away from me again. Ever."

"I—I don't want you to leave," Chloe murmured.

He slipped his arm around her waist and pulled her against him, his mouth descending over hers in an act of pure possession. A soft moan of protest tore from her throat as he kissed her, long and deep. Her first instinct was to pull away, yet she couldn't. To deny his desire might be possible, but to deny hers was a lost cause. She wanted him more than she'd ever wanted a man in her life.

It suddenly made no difference whether it was for one night or the rest of her life, her need overwhelmed all common sense, all thought of commitment and the future. Her determination to tell him about her daughter melted in her mind as she reveled in the feel of his mouth, the taste and smell of him.

She grasped his forearms as he cupped her face in his hands, certain that if she let go she might sink to the floor, or, worse yet, turn and run. With tiny steps, he backed her up against the edge of the bed, and the reality of what they were about to share suddenly pierced through her hazy mind.

Could she do this? Could she let go of all her inhibitions and give herself freely to this man? Could she forget all her fears and make love to him with all the abandon and the emotion that she felt in the depth of her soul?

Slowly, she lowered herself to sit on the edge of the bed, never allowing herself to slip out of his embrace for fear that to break their connection might mean breaking the spell between them. She braced her hands behind her, splaying her fingers over the satin coverlet. He bent over her, burying his face in the curve of her neck, softly nibbling as he traced a path to her ear.

"This is just us now, sweetheart," he murmured, his breath soft against her ear. "No one else."

She knew if she was going to pull away, she should do so now. But she felt as if she'd been drugged by his kisses, unable to muster the resistance she'd managed in the past. She couldn't fight him anymore. She didn't want to. Instead, she wanted to escape into this secret world with him, to shut out the rest of the world and live out the fantasy.

Slowly, she let her arms buckle behind her, and in an instant he was above her, dragging her alongside him and pressing her back into the softness of the bed. He moved his hips against hers. Her limbs slowly went liquid and her blood warmed as she became aware of his arousal.

His fingers fumbled with the tiny buttons of her cotton sweater, and finally he abandoned his attempt and simply slipped his hand beneath the hem, sliding his palm over her belly. He massaged gently and she closed her eyes, her mind focusing on the path of his exploration.

A soft sigh escaped her lips as he cupped her breast, his thumb rubbing at her pebbled nipple through the fabric of her bra. Then she became aware of his mouth again, trailing along her stomach, his lips cool on her hot skin. He nuzzled her breast, then pushed the fabric aside and teased the hard peak with his tongue.

Her body belonged to him and her soul cried out for his touch. Wild, unbidden sensations coursed through her veins until her fingers and toes tingled. She surrendered herself to the feelings, riding each wave of desire until her hands moved across his body of their own will, wanting to return the pleasure that he gave so freely.

She tugged at his shirt, desperately needing to feel his skin beneath her hands. He rolled away for a moment and yanked it over his head, tossing it aside.

Chloe languidly drew her fingers over the muscles of his chest, raking her nails through the dusting of dark, silky hair. He rested his hand on her hip and watched as she touched him, sucking in a sharp breath as she kissed his nipple. Hesitantly, she stopped just above the waistband of his jeans. But then, she brushed her fingers over the hard ridge beneath the faded denim. He moaned, almost as if in pain, and at that instant she became aware of the incredible power she had over him.

It was as if a floodgate had been opened, as if the final shreds of her doubt had been tossed aside in a rush of passion. She reached for the button on his jeans and soon they were tugging at each other's clothes with urgent words of encouragement.

When the last bit of clothing was tossed aside, Sloan dragged the satin coverlet around them, pulling her over him along with it. She felt him all along the length of her, his legs twisting around hers, her breasts flat against his hard chest, his erection pressing between them.

Gone was her apprehension, and she rolled off him, then reached between them, stroking and wrapping her fingers around his length. She remembered nothing of any other man in her life; in her mind, Sloan was the first.

He touched her as she touched him, in places so intimate his fingers caused frissons of wild sensation to shoot deep into her core. Her gaze locked with his and he smiled lazily, rubbing his forehead against hers, his quickened breath soft on her lips.

"What you do to me," he whispered, "no one has ever done before. You have a power, a hold over me that I can't explain. Tell me what it is, Chloe. Tell me why I feel this way."

She reached up and traced his lower lip with her finger. "I don't understand it," she said. "Maybe it's not supposed to make sense. It's like a dream."

"A fantasy."

"Make it real," she murmured.

He smiled seductively. "Ask me, Chloe."

"Make love to me," she said.

He rolled her with him as he reached over the edge of the bed, fumbling through the pocket of his jeans. He pulled a foil packet from his wallet and handed it to her, then pulled her up to sit on his thighs.

Chloe stared down at the condom and forced a smile. "I'm afraid I've never done this before."

He frowned. "You haven't?"

"I mean, I've had sex with a man before, but never with one of these—not that I've had unprotected sex, I just haven't had *any* sex for a long time, protected or otherwise, which doesn't mean I don't want to have sex with—"

Sloan slipped his hand around her nape and pulled her mouth down on his. "I wouldn't worry," he murmured against her lips. "You're doing just fine so far."

With nervous fingers, she sheathed him, letting her touch linger over him until he groaned impatiently. He shifted her above him and gently probed at her entrance. Slowly, deliciously, she sank on top of him, opening herself until she could feel him buried deep inside her.

Their joining took her breath away, and for a moment she couldn't move for fear that she'd lose her grasp on reality. Then, his gaze fixed on hers, he lifted her slightly and pressed down on her hips. She took his cue and began to move above him, slowly at first, then faster, his soft voice urging her on.

Nothing had prepared her for the intensity of their love-making, for the utter rush of need and passion and hunger that overwhelmed them both. Pleasure suffused every nerve in her body, building at her core until she knew her release was near.

His hands slid around her hips and he touched her where they were so intimately joined. Suddenly, the sensations intensified, hot and pulsing. She cried out and then felt herself tumbling over the edge. And through the surge of ecstasy, she knew he was with her, shuddering with his own release.

With a gasp, she fell to his chest and he wrapped his arms around her, pulled her face into the curve of his neck.

"This was definitely no mistake," he said in a sleepy voice.

"Mmm," Chloe replied, closing her eyes and breathing deeply of his scent.

She wasn't sure how long she'd slept or what woke her, whether it was the security guard's footsteps outside the door or the sound of a passing conversation on the street.

Carefully she crawled out of bed and began to gather her clothes. If they stayed here much longer, they were sure to be discovered. She watched him as she dressed, smiling at the look of boyish innocence on his relaxed features. When she'd pulled her shoes on, she quietly approached the bed and gazed down at him, staring at the gentle rise and fall of his chest.

She reached out to touch his shoulder, but suddenly she couldn't bring herself to wake him. What had happened between them had happened in a world of their own making. Would it survive in the real world, or would they both regret giving in to their desire? Would all the doubts return once they stepped outside of this room?

Slowly, she backed toward the door, watching him all the while. She turned the latch behind her, then took one last look at him, the satin coverlet twisted around his waist, his arm thrown across his eyes.

"I have a daughter," she whispered. "Her name is Audrey and she's eleven years old and she's the most important person in my life. I've wanted to tell you about her for a long time and I will, I promise. And I hope, if you really love me, that someday you'll come to love her, too."

With that, Chloe pushed open the door and stepped out of the display window, knowing that no matter how he took the news, she'd never regret what they'd shared this night.

CHLOE SAT ON THE FLOOR of her bedroom and stared into the dark interior of her closet. The apartment was silent, the only sounds drifting through the open windows from the street five stories below. She glanced down at her watch and then at the piles of shoes scattered around her. Audrey would be home any minute and would most likely be anxious for dinner. A mental inventory of the refrigerator revealed not much more than a frozen pizza and a half gallon of milk.

She had forgone grocery shopping and spent most of the morning and the entire afternoon cleaning her closets in a futile attempt to keep her mind off the events of the previous evening. She'd arranged all her clothes by color, then rearranged them by type, then put them back the way she'd originally had them. Accessories came next, and finally she had started on the shoes. But no matter how hard she worked at organizing her closet, she couldn't organize her thoughts. Time after time she would catch herself drifting from her task, the memory of their lovemaking too strong to deny.

Even now she felt a blush creep up her cheeks at the memory of their uninhibited passion. They'd made love in the display window of a Fifth Avenue department store! While people strolled the sidewalk on the other side of the glass and security guards prowled the interior of the store!

In all her life, she'd never made love the way she had with Sloan—with such reckless abandon. Julien had always exacted a properly passionate response from her, but never any true passion. She'd been so young and so naive, she'd just assumed that what she was feeling was what every other woman felt in bed.

But what she'd experienced with Sloan had been fun, exciting, exhilarating and more than just a little naughty. She knew that Sloan was accustomed to this element of danger and adventure, but to find the same quality in herself came as a bit of a shock. When she was with Sloan, she seemed to forget who she was. And who *they* were, as well.

What had started out as sex, as two people slaking their physical desire for each other, had turned into something more. She and Sloan had made love, had expressed their feelings for each other, feelings she'd never suspected he harbored, feelings she was almost afraid to admit to herself. She had opened herself to him both physically and emotionally, something that she never thought she'd be able to do again after Julien.

She reached out for the glass of wine she'd poured and took a sip, hoping it might calm her quickened pulse.

Though their feelings had seemed so clear last night, in the light of day, the future was less certain. Had they made a commitment to each other by making love? Or had they simply decided to admit their passion and act on it?

She knew where Sloan might belong in her life, but where did she belong in his? And even more important, where would Audrey belong? Chloe closed her eyes and hugged her legs against her chest. There would be no telling what the future held for them until she told him about her daughter. Only then could she contemplate a future with him.

"Mom! I'm home!"

Chloe leaned over and looked out the bedroom door as her daughter stepped inside the apartment. "I'm in here, honey."

Audrey walked into the bedroom and immediately tossed her backpack on the floor and flopped onto Chloe's bed. She lay there, silent, but the apartment suddenly seemed right again. Her daughter was home, safe and sound, and the little corner of her mind that kept a constant vigil could now relax.

"So? Did you have a good time at Lindsay's house?" Chloe asked.

Audrey stared at the ceiling and idly picked the bright red nail polish off her fingernails. "It was okay," she said. "We went to the park with her dad. And her mom let us stay up until midnight and use her makeup. Lindsay's dad doesn't live with her and her mom, so her mom kind of lets her do whatever she wants."

"Are they divorced?" Chloe asked.

"I guess," Audrey replied with a sigh.

Chloe glanced over at her daughter and wondered what was going through the little girl's mind. She could tell something was bothering Audrey, and once again she suspected it had to do with her own family situation, with Julien, or the absence of Julien, or maybe even fathers in general.

Chloe crawled across the carpet, then reached out and smoothed her hand through Audrey's long hair. "You look a little tired, Claude. Are you feeling all right?"

Audrey nodded.

"Is there something you'd like to talk about? Did you and Lindsay have an argument?"

Audrey shook her head.

Chloe watched her for a long moment, then reluctantly returned to her spot on the floor. She knew from past experience that it was no use pushing Audrey into a discussion. Her daughter would talk when she wanted to and no sooner.

Reaching into the depths of the closet, Chloe pulled out another shoe box that had been tucked into a dark corner. She pulled off the top, expecting a pair of shoes, but getting instead a jolt from her past.

"Oh, my," she murmured. "Look at this."

Audrey flipped over on her stomach and watched her mother. "What is it?"

"Come and look."

Audrey scrambled to the floor and plucked a wrinkled tube of acrylic paint from the box. "Wow. What are these?"

"My paints," Chloe said.

Audrey blinked and regarded her mother with surprise. "*Your* paints?"

"Mmm-hmm," Chloe replied. "When I was younger, long before I had you, I was a painter. At least, I wanted to be."

"Like my dad?" Audrey asked.

Chloe smiled, then suddenly realized that this was the first time she'd been able to think of Julien without an accompanying trace of bitterness. Had she finally put her past in the past? And why now? Somehow she suspected it had to do with Sloan DeWilde.

"Yes," she said, "like your dad. Only your father was much more passionate about his painting than I was. He used to stay up for days, pacing and painting. Once, he got so angry he threw a painting out the window."

"My dad did that?" Audrey asked.

"He was very temperamental. I didn't stick with my painting, but I knew someday he'd be very famous."

Audrey stared at her, wide-eyed. "How come you're talking about him now?" she asked bluntly.

Chloe shrugged. "I don't know. I guess I was just answering your question."

"But you don't like to talk about my dad," Audrey accused. "You never want to talk about him."

Chloe drew a deep breath. "Well, maybe it's time we did."

And so they did, over the next hour, Chloe sitting on the floor among her shoes and paints, and Audrey beside her, her head resting in Chloe's lap. She asked all the questions she'd kept to herself for so long, revealing a curiosity that Chloe had never known she possessed.

In the end, it wasn't as difficult as Chloe had expected, for Audrey had guessed at most of the story and filled in the rest with her imagination. Reality turned out to be much more palatable than her imagined scenarios, so she seemed quite happy once in full possession of the facts.

"Maybe someday, when I'm older, I can go see my dad," Audrey said, her voice wistful.

"Not now?"

She shook her head. "I kinda like it just you and me."

Chloe pressed her lips to Audrey's forehead. "Me, too, sweetie. Me, too."

"I'm hungry," Audrey finally said, signaling the end of their conversation and the exhaustion of her curiosity. "Can we go get piroshki for dinner?"

They were just a short walk from Audrey's favorite Ukrainian restaurants on Cooper Square. But Chloe didn't want to spoil the evening by venturing out into the noisy East Village. "Why don't we send out for Chinese food?" she suggested. "We can keep talking if you want. Or we can watch a video."

Audrey picked up a tube of burnt umber and stared at it. "What are you going to do with these paints?" she asked.

"I don't know," Chloe said. "Maybe I should try to find my palette and do some painting. What do you think about that?"

"But you haven't painted a picture since before I was born," Audrey said. "What if you don't remember how?"

"I won't know until I try." She picked up a tube of cerulean blue. "But I think I'd like to try again. I used to be pretty good. In fact, one of my teachers once said I was the best she'd ever taught."

"I know why you want to paint again," Audrey said. "It's because you're in *love.*"

Chloe stared down at her daughter in surprise. "Where would you get an idea like that?"

"Come on, Claude, we live together. There's not much that gets by me. You've been getting up early every morning so you can do your hair and makeup before I get up. You're always walking around with that moony look on your face. And you talk about that Sloan guy all the time."

Chloe groaned inwardly. If she'd been this obvious to her own daughter, no wonder the whole store knew by now. "And what if I was in love?" she asked. "How would you feel about that?"

Audrey shrugged. "It depends how dweeby the guy is, I guess."

Chloe pinched her daughter's nose playfully. "The guys I date are not dweebs," she said. Audrey's eyebrows shot up dubiously. "All right," she conceded. "A few have been a little strange. But not all of them." Audrey shook her head slowly. "All right, most of them have been strange. But it's not as if there have been that many."

"Five," Audrey said, scrambling up to sit next to Chloe. "Dave, Charles, Andy, Steve and Harold." She ticked them off one by one, then wiggled her fingers in Chloe's face.

"Yes, five. We're not talking the Sixth Fleet here. I can count my previous boyfriends on one hand. Five boyfriends in ten years. That averages out to one every two years. And three of them lasted a grand total of one date, so they don't even qualify as boyfriends. This is not going to put me in the *Guinness Book of Records,* Claude."

"What about this new guy?" she asked. Though she feigned indifference, Audrey was obviously worried. It showed in the slight frown creasing her brow and the stubborn set of her mouth.

"What new guy?" Chloe asked. "Who says there's a new guy?"

"You tell me," Audrey challenged.

Chloe reached out and smoothed her fingers along her daughter's temple. "This is nothing you should worry about," she said. "At least not now. Not yet. You'll be the first to know if I decide to make Sloan my boyfriend."

Audrey shrugged. "I'm not worried. I just wish you would find a nice guy, someone who would make you happy. Someone who will stay with you and not leave, like my dad did."

"I'm very happy right now. I don't need a boyfriend to make me happy. I have you and that's all I need."

"Mom, get real. Someday I'm gonna go to college and you're not going to have anyone to take care of. I was kinda thinking if you found someone who you really liked, you could get married. Then maybe I could have a father and you could have someone to keep you company when I grow up."

"Is that what you want?" Chloe asked.

Audrey nodded.

Chloe reached out and pulled her daughter into her arms. "Honey, I can't tell you how this is going to go. I don't even know myself." She ruffled Audrey's hair. "Besides, I just kind of figured I'd come and live with you when you grew up."

Audrey turned her face up to Chloe's. "We could live together," she said. "That would be all right with me."

Chloe smiled warmly and gave her another hug. "We'll see, sweetheart. "We'll see."

"OH, HELL!"

Sloan pulled the sales report off his desk and heaved it in the direction of his trash basket, then pushed back in his chair until it rolled to a stop against his credenza.

Another week, another 2.4 percent rise in gross sales. At this rate, they'd hit a new sales record sometime before Christmas. He'd known the end was coming for some time now. In fact, he could trace the demise of his carefully laid plans all the way back to the moment he'd met Chloe Durrant.

She had barged into his world and turned it completely upside down, and now, after making love to her, he knew he'd never had a chance in the first place. She was destined to change his life, to capture his heart and lay claim to his soul. No matter how many times she pushed him away, he knew she'd be his, sooner or later.

And she had been. Never mind that she'd left him sound asleep, and naked, in the display window of DeWilde's. And forget the embarrassment at being discovered by a very surprised security guard. She'd run out on him for the last time. From now on, he'd make sure she stayed in his bed all night, every night.

Sloan punched the intercom button and Miss Crenshaw answered. "Is Ms. Durrant in yet?"

He heard Edna sigh. "It's only been three minutes since you last asked," she replied.

"Well, is she?"

"No," Edna said calmly. "But I'll ring you as soon as she walks in the door."

Sloan got out of his chair and began to pace the office restlessly. All his carefully laid plans were in a shambles. His brother was ready to boot him out of the family, his family was ready to have him committed, and he was about to throw away a multimillion-dollar deal. And he didn't really care!

All he cared about was Chloe—and, strangely enough, he cared about DeWilde's Fifth Avenue. Until he'd met Chloe, he'd never had a true sense of who he was, of where he belonged. DeWilde's was the last place he'd ever expected to find himself. But here, with Chloe pushing and challenging and testing him, he'd discovered that he actually enjoyed retailing—once he'd learned to read the damn sales reports.

Sloan groaned inwardly. Oh, Lord! Could it possibly be? Could there be DeWilde blood running through his veins? Sure, his father had hated the store, but then maybe the retailing gene had skipped a generation. Once his family found out, they *would* have him committed!

The sound of his intercom buzzer pierced through the jumble of his thoughts and he strode to the door and flung it open, expecting to see Chloe standing there. But instead of a willowy blonde, the only occupant of the reception area was Nick Santos. Edna stepped out from behind her desk and hurried to his side.

"Mr. Santos is here to see you again," she whispered. "He doesn't have an appointment, but he said you'd want to see him."

Sloan released a tightly held breath and nodded in the detective's direction. "Come on in, Mr. Santos," he called.

He stepped aside as the investigator entered the room, then pointed to a chair. "Please, sit down."

"Thanks," Santos said, folding his frame into the chair. He ran his fingers through his thick, dark hair and tugged at the knot in his tie until he'd loosened it enough to unbutton the top button of his shirt. Unlike their first meeting, he seemed to be more relaxed this time around.

"I understand you had an opportunity to speak with my mother," Sloan remarked, returning to his desk. "Was she able to provide you with any new information?"

"Some. I've got a few more promising leads to follow."

"Good," Sloan said. "I hope you solve this little family mystery before the press gets hold of it. I'd hate to see it have a negative effect on our stock price. Now, what else can I do for you? Why are you here?"

He looked a bit surprised at Sloan's blunt question. "I have something for you." He tossed a manila file folder on the desk.

Sloan stared down at it. "What's this?"

"The little girl," Santos said. "I found out who she is."

"Madeline?" Sloan asked, snatching up the folder. He blinked, then shook his head. "I'd forgotten that I'd asked you to find her. What did you learn?"

"She's the daughter of one of your employees," Santos continued efficiently. "From what I can tell, she comes here every day after school and waits for her mother in the sixth-floor ladies' lounge. But her name's not Madeline. It's Audrey. Audrey Durrant.''

Sloan gasped. "Durrant? Her last name's Durrant? You must be mistaken."

Santos raised a brow. "I'm afraid not. It's all there in the folder. But then, there's nothing you couldn't have found in your own personnel files."

The typewritten pages of Santos's report seemed to blur together as the full impact of the revelation hit Sloan. Good God, Chloe had a daughter? Little Madeline, ersatz street urchin, was the child of his merchandising manager! And even worse, the child of his lover!

Sloan didn't know whether to be relieved or angry. He decided to be both. He glanced up at Santos. "What do I owe you?" he asked in a tense voice.

The investigator shook his head. "Nothing. It was a fair trade. The little girl in return for a few new leads. Besides, it didn't take me more than a few hours of digging once I finally caught sight of her inside the store. I just didn't have a chance to get back to you till now."

Santos rose from his chair and held out his hand. Sloan stood and shook it. "Thanks for your help," Santos said.

"And thanks for yours," Sloan replied. As Santos walked out, he stared after him in disbelief. If it were anyone else, he'd question the authenticity of the information, but Nick Santos didn't seem the type to make mistakes.

Sloan snatched the folder from his desk and began to pace the perimeter of the office as he read. How the hell could she have kept this from him? An ex-husband, maybe. Even a current husband he would have understood. But neglecting to mention the existence of an eleven-year-old child was going too far!

And what kind of mother was she, anyway, to allow her child to wander all over the city on her own? Geez, for all *she* knew, he could have been some sick pervert, leading Madeline on, taking advantage of her.

An overwhelming anger surged through him. All this time he'd been feeling guilty about his own secrets, when she'd been keeping a secret of her own. Suddenly, it all made sense—her strict adherence to a nine-to-five schedule, her inability to accept a spontaneous invitation, her reticence when it came to any discussion of her personal life.

He'd just assumed she had no personal life, that her job *was* her life. But now he'd come to find that she was living two separate lives—one with him at the store and the other at home, with her daughter.

And then there was Madeline—or Audrey. He wasn't sure what to call her. She'd deliberately lied to him, hidden her real identity, led him to believe she was some street kid, and all to protect her mother from the repercussions of using DeWilde's as a baby-sitting service.

Sloan swore softly. He should be glad that Audrey had a warm place to live and food on the table. How many times had he wondered where she was, whether she was safe? But his sense of relief was overwhelmed by the betrayal he felt.

What did Chloe expect from him? Did she think that having a child would make him feel differently about her? Or did she consider him such an inconsequential part of her life that he didn't warrant an introduction to her daughter? And where the hell was Audrey's father in all this?

Damn it, he deserved answers! In the short time he'd known the little girl, she'd become an important concern in his life. He cared about her. And then there was Chloe. He had managed to fall in love with her! Only to learn that he really didn't know her at all.

Well, he was going to learn a helluva lot more pretty quickly. Sloan crossed the room and pressed his intercom button. "Edna, is Ms. Durrant in her office yet?"

"Not yet," Edna replied, her voice strident through the speaker.

"Then track her down, Miss Crenshaw," he ordered. "I want to see her now!"

CHAPTER TEN

CHLOE WALKED BRISKLY down Fifth Avenue, dodging and darting around Monday-morning pedestrians who were less anxious to get to work than she was. The weather had finally cooled and a fresh breeze buffeted between the skyscrapers, lofting bits of paper into the air and sending them swirling up with the currents.

Autumn was in the air, and it was as if the new season signaled a new time in Chloe's life, as well. She still couldn't comprehend the changes that had taken place since the day she first met Sloan.

Though she'd tried to resist him, she'd never really had a chance. She'd been right about him from the start—Sloan DeWilde was a man who got exactly what he wanted. And he had wanted her.

A secret thrill shot through her. It was odd how her strict adherence to propriety now seemed almost prudish. Sloan had been right—the fact that they worked together had nothing to do with their attraction, it was just coincidence. Somehow, she knew that even if she'd never gotten the job at DeWilde's, she would have met him. They were destined to be together.

As she passed the wide display windows of the store, she stopped and smiled to herself, her thoughts drifting back to Saturday night, to the events that had taken place behind the opaque paint.

Since those hours they had spent together, she'd thought about what they had shared...and what it all meant. In the end, she decided that she was in love with Sloan DeWilde, and deep in her heart, she hoped he was in love with her. Though he hadn't said the words, she'd felt it—in the throes of their desire and in the quiet aftermath, in his whispered urgings and his soft moans.

Still, underneath this flood of feeling, a niggling guilt pierced her thoughts. She had yet to tell him about Audrey, and that prospect had kept her up most of last night. In the endless early morning hours, Chloe had agonized over how to tell him she had a child. Finally, as the sun had begun to turn the sky gray over the East River, she decided that if his feelings for her were true, he'd understand her silence.

She'd always been up front about Audrey in the past, introducing the men in her life to her daughter. But then, when the relationships didn't work out, Audrey was the one who was hurt and confused, believing that she had somehow been the cause of the breakup.

This time, though, Chloe had done it right. Besides, of the men she'd dated, Sloan had seemed the least likely candidate for a long-term relationship. So she'd protected her daughter's feelings first. And she'd waited until she was sure about her own feelings—and nearly sure about his. True, Sloan might feel hurt or betrayed by her secrecy, but if he really cared about her, he would understand.

As she walked inside the store and took the elevator up to her office, she repeated this to herself like a prayer, hoping that her instincts about him would prove to be right.

"Mr. DeWilde has been asking for you," Edna said as Chloe breezed through the reception area of the executive suite.

Chloe took a deep breath and marshaled her courage. "Has he?" she asked.

"He'd like to see you immediately," Edna continued. "In his office."

Chloe dropped her portfolio beside Edna's desk and stepped over to Sloan's office door, knocking softly before she entered.

He was standing with his back to her, looking down at the street from a narrow window. For a moment, she didn't think he had heard her enter. Finally, she decided to speak.

"You wanted to see me?"

"I did," he said in a flat voice, still not turning around.

His reaction surprised her. Somehow she'd imagined that their first meeting after making love would be different, warmer, more intimate. But maybe he was determined to keep their personal life out of the workplace. Her heart suddenly twisted in her chest as another thought crossed her mind. Maybe he already regretted what had happened between them.

"Is something wrong?"

He braced his hands on either side of the window and she could see the tension in his posture. "You left the other night without saying goodbye," he said.

"I know," she replied. "I'm sorry. I just thought it would be better to go, before someone discovered us."

"Would you like to tell me the real reason?"

Chloe slowly approached him and put her hand on his shoulder. His muscles tensed under her fingers, the movement almost imperceptible through the fine fabric of his jacket. "Actually, I would," she said. "We have a lot to talk about."

He turned around and faced her, a cold smile curving his lips. "I assume you've finally decided to tell me about Audrey."

Chloe gasped. "Audrey?"

"Your daughter? That is her name, isn't it?"

"You know about Audrey?"

Sloan strode over to his desk and picked up a manila folder, then held it out to her. "Audrey and I are good friends. We've known each other for quite some time now." He slapped the folder down on his desk and fixed her with an angry glare.

She watched him warily. "I don't understand."

"You heard me," he said. "I know all about Audrey."

Chloe bit her bottom lip and winced. The personnel files. He'd obviously seen Audrey's name listed on the insurance forms. She should have known that sooner or later he'd have reason to peruse her file. But had he sent for them immediately after they'd made love? Or had he known all the time? "I'm sorry I didn't tell you sooner, but I had my reasons for not being more up-front. I—"

"I don't care about that! You kept your daughter a secret from me and that was your right. You probably should have told me before we made love, but I can see why you didn't."

His words suddenly made no sense. "I don't understand. Why are you so angry, then?" She watched as Sloan battled his temper, his jaw tight with repressed emotion, his fists clenched.

"How the hell could you allow her to run around the store with absolutely no supervision?"

Chloe groaned inwardly. Not only did he know about Audrey, he knew about her improvised child-care arrangements. "She was only supposed to be here for a week," she explained. "And then a week became two, and three. I finally found a sitter and she had to quit after two days. And she wasn't running around the store, she stayed in the ladies' lounge on the sixth floor the whole time."

"Oh, really?" Sloan said, a sarcastic arch to his brow. "That's very interesting, because Audrey and I have spent some lovely afternoons together in Central Park. We're regulars at Rumpelmayer's. She prefers their triple fudge sundaes with extra nuts.''

"She left the store?" Chloe cried. "You took her out of the store without my permission?"

"I didn't know she was your daughter, remember?"

"Well, didn't you think to ask her where her parents were?" Chloe accused. "You can't just walk off with someone's child."

"Audrey didn't want to talk about her family. The first time I met her, I just assumed she was a street kid, a runaway without a home. She was dressed in a ragged old jacket and she told me her mother had been killed in a bus crash in Mexico."

Chloe pinched her eyes shut and rubbed her temples with her fingers. "The bus story. She told you the bus story. And her jacket wasn't ragged. It's called grunge."

"Grunge or not, that doesn't change the fact that she left the store with me on a number of occasions. I could just as easily have been some pervert rather than a friend of the family." The last was said with more than a trace of accusation.

Chloe paced the length of Sloan's office, trying to calm her anger and assuage her growing anxiety at the realization that something *could* have happened to Audrey. "She should never have left the store," Chloe said. "She promised me she'd stay put."

"You're damn right she shouldn't have left! *You* should have been keeping better track of her."

Chloe stared at him, speechless. "Me?" she finally said.

"Yes, *you*. You're her mother. The person who's supposed to take care of her, to protect her."

Chloe shook her head in disbelief. "You don't have a clue, do you."

"I think I know what makes a good parent."

Chloe laughed bitterly. "You don't know anything. I thought I could trust her with this. I was wrong. It's not the first time she's disobeyed me, and I don't expect it will be the last. It's part of growing up and it's something you have to accept if you're a parent. I can't be with her one hundred percent of the time."

"Well, maybe you should be," Sloan said.

"Oh, now there's an idiotic suggestion if I ever heard one. How would you have me support my daughter? Who do you think pays for the baby-sitters and the private school tuition and the clothes she seems to grow out of every two weeks? And what about the rent and the doctor's bills, not to mention saving for college?"

"You're the merchandising manager of DeWilde's," Sloan said. "You make a good salary."

Chloe stopped her pacing and faced him. "It's not just the money. I can't leave Audrey with any old stranger. Until I could find a sitter I could trust, I thought she was safer right here, with me only a few floors away."

"That doesn't change the fact that your daughter was wandering around New York while you thought she was safe and sound three floors below you."

"Don't you lecture me about parenting!" Chloe snapped. "You're not a parent, so what do you know? Audrey and I have done just fine on our own."

"I disagree," Sloan said.

"I don't care what you think," Chloe shot back.

He grabbed her shoulders and stared down at her. "You don't have to worry anymore. I can take care of you and Audrey. I have the money to make your life easier...and safer. You won't have to leave her alone ever again."

"So your money is going to solve all my parenting problems, is that it?"

"Well, it would certainly help."

Chloe pulled out of his grasp. "Just what are you offering, Sloan?"

Sloan sighed and raked his fingers through his hair. "I care about both of you. And Audrey deserves a secure future. I can do that for her...and you."

"Then you're offering marriage?" she asked in a cold voice, her anger overcoming all her reticence.

He blinked in surprise and stepped back. "Marriage?"

Chloe smiled humorlessly. "Go ahead. You can turn and run right now." She watched as he began to pace the width of his office, clearly disturbed by her statement. "Well, what's it going to be?" she asked. "There's the door. If I were you, I'd bolt now while you have the chance. After all, what man in his right mind would want a ready-made family?"

He turned and stared at her, his eyes filled with anger. "I'm not running, Chloe. You just—took me by surprise."

"But you want to run," she said. "It's not just coincidence that you've avoided marriage for this long."

"I'm not going anywhere," he repeated more firmly.

Her jaw tightened. "So then you'll marry me?" she asked, her tone challenging. "Because that's what it's going to take. Total commitment. I won't settle for anything else. I can't...for Audrey's sake." She straightened. "And mine."

"All right," Sloan said reluctantly. "We can discuss this. And when the time is right, we'll get married. But until then, I want to help you and Audrey. I want to learn how to be a good father to her."

"You're not her father," Chloe said.

Chloe didn't expect the flash of hurt she saw in his eyes. "I *can* be," Sloan said. "I care about your daughter, Chloe. Nothing will change that."

She swore softly and shook her head. "You live in a world where money will buy anything. I live in a whole different world. We're used to making do on our own. Just because you want to be part of our lives won't make it all perfect. You can't just buy yourself a family."

"Damn it, Chloe, money is not the issue here."

"Oh, no? Isn't that what you're trying to do? Just because you can pay Audrey's college tuition with the spare cash in your wallet does not make you father material. There are other things I have to consider."

Sloan crossed the room in three short steps and pulled Chloe against him, gazing down into her eyes. "Listen to me. I *can* make your life easier. I *can* give Audrey the father she needs. You'll never want for anything, I promise."

"And you think this is why we should get married? Because you can provide for us?"

He nodded. "What better reason?"

"What about love?" she asked flippantly.

He stared at her for a long moment then looked away, his gaze faltering for an instant. In that moment, Chloe knew. She knew that he didn't love her.

He drew a deep breath and met her eyes once more. "If we loved each other, that would be good," he said. "But I don't think it's necessary, at least not right away. We'll be a family and that's what matters most."

Chloe wrenched out of his grasp. "I was right. You *are* an idiot." She spun around and made for the office door, then yanked it open and turned back to him. "And I was an even bigger idiot to sleep with you!" She slammed the door behind her, then grabbed her portfolio from Edna's desk.

"Don't look so surprised, Miss Crenshaw," she said. "You heard right. I slept with Sloan DeWilde. Deal with it."

Chloe didn't take refuge in her office but headed straight for the peace and solitude of her workroom. On her way through the door, she spotted a mannequin that resembled Sloan DeWilde and gave it a shove. The mannequin tipped over and crashed to the floor, its head tumbling off and rolling under her worktable.

"How could I have been so stupid?" she muttered. Over and over again, she'd told herself to be careful, to protect herself against him and the hurt she knew he'd eventually cause. But instead, she'd rushed headlong into a relationship, forgetting all her common sense.

Of course he didn't love her! Sloan DeWilde was the type of man who backed away from any commitment to a woman. She'd known that from the start.

And how dare he lecture her on parenting? The man knew nothing about children! Chloe cursed softly. In her heart, she knew he'd been at least a little right. She shouldn't have trusted Audrey as she had. She should have checked on her more often, or made a greater effort to find a sitter, or—

Chloe groaned. She'd been through this before. The first time Audrey crossed the street on her own, the first time she climbed the fire escape to the roof, the first time she went home with a school friend without asking permission. Audrey constantly pushed her boundaries and Chloe should have known she'd do it again.

But to walk out of the store with a complete stranger was something that even Chloe couldn't easily forgive! She was tempted to leave work, to show up at Audrey's school and pull her out of class just to have a talk with her. Chloe drew a deep breath. She also knew that in her state of mind, her temper would take over. It would be better to wait and talk to her daughter when she'd calmed down.

As for Sloan, she wasn't sure she ever wanted to talk to him again. She'd made a big enough fool of herself already, falling in love with a man who could never love her.

SLOAN CURSED AND KICKED his wastebasket across the room, scattering crumpled paper in its path. What the hell had happened here? He hadn't planned to get so angry. And he certainly hadn't intended to make such a mess of things.

After the initial shock of learning about Audrey—"Madeline"—he'd actually decided he liked the idea. And Chloe was probably right to have kept her daughter's existence from him.

If he had known, he wouldn't have bothered to get involved with her in the first place. He'd always preferred unencumbered companions. But he had gotten to know them separately, and he'd fallen in love with them both.

So how the hell had he managed to screw up her proposal of marriage? Or had it been his proposal? Sloan shook his head in disgust as he tried to determine what had gone wrong.

He flopped down at his desk. She didn't love him, that's what was wrong! Chloe had been the one who'd brought up the subject of love, and it was obvious that she wanted to marry a man she loved. All that his money could offer made absolutely no difference to her.

But hell, *he* loved *her*. She must know that. It should count for something, after all, and he'd told her he was willing to wait. Sloan winced and shook his head. "This one is for the books," he muttered. "I fall in love for the first time in my life and she doesn't love me. Sloan, old boy, I think this is what they call poetic justice."

There was a perfectly good reason he'd avoided marriage up to this point. He'd never found a woman he could imagine spending his life with. But he knew he loved Chloe. He couldn't fathom life without her—or Audrey.

But she'd obviously been hurt by love before, most likely by Audrey's runaway father. From what Audrey had told him, the guy had run out on both of them before she was born. And then there were the other men.

Sloan gripped the arms of his chair with white-knuckled hands. Well, he wasn't about to give up on Chloe. He'd *make* her fall in love with him. And then he'd marry her.

After all, Sloan DeWilde always got what he wanted. And he wanted Chloe and Audrey to be a part of his life.

"You've certainly made a mess of things now!"

Sloan didn't need to look up to know that Edna Crenshaw had decided to add her two cents to the matter. "Come in, Miss Crenshaw, and have a seat. I've been expecting you." He ran his hands through his hair and forced a smile. "So, have you heard any good gossip lately?"

Edna crossed her arms, clutching an envelope to her chest as she slowly walked up to his desk. She stood over him silently, looming like an angry schoolteacher. "I'd appreciate an explanation, although for the life of me, I can't imagine how you're going to explain this."

"I can't, either," Sloan said wearily, leaning back in his chair. "So don't ask me to. I'm a little confused right now."

She primly took a seat across from him. "You've broken all the rules and shown yourself to be absolutely lacking in good judgment. Mixing business with pleasure is never a good idea."

Sloan looked at her through hooded eyes. "Tell me, Miss Crenshaw, have you ever been in love?"

Edna looked at him as if she wanted to answer but didn't think it proper. Instead, she shifted in her chair, straightening her spine and her cuffs at the same time.

"Well, I haven't," Sloan continued. "I used to think I had been, but now I know I haven't. At least, not until now. Now I know... that I'm in love, I mean." Sloan rubbed his forehead. "Hell, I'm starting to sound like her."

"Miss Durrant?" Edna asked.

"Miss Durrant."

"You're in love with Miss Durrant?"

"I am. And because of her, I've learned one thing about love. It completely defies common sense. Did you know she has a daughter?"

Edna nodded. "It was in her personnel file. I believe the girl is eleven. Audrey is her name."

Sloan frowned. "If you knew about Audrey, why didn't you tell me?"

"I didn't think it was important. Having a child has no bearing on a woman's ability to do her job. I have three children."

Sloan sat up in his chair. "You? You have children?"

"Does that suddenly change your opinion of me?"

He shrugged. "Only for the better."

"They're all grown now," she said. "But they weren't when I started working here. It was very difficult. My husband walked out on us before my youngest was born. I had no choice, I had to work. And I know there were times when I wasn't there for my children, but I did my best, and I think they knew that."

"It was hard?"

"I think I understand what Miss Durrant is going through, being a single working mother," Edna said.

"Better than I do," Sloan replied quietly.

Edna folded her hands on her lap. "So what do you plan to do?"

Sloan took a deep breath. "First, I plan to let Ms. Durrant cool off. Then I plan to find her and work this out. I'm not about to let a little argument get in the way of our future."

Edna stood up. "Good luck." She started for the door, then turned back around. "I almost forgot. This was delivered a few minutes ago. It's from your brother Mason."

Sloan took the envelope from her hand and tore it open. Inside was a formal proposal for the sale of DeWilde's with Sloan's name attached as the document's author. Mason had obviously gone over Sloan's head with the board, providing a prospectus before next week's board meeting.

Sloan flipped through the pages and laughed dryly. "Do you know what this is, Miss Crenshaw?" He didn't wait for an answer. "It's a proposal. To sell DeWilde's Fifth Avenue." He glanced up to see an expression of shock on her face. "Don't worry, we're not going to sell. Not if I have anything to say about it."

Relief flooded her features. "I'm happy to hear that."

"I thought it would be so easy. I never wanted to run this place and the store's been losing money for years. I wanted out. And with the problems between Grace and Jeffrey, the time was right for an infusion of capital."

"What changed your mind?" Edna asked.

"It's really *who* changed my mind," Sloan said, smiling. "I used to hate coming to this store. Now I can't wait to walk in the doors, can't wait to pore over the flash report. This is an addictive business, Miss Crenshaw. A little taste of success is enough to hook you for life."

"I understand that feeling," Edna said. "I remember the first time I walked through the front door of DeWilde's. I knew this was where I belonged. Every day is a different challenge, nothing ever stays the same."

"I want to see this store succeed," Sloan said. "I want to make it as good as the other four stores. I want to prove to every last DeWilde that this branch of the family is as talented and dedicated as they are. I'm going to make it happen, mark my words."

"Miss Durrant can help you do that," Edna said.

"I thought you didn't have much faith in her abilities," Sloan remarked.

"I may have been wrong about her," Edna admitted. "Sales have been rising and I believe it's because of her work. She has a natural aptitude for retailing. You were right to promote her."

Sloan chuckled. "I promoted her to get her out of my hair. I thought if she stopped doing the displays, sales would fall again. I guess I underestimated her."

"So, would you like me to order white or red roses?" Edna asked.

Sloan grinned. "I think red would be appropriate, don't you? In fact, order enough roses to fill her office. Then let me know when they'll be delivered."

"Is there anything else?" Edna asked.

Sloan thought about it for a moment, then nodded. "There is one more thing," he said. "Do you know where I might be able to order a pony?"

Edna chuckled, and he realized it was the first time he'd ever seen her show the slightest trace of good humor. The wall between them had been breached and somehow they'd managed to forge a new respect for each other. Edna wasn't his enemy, she was the best ally he had.

"A pony? Not offhand," Edna said. "But then I don't own a horse farm."

The absurdity of his question slowly hit him and he smiled. "Right," he said. "Call Mason and get a name and number from him. Better yet, tell him I want the best pony money can buy and I want him to arrange the whole thing. And I want it delivered to the farm by tomorrow."

"I'll get right on it," Edna replied.

"And I'll get to work calling the board members and putting out the fire that Mason set with this damned proposal."

"Would you like some coffee?" she asked.

"I can get it myself," Sloan said, rising from his chair. "And I'll get you a cup while I'm at it."

Sloan spent the next hour on the phone with various board members, undoing the damage that Mason had caused with his prospectus. Though most of the board members claimed they still intended to vote for the sale, Sloan knew that without his vote, there was little chance of the sale going through. As long as he could hold on to his vote, the store would be safe.

A few minutes after he hung up on the last call, Edna buzzed his intercom and informed him that Chloe had returned. Sloan strode out of his office to meet her, but by the time he got out to the reception area, she'd already walked inside her office. He stood in the doorway, leaning up against the doorjamb as he watched her take in the huge bouquets of roses.

"I'm sorry," he said softly.

She spun around to face him, her expression wary.

He slowly approached, then reached out and cupped her cheek in his palm. "I was wrong. I never meant to get angry with you or question your devotion to your daughter. I guess I just felt . . . left out."

Chloe's expression softened slightly. "I suppose I should be happy that you care so much about Audrey. Not many men would."

"She's quite a little girl," Sloan said. "Stubborn, opinionated . . . and beautiful, just like her mother."

He watched as a multitude of emotions flickered in her green eyes.

"Can we forget what happened and start again?"

After a long moment, she nodded hesitantly. "I'm sorry I didn't tell you right away. I should have. The time just never seemed right."

"No," he said. "If you had told me, I probably would have stayed as far away from you as I could. I wasn't the sort to get involved with someone's mother."

"And now? I'm still someone's mother," she said.

"You're Audrey's mother. That's different." He pulled her against him and kissed her forehead. "Am I forgiven?"

Chloe stiffened, then gently pushed him away. "Sloan, this isn't just a matter of forgiveness. I think things go much deeper than that. We've only known each other a month."

"Exactly six weeks," he corrected her.

"That's my point. Six weeks. You can't make decisions like these after just six weeks."

"*I* can," Sloan said. "I know exactly what I want."

"But *I* can't," Chloe replied. "If it were just me, maybe. But I have Audrey to think about, as well."

"So when are you going to introduce me to your little girl?"

Chloe looked up into his eyes. "I'm not sure. I want to be careful about this. She's so vulnerable right now."

"She once suggested that I date you," Sloan said. "She wanted to set us up because she thought you were in love with some dweeb."

"Audrey told you this?" Chloe shook her head in disbelief. "Sometimes I don't know what goes on in her head."

"She just wants you to be happy. And so do I." Sloan kissed her, his lips lingering over hers until she couldn't help but smile. "I bought Audrey a gift. I guess I'll have to wait to give it to her."

"She won't expect gifts," Chloe said.

Sloan reached into the breast pocket of his suit jacket and pulled out a fax. "Here. Tell me what you think."

Chloe unfolded the paper and stared at it, a confused frown furrowing her brow. "This is a picture of a pony."

"Actually, it's a real pony. It's being delivered to my family's farm tomorrow. I thought I might teach Audrey to ride. She'll love the farm. And my family will love her. I thought we might—"

Chloe placed her finger over his lips then stood on her toes and kissed him lightly. "Let's take this one day at a time," she said. "Audrey and I have been on our own for a very long time. It's going to take a while to get used to this."

Sloan grinned. "I can wait."

"We'll get to know each other a little better. And then you can get to know her."

"I know all I need to know," he said, nuzzling her neck.

"We'll start fresh. With no more secrets between us, all right?"

Sloan bent down and brushed his mouth over hers. "No more secrets," he agreed, pushing her back against the edge of her desk. Drawing her body against his, he kissed her deeply, moving his hands over her body in a gentle sign of possession and intimacy.

"The door's still open," Chloe murmured against his mouth. "What about Miss Crenshaw?"

"Don't worry," Sloan replied. "Miss Crenshaw approves."

"SLOAN, DO YOU HAVE YOUR copy of the—"

Chloe stepped into Sloan's office, only to find it empty. She glanced back at Edna's desk, but Sloan's assistant had also disappeared.

She paused for a long moment and drew a deep breath. The spicy scent of his cologne still lingered in the air, causing an unbidden memory to spring to mind. She could almost imagine his lips on hers, the feel of his hands stroking her body.

He cared about her—and for now, that was enough. After all, they'd only known each other six weeks. How could she expect him to love her? And he'd only just found out about Audrey. Real love, deep and abiding, took time. No one knew that better than her.

She'd rushed into a relationship with Julien and look where it had left her. She needed to be patient, to give her relationship with Sloan more time. "More time," she murmured to herself.

Chloe walked across the office to his desk and searched the surface for the merchandising report she'd prepared for the upcoming DeWilde board meeting. They'd worked on it together, combining her retailing savvy with his knowledge of board politics to develop a plan that would start DeWilde's Fifth Avenue on the road to profitability.

Chloe riffled through a teetering stack of papers. As always, Sloan had his own problems with organization and his desk was a mess. She picked up a report in a navy blue DeWilde cover and scanned the title. She was about to toss it back on the desk, when she looked at it more closely.

"Strategic Plan for the Divestiture of DeWilde's Fifth Avenue," she read out loud. "Presented by Sloan De-Wilde." His name was there on the cover, in black and white. Slowly, she lowered herself into his huge leather chair and paged through the official-looking document.

At first, she couldn't believe what she was reading—outlines for the sale of property, the layoff of employees, the liquidation of assets. It was all there, right in front of her, along with the basic requirements for the sale.

The store had to show a consistent decrease in sales for a six-month period before approval would be granted. She frowned. But the store hadn't shown a decrease in sales in the past month. In fact, sales had been going up.

Slowly, as she read through the prospectus, it all began to make sense to her. His insistence on approving her display designs, his choice of the very worst schemes for the Fifth Avenue window, his continuing presence at the store and—her heart twisted in her chest—her promotion.

All this time, he'd been keeping his own secrets, encouraging her, telling her how much he wanted the store to succeed, how much he appreciated her help, when he'd been planning to sell the store right out from under her, from under *all* the employees and their families.

Chloe covered her eyes with her hands, then shook her head, trying to muddle through the turbulent emotions spinning in her mind. Could she have misread him so badly? Could he really intend to sell DeWilde's? Or had she happened upon an old document?

"That's it," she murmured. "It's just an old document." She searched the cover for a date, her hope destroyed when she saw that the plan had been prepared for next week's board meeting.

Her suspicions about her promotion were not unfounded, after all. He'd promoted her to merchandising manager, knowing full well that she'd be able to make little impact on the store. The buyers had already spent their open-to-buy for the current season and most of the next. The best she could do was make changes on the sales floor, since the merchandise selection would not be affected for at least a year.

Still, her window designs had an impact *now*. And he'd done everything he could to try to convince her to hire a new display manager.

Chloe squeezed her eyes shut, trying to stem the sting of tears. No! She had to be mistaken. The man who professed to care for her, the man who had made love to her just two nights ago, couldn't have betrayed her like this. He knew how much her job and the store meant to her.

Business is business. Isn't that what he'd always said to her? And if he wanted to sell DeWilde's, then he'd do whatever it took to accomplish his goal.

But had making love to her been part of his plan? Had he intended to draw her into a relationship and then break it off, hoping she would quit her job rather than face the prospect of seeing him every day at the store? And why hadn't he let their fight over Audrey be the end? Why the roses and the apologies?

She honestly couldn't say, for certain. Beneath that smooth, seductive exterior was a man she really didn't know at all. She had thought she'd sensed honor and goodness in him, but then, she'd thought the same of Julien and been sadly mistaken.

Chloe stood up and walked around Sloan's office, trying to recall all that had passed between them, every nuance of conversation, every fleeting expression. Had she somehow missed his true motives in the midst of her fascination with him? Had her infatuation blinded her to the man he truly was?

Her mind screamed "yes" at the same time her heart cried "no!" What she wanted to believe and what she was forced to accept were two very different things.

She had only one choice—she'd have to confront Sloan with what she knew. He owed her an explanation and she intended to get one. Drawing a deep breath, she turned and started out the office. But Sloan suddenly appeared in the doorway, blocking her escape. Her heart leapt into her throat and she stopped short.

"Here you are," he said warmly. "Are you almost ready to leave?"

Chloe opened her mouth, but she couldn't speak.

"What's wrong?" he asked, concern creasing his brow.

"Wrong?" Chloe croaked, forcing back her emotions, suddenly afraid to hear the answers she sought.

"You seem a little...upset."

The spark of anger she'd held in check burst into a flame. "Oh, I am just a *little* upset," she replied, her voice wavering. "But I think I have good reason. I just discovered that you plan to sell DeWilde's."

"What—" Sloan began.

She turned around and snatched the report off his desk. "This. You're going to sell the store, aren't you." Her words weren't a question but a statement of fact, one he couldn't possibly deny when faced with the evidence.

He stood mutely, staring at the report clutched in her hand.

"Aren't you!" she repeated. "Go ahead, answer me. Tell me that it's all business. Tell me that the decision has nothing to do with us."

"It *was* business," he replied, his voice purposely calm, "and it has absolutely nothing to do with us."

"So much for honesty," she said, tears flooding her eyes. She headed toward the door, but he grabbed her arm as she passed.

"All right, it's true," he admitted. "I planned to sell the store."

"When did you intend to tell me? When they tacked up the For Sale sign on the front of the building?"

"I didn't intend to tell you," Sloan said. "There was no reason. I'm not going through with the sale."

"You expect me to believe that?" Chloe cried. "I read the prospectus, I know what it means."

"If you read the prospectus, you know that the sale is contingent on posting a loss in the last two quarters of this year. I don't think that's going to happen in this quarter."

"Not for lack of trying on your part," she accused.

"What's that supposed to mean?"

"Tell me, Sloan, why did you promote me? And tell the truth, because I'll know if you're lying."

Sloan cursed and turned away from her. "I promoted you because you were ruining my plans. I thought if I occupied your time with administrative tasks, you wouldn't have time to design the windows and displays."

At his admission, Chloe knew she couldn't stay in the room with him any longer. All the confidence that had filled her over the past month had been shattered in a single moment. Everything she'd accomplished meant nothing in the face of the truth. Just like Julien, he'd stolen her heart and then her self-esteem.

She freed her arm from his grasp. "Go ahead," she said. "Sell your store. Just don't expect me to stick around and watch." With that, she turned and walked out of his office, walked out the front door of the store, walked out of Sloan DeWilde's life without once looking back.

In the end, she went straight home to Audrey. But she couldn't bring herself to scold her daughter for disobeying her orders. In fact, she couldn't bring herself to even mention Sloan's name. Instead, she took her daughter shopping at Macy's and then out for ice cream.

And later that night, when sleep continued to evade her, Chloe crawled into Audrey's bed and held her daughter close as she slept, unwilling to let go of the only real constant in her life, the only person she would ever be able to count on for unconditional love.

CHAPTER ELEVEN

SLOAN STOOD ON the sidewalk across from Chloe's Greenwich Village apartment building, his shoulder braced on a lamppost. He'd been waiting there for almost an hour, watching as tenants walked out into the Saturday-morning sunshine. But the two people he most wanted to see had yet to appear.

He wasn't sure what he'd say to Chloe, he just knew he had to explain. The past few weeks without her had been unbearable. He'd walked the aisles of DeWilde's, hoping to see her around the next corner but knowing she was gone for good.

Discussion of the sale had never materialized at the October board meeting, much to his brother's chagrin. Sloan had finally convinced the board members that neither he nor Jeffrey would support the sale and a vote on the subject would be useless. And now, Sloan was determined to finish the work that Chloe had started—turning DeWilde's Fifth Avenue into the retailing power it was meant to be.

She'd taught him to enjoy the excitement and the challenge of the business, but now that she wasn't there to share in it, the luster had somehow faded. But he wasn't ready to give up yet. He'd stay at the store until all hope of winning her back was gone. For if they were to have a future together, it would be at DeWilde's.

She might never love him as he loved her, but maybe, with a little luck, he would be able to convince her to return to her position at the store. They could still work together, putting past mistakes behind them in the quest for a common goal. And he was prepared to offer whatever it might take to get her back into the office next to his—a salary increase, benefits, vacation, whatever she wanted.

Sloan pushed away from the lamppost and shoved his hands into his jeans pockets. He began to pace the length of the sidewalk, keeping one eye on the doorway to Chloe's building.

It wasn't just Chloe he missed, it was Madeline—or Audrey. Both mother and daughter had carved out their own special place in his heart. He wanted Chloe to be a part of his life again, but he wanted to be a part of Audrey's life, as well. Audrey needed him, and he could only hope that Chloe might come to realize that she needed him, too.

He'd never thought about fatherhood, always assuming that when the subject presented itself, he'd know what to do. But the instinct to protect Audrey, to make her life safe and secure, had grown within him, overwhelming him until he found himself worrying about the silliest things—whether she was looking both ways before crossing the street, whether she had her umbrella when it rained, whether she was doing well in school.

He'd assumed the paternal feelings would go away once he'd learned her true identity. But that hadn't happened. Knowing she was Chloe's daughter only strengthened his feelings for her. He could imagine loving Audrey for the rest of his life just as easily as he could imagine spending his life with Chloe.

They *could* be a family.

Sloan forced the thought from his mind. They were all a long, long way from setting up housekeeping. Audrey probably didn't even know who he really was. And Chloe wouldn't talk to him. She refused to answer his phone calls, had turned down bouquet after bouquet of the flowers he had sent, and had scribbled "return to sender" on the one official letter he'd written offering her her job back.

Sloan tugged his Yankees cap lower over his eyes, then glanced back at the apartment building once more. A tiny figure sat on the steps, a book in her lap, the breeze toying with her long, dark hair. A smile touched Sloan's lips and he fought the urge to call out to her.

Chloe was nowhere to be seen. He watched Audrey for a long time, but her mother didn't appear, nor did Audrey make a move off the front steps. Satisfied that he could talk to her alone, he crossed the street and slowly approached the steps.

"Hi there, Madeline."

She looked up from her book and frowned. "What are you doing here?"

"I just wanted to see how you were doing," he said. "I've really missed you around the store. And I've missed our afternoon treats at Rumpelmayer's."

"I'm not going to be getting much ice cream in the next few months. 'Cause of you I'm grounded. I can't go to the park, I can't watch television, and I have to read a whole book every weekend for the next month. How come you had to tell her I left the store with you?"

"Well, we got into a little bit of an argument and I said a lot of things I didn't mean to. I'm sorry I got you into trouble."

She shrugged. "You're in as much trouble as I am. My mom is really mad at you."

"She told you about us?"

"She told me that you were the guy she was going out with and that you were her boss. Why didn't you tell me you were seeing my mom?"

"Why didn't you tell me your real name?"

"You didn't tell me your name, either," she challenged.

Sloan sat down beside her. "Sounds like we both messed up pretty bad. You think your mom will ever forgive us?"

"She'll forgive me," Audrey said. "She has to. I'm her daughter. But I don't know about you. What did you do to make her so mad?"

"I lied to her. And I deceived her. I was planning to sell the store and I didn't tell her. At first, I didn't want to tell her. Then later on, I couldn't tell her. In the end, I had to tell her, and that's what got her angry."

Audrey nodded sympathetically and patted him on the arm. "That happened to me once. I wore her jade necklace. It broke when I was turning cartwheels on the playground. I tried to put it back together, but it looked really bad. Then I tried to hide it in my closet. And then she found it and I had to tell her the truth. She was mad for a while, but she got over it."

Sloan bumped against Audrey's shoulder and smiled dubiously. "I'm not sure your mom will be as forgiving of me."

Audrey glanced up at him hesitantly. "Do you love my mom?"

Sloan considered her question for a long time, knowing he owed her an honest answer. "Yeah," he finally said. "I really love her."

"Do you want to marry her?"

"We have a lot to work out before that happens, sweetheart. I wouldn't get my hopes up just yet."

"Is it 'cause of me?" Audrey asked.

Sloan frowned at her. "What do you mean?"

"When you fell in love with my mom, you didn't know about me."

"No, I didn't know you were Chloe's daughter," he said. "But I was already in love with *you*, anyway... Madeline."

A wide smile lit up her face and she blushed, her freckles standing out even more across the bridge of her nose. "Really?" she asked.

He put his arm around her shoulder and hugged her against him. "Really."

"What if you and my mom don't make up?"

"I don't know. I'd like to say we could still be friends, but I'm not sure your mom would like that."

"We wouldn't have to tell her," Audrey suggested.

"No way. I don't know about you, but I've learned my lesson. No more lying."

"That might be easy for you, but I've got my whole life ahead of me, Jack. I might have to lie sometime. Like, what if someone breaks into our apartment? I'd have to tell him we have a Doberman chained up in the bedroom. Or what if my science teacher, Mrs. Florsheim, asks if we like her new dress and it's really, really ugly?"

Sloan chuckled. It wasn't hard to see that Audrey had inherited her mother's colorful imagination and her talent for babbling. Lord, he could listen to her chattering forever. "No more lying to your mother."

"But what if—"

He held up his hand to stop her next words. "No 'what-ifs.' No more lying to your mom, okay?"

She nodded reluctantly as she riffled the pages of the book on her lap. "So, did you sell the store?"

Sloan shook his head. "No, I decided to keep it. I was kind of hoping I could convince your mom to come back and work there."

Audrey's expression brightened. "We should ask her! You wanna talk to her now? She's upstairs. I bet if you go up, she'd talk to you."

"I think I'd better wait. I'm not quite sure what I want to say. And maybe I should give her some more time to cool off."

"That might be best. My mom can't stay mad very long. Besides, she just got another job."

Sloan's heart twisted in his chest. "Where?"

Audrey shrugged. "Some store on Madison Avenue. I don't think she likes it as much as the job at DeWilde's. And I might have to leave Wellton Academy after the semester is over, 'cause the tuition's too high. But she still buys Twinkies and strawberry soda, so we must be doing okay."

Sloan reached into the breast pocket of his sports jacket and withdrew one of his business cards. "Here," he said, handing it to Audrey. "No matter what happens, if you ever need anything, including tuition for Wellton, I want you to call me. Even if your mom and I don't work things out, that doesn't mean that we can't be friends. Promise me, Audrey."

She took his card and tucked it between the pages of her book. "I promise," she said softly.

Sloan pulled her close and kissed her on the top of the head, then stood. "We'll talk again, soon. And you promise to take care of your mom?"

Audrey nodded, her blue eyes wide. As he stepped back onto the sidewalk, she gave him a timid wave. "Bye, Jack."

Sloan took off his baseball cap and pulled it down on Audrey's head, the brim low over her eyes. "See ya, Madeline."

He left her there, all alone on the steps, her book clutched to her chest, the oversized Yankees cap shadowing her face. And as he walked away, he made a vow that he and Audrey would talk again... and again... every day and every night for a very long, long time. And when she fell asleep at night, he would speak in quiet tones to her mother, and hold Chloe in his arms, and make love to her.

He would do all that and more. He'd let nothing stand in his way.

THE APARTMENT WAS QUIET, the only sounds coming from the traffic on the street outside. Lacy curtains moved in the nearly nonexistent breeze that stirred the air five stories up. The smells from an Italian restaurant down the block drifted in, garlic and fresh-baked bread and oregano.

Chloe pulled the bedsheet up around Audrey's chin and gave her daughter a kiss on the forehead. "'Night, Claude," she murmured, brushing a dark strand of hair from Audrey's cheek. "Sleep tight." She rose from the bed, reaching for the lamp, but her daughter's words stopped her.

"I saw Jack today," Audrey said in a small voice.

Chloe dropped back down on the bed. "You mean Sloan? You saw Sloan today? Where?"

"He was outside, on our steps. I think he was going to come up and talk to you, but then he decided not to."

"But he talked to you?" Chloe asked, her voice trembling slightly.

Audrey nodded, snuggling under the covers a bit more.

Chloe felt her anger rise. How could he do this? How could he put Audrey in the middle of all of this? Her daughter's feelings were fragile enough. She didn't need to be dragged through the middle of their fight. "I'm sorry, Claude."

"You don't have to be sorry, Mom. Jack's a nice guy. He told me that it didn't matter what happened between you and him. That he still liked me, anyway."

"He said that?" Chloe asked. A surge of relief washed over her. Audrey was taking this a heck of a lot better than she was.

Not an hour went by that Chloe didn't think of him, didn't wonder whether he still thought of her, even for just an instant. Everything had been so close to perfect with them. And then, just as suddenly as it had started, it all went bad.

"He told me he loved you, Mom," Audrey said, interrupting Chloe's thoughts.

Chloe smiled indulgently. "I'm sure you misunderstood him, honey."

Audrey's head wagged back and forth on the pillow. "Uh-uh."

"You may have wanted him to say that, but I don't think he did."

"He told me I wasn't supposed to tell any more lies, and I'm not. Couldn't you just talk to him? He seemed like he was really sad about what happened."

Chloe fussed with the sheets, straightening and smoothing and all the time avoiding her daughter's inquisitive gaze. "I think it's time for you to go to sleep. Whatever happens will happen, and all your worrying about it won't make any difference."

To stop any further protest from her daughter, Chloe quickly turned off the light and stood. "Sleep now. We can talk about this tomorrow."

"Okay," Audrey said. "But I still think you should—"

"Claude," she said, a warning tone in her voice.

Audrey went silent and closed her eyes, pulling the sheet back up to her chin. With a silent sigh, Chloe left her daughter to her dreams and stepped out into the quiet living room to deal with her own demons.

Flopping down into an overstuffed chintz chair, Chloe let out a tightly held breath. Conflicting feelings tumbled around in her mind, causing a tight knot of apprehension in her stomach. She didn't know whether to be angry or upset or overjoyed.

He'd come to see her, to talk. It didn't matter that he hadn't made it up the five flights. At least he had tried. But would he bother with a second attempt, or was it really over between them? Audrey tended to be optimistic, and it was clear how much she liked "Jack." Chloe suspected her daughter would say just about anything to smooth the rift between them.

No matter how much she wanted to give Audrey a father, she wasn't sure that Sloan DeWilde was the right man. The fact that he was rich as Croesus didn't hurt his cause, especially since she'd been forced to take a job that paid half the salary of her position at DeWilde's. And he did care about Audrey, or at least he seemed to. But these were not reasons to resume their relationship.

She had more than just her feelings to consider. Audrey had grown way too close to the man for Chloe to accept anything but total commitment. And though he'd offered marriage, he'd never once mentioned love.

Besides, she wasn't entirely sure she could ever trust Sloan again. Discovering his plan to sell DeWilde's Fifth Avenue was bad enough, but knowing that he'd carried on a lie for so long, playing her for the fool, was impossible to accept.

It all went back to his character, the inbred arrogance, the supreme confidence, the knowledge that he would, in the end, get exactly what he set out to achieve. Yet her mind constantly wandered back to the time they'd spent working together at the store, poring over sales reports, outlining new merchandising strategies, arguing over creative control.

Over time, he'd come to love the challenge as much as she had, there was no hiding that fact. And in the end, he hadn't sold the store. Word on the street was that Sloan DeWilde was firmly in control of the store and that plans for the in-store boutiques were still on track.

She'd watched for the ad for a merchandising manager in the trades and wondered when he'd find someone to replace her. No doubt the replacement would be pretty, the kind of woman Sloan could charm, the kind who would accompany him to dinner and gallery openings.

A flood of jealousy washed over her, an unbidden and unwelcome reminder that she still had strong feelings for him. "Admit it," she muttered to herself, "you're not over him. You may want to think you are, but Sloan is a hard man to forget."

With a groan, Chloe sank back into the soft chair and covered her eyes with her hands. What was she supposed to do? She knew that Sloan could only be trouble. She'd always imagined herself with a nice, dependable, steady man, the kind who would work hard and provide a stable environment for her daughter.

But now, as she looked back on this old image, she realized that this was not the kind of man she wanted. The man she wanted had become Sloan DeWilde. There was nothing dependable about him. He was irresistible, with a hint of danger always lurking beneath that smooth, sophisticated exterior. With Sloan, every day would be an adventure, filled with passion and excitement and challenge.

Chloe shook her head and swore softly. "I *want* a dull man," she said out loud. "I want a man who eats crackers in bed, a man who lives with the remote control in his right hand, a man who leaves his socks on when he makes love."

Sloan would settle for nothing less than caviar in bed. And the only thing he might keep in his right hand would be a glass of very expensive champagne. And she had proof positive that when he made love, he didn't wear a single stitch of clothing, not even his socks.

Her mind flashed an image of them in bed together, their limbs twisted in the satin coverlet, and she remembered the depth of the passion they had shared. And in that instant, she knew there would never be another man in her life like him.

SLOAN STOOD ON the sidewalk and stared into the window of the Madison Avenue boutique. He wasn't quite sure what had caused him to stop and look, but a quick glance at the window had suddenly drawn his full attention.

The display was unique—outrageous, in fact. And as he studied it, he realized why it had caught his eye. The window had Chloe Durrant written all over it. Mannequins dangled upside down from a line of trapezes, their dresses hiding their heads but revealing their brightly colored underwear.

Sloan chuckled to himself. Chloe did have a way with underwear. He glanced up at the name of the boutique, then peeked through the door, wondering if she was working. But it was Saturday, and he doubted that she'd spend such a beautiful day inside.

It had been nearly two weeks since he'd seen Audrey, and in all that time, he'd never stopped thinking of her...or her mother. He couldn't count the number of times he'd picked up the phone and dialed Chloe's number, then hung up. Or the times he'd driven past her building, hoping he might catch them both outside. He'd even strolled down Madison Avenue, his gaze searching the crowds of pedestrians for a tall, slender blonde and her pretty, dark-haired daughter.

Even at night, Chloe haunted his dreams, and he'd wake with the feel of her skin beneath his fingers, the scent of her hair teasing at his nose, the sound of her soft voice in his ears. He'd tried to forget, but he couldn't.

He turned to walk away, but a small voice stopped him.

"Jack?"

Sloan spun around and searched the sidewalk, but she was nowhere to be seen. He rubbed his eyes and swore, certain that he'd imagined the sound, but then the voice called his name once more.

"Jack!"

Sloan frowned, then saw a dark head peeking around the corner of the display window. He stepped into the recessed doorway of the shop to find Audrey standing there, a wide smile beaming from her face.

"I knew you would come back," she said.

Sloan smiled. "What are you doing here?"

"My mom works here now. She had to stop and drop off some sketches before we go to the park. Are you going to the park with us? Mom says we can ride the carousel. What ever happened to that horse at the store? Will you ride the carousel with me?" She couldn't hide the excitement in her voice and Sloan couldn't bring himself to disappoint her.

"I don't know, sweetheart. Your mom might not want my company."

Her smile faded and he felt his heart twist in his chest. Damn, if Chloe didn't want him around, Audrey sure did! "Would you really like me to come?" he asked.

She nodded her head enthusiastically. "And after, we could go to Rumpelmayer's again."

Sloan knew he should make a graceful exit before Chloe came out of the shop. But somehow he also knew his chances with Chloe were much improved with Audrey there to back him up. So what if the mother didn't have a high opinion of him, he could count on the daughter for a few good words.

"Yeah," he said. "We'll go to Rumpelmayer's and have a triple fudge sundae."

"With nuts," Audrey said.

"Lots and lots of nuts," Sloan added.

Audrey grabbed his hand and smiled. "This will all work out," she said knowingly. "You just wait and see." She gave his fingers a gentle squeeze and they stood there, hand in hand, staring at the entrance to the boutique.

A minute later, Chloe pulled the door open and stepped outside. She glanced up, clearly expecting to find Audrey waiting for her. And it was just as obvious that she didn't expect to see him. She froze, her gaze locking with his, her expression tense.

Audrey stepped forward and smiled at her mother. "Look, Mom. I found him out here on the street."

"I can see that, Audrey," Chloe said, forcing a smile in return. "I guess you forgot our little chat about picking up stray animals."

"Mom," she chided. "That's not very nice."

A blush rose in Chloe's cheeks. "You're right, it's not. What are you doing here, Sloan?"

Sloan shrugged and grinned, trying hard to melt her icy facade. But she wouldn't have it and continued to stare at him without a trace of warmth or forgiveness. "I was just passing by," he said, "and noticed your windows. They're very...unusual."

"Yes," she replied. "They are."

His gaze skimmed over her face, drinking in her beauty, her luminous skin and her wide eyes, her perfect nose and her soft hair. "I've been looking for someone with exactly your talents to work at DeWilde's."

"Hear that, Mom?" Audrey piped in. "You could go back to DeWilde's."

"The store hasn't been the same without you," Sloan said.

Chloe drew a long breath and shook her head. "I can't go back there, Sloan. I won't go through it all again."

"You don't have to," Sloan replied, sensing a weak spot in her defenses. "You can have your job back. I'll stay out of the store and let you run it. I want you back at De-Wilde's, Chloe. You belong there."

"No," Chloe said. She grabbed her daughter's hand and tugged her along. "Come on, Audrey, we're going to be late."

Audrey turned and looked over her shoulder at Sloan. "Why don't you tell her that you love her?" she shouted.

"Audrey, hush!" Chloe cried.

"She knows I love her," Sloan called back.

Chloe stopped in the middle of the sidewalk, still clutching Audrey's hand, but didn't turn around.

"No, she doesn't," Audrey insisted. "Tell her!"

"Chloe Durrant," Sloan shouted, "I love you!"

Slowly, she faced him, her green eyes wide. Audrey beamed, her gaze darting from one to the other. "You love me?" Chloe asked.

"Of course I love you. I think I fell in love with you the moment we met. Hell, I wouldn't have proposed marriage if I didn't love you."

"You didn't propose marriage. I did," Chloe said.

"I don't care who said the word first," he replied.

"But you never told me that you loved me."

"Damn it, Chloe, I offered to take care of you and Audrey. And I wouldn't have considered that commitment unless I was sure I loved you both. I thought that was understood."

"Ask her again!" Audrey urged. "I think she'll say yes now."

Sloan chuckled. "All right," he said. "I will. Give me a chance!"

Sloan slowly walked up to Chloe, then grabbed her hand and bent down on one knee. Pedestrians who had heard all the shouting stopped to stare, and a small crowd gathered around them on the sidewalk.

"Chloe Durrant," Sloan said, "I love you. And I love your daughter. I want to make a life for the three of us. And I promise, I will make you both happy. I'll take care of you both and keep you safe. And I'll never, ever lie to you again. Will you marry me, Chloe?"

Her eyes bright with tears, Chloe looked at him as if she wanted to believe his words but wasn't quite sure.

"Answer him, Mom," Audrey urged, giving her a nudge. "Say yes."

"Listen to your daughter, Chloe," Sloan said. "She knows what she's talking about."

A tiny smile quirked the corners of her mouth. "You didn't sell DeWilde's," she said.

"I couldn't. It's your store ... and mine. And someday it will be Audrey's to run, if she wants. Come back and make it great, Chloe. I need you, at the store and in my life."

"Say yes, Mom," Audrey demanded.

Chloe looked at her daughter and then smiled down at Sloan. "All right," she said with a sigh. "Yes! Are you both satisfied now? Yes, I love you, and yes, I'll marry you, Sloan DeWilde!" As she shouted the last words, the crowd of pedestrians broke out in wild applause and shrill whistles.

In that instant, the man who had always got what he wanted knew that he'd stumbled upon something more valuable than anything he'd ever coveted before. Worth more than all the jewels in the DeWilde family vaults.

He had found love.

Sloan stood and pulled Chloe into his arms, kissing her thoroughly to the cheers of the Saturday-morning crowd. Then he bent down and drew Audrey into his embrace, hugging them both to him and making a silent vow never to let them go.

WEDDINGS BY DeWILDE

continues with

WILDE HEART

by Daphne Clair

Available in July

Here's a preview!

WILDE HEART

RYDER DIDN'T MOVE from the door. "Come here," he said, looking straight into her eyes.

Natasha walked slowly toward him and he reached out a hand, drawing her closer, leaning back against the door as he folded her into his arms.

Natasha returned his kiss, locking her own arms around his neck, her body curved into his, her lips parted and welcoming.

He lifted his head, rubbed his cheek against hers and let out a long sigh. "I've been dying to do that for hours."

Natasha rested her head against his shoulder. So had she, but she'd tried to hide it. She also tried to remember all the reasons why this was not a good idea, only it was difficult to call them to mind when his fingers were playing tantalizing little games—stroking, exploring, gently kneading—so that her breath suddenly caught and her spine went rigid.

"What?" he murmured, drawing away a little. "I didn't hurt you, did I?"

"No." She lifted her eyes to his. "Oh, no!"

His smile widened, as though her naked desire for him were an unexpected compliment, as if he'd expected her to reject him, after all.

Behind the successful, polished exterior that Ryder presented to the world, she glimpsed the lonely, scared boy who had been sent halfway across the world by seemingly uncaring parents. And whose second family—the people he felt closest to in all the world—was breaking apart, Jeffrey and Grace separated, their children perhaps taking sides, straining his relationship with all of them.

In that moment she stopped fighting her emotions, stopped considering consequences or trying to weigh possible advantages against probable risks.

He wasn't asking, and he'd never force the issue. If she got up and walked away, he'd take her home without a word of protest or disappointment.

But he needed her, needed to be close to someone. His relationship with Jeffrey had changed, and that was hurting him. The disintegration of the DeWildes' marriage, of the perfect family, was hard for him. Maybe even his friendship with Gabe was threatened. And anyway, Gabe was far away in England.

But Natasha was here. She could at least give him the comfort of knowing that she cared. She could love him.

HARLEQUIN®

Don't miss these Harlequin favorites by some of our most distinguished authors!
And now, you can receive a discount by ordering two or more titles!

HT #25663	THE LAWMAN by Vicki Lewis Thompson	$3.25 U.S.☐/$3.75 CAN. ☐
HP #11788	THE SISTER SWAP by Susan Napier	$3.25 U.S.☐/$3.75 CAN. ☐
HR #03293	THE MAN WHO CAME FOR CHRISTMAS by Bethany Campbell	$2.99 U.S.☐/$3.50 CAN. ☐
HS #70667	FATHERS & OTHER STRANGERS by Evelyn Crowe	$3.75 U.S.☐/$4.25 CAN. ☐
HI #22198	MURDER BY THE BOOK by Margaret St. George	$2.89 ☐
HAR #16520	THE ADVENTURESS by M.J. Rodgers	$3.50 U.S.☐/$3.99 CAN. ☐
HH #28885	DESERT ROGUE by Erin Yorke	$4.50 U.S.☐/$4.99 CAN. ☐

(limited quantities available on certain titles)

	AMOUNT	$
DEDUCT:	**10% DISCOUNT FOR 2+ BOOKS**	$
ADD:	**POSTAGE & HANDLING**	$
	($1.00 for one book, 50¢ for each additional)	
	APPLICABLE TAXES**	$
	TOTAL PAYABLE	$
	(check or money order—please do not send cash)	

To order, complete this form and send it, along with a check or money order for the total above, payable to Harlequin Books, to: **In the U.S.:** 3010 Walden Avenue, P.O. Box 9047, Buffalo, NY 14269-9047; **In Canada:** P.O. Box 613, Fort Erie, Ontario, L2A 5X3.

Name: _____

Address: _____ City: _____

State/Prov.: _____ Zip/Postal Code:_____

**New York residents remit applicable sales taxes.
Canadian residents remit applicable GST and provincial taxes.

HBACK-JS3

Look us up on-line at: http://www.romance.net

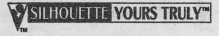

WAYS TO *UNEXPECTEDLY* MEET MR. RIGHT:

♡ Go out with the sexy-sounding stranger your daughter secretly set you up with through a personal ad.

♡ RSVP yes to a wedding invitation—soon it might be your turn to say "I do!"

♡ Receive a marriage proposal by mail— from a man you've never met....

These are just a few of the unexpected ways that written communication leads to love in *Silhouette* Yours Truly.

Each month, look for two fast-paced, fun and flirtatious Yours Truly novels (with entertaining treats and sneak previews in the back pages) by some of your favorite authors—and some who are sure to become favorites.

YOURS TRULY™:
Love—when you least expect it!

Harlequin®
Historical

If you're a serious fan of historical romance,
then you're in luck!

Harlequin Historicals brings you
stories by bestselling authors, rising new stars
and talented first-timers.

Ruth Langan & Theresa Michaels
Mary McBride & Cheryl St. John
Margaret Moore & Merline Lovelace
Julie Tetel & Nina Beaumont
Susan Amarillas & Ana Seymour
Deborah Simmons & Linda Castle
Cassandra Austin & Emily French
Miranda Jarrett & Suzanne Barclay
DeLoras Scott & Laurie Grant...

You'll never run out of favorites.

Harlequin Historicals...they're too good to miss!

HH-GEN

HARLEQUIN®
I N T R I G U E®

THAT'S INTRIGUE—DYNAMIC ROMANCE AT ITS BEST!

Harlequin Intrigue is now bringing you more—more men and mystery, more desire and danger. If you've been looking for thrilling tales of contemporary passion and sensuous love stories with taut, edge-of-the-seat suspense—then you'll *love* Harlequin Intrigue!

Every month, you'll meet four new heroes who are guaranteed to make your spine tingle and your pulse pound. With them you'll enter into the exciting world of Harlequin Intrigue—where your life is on the line and so is your heart!

Harlequin Intrigue—we'll leave you breathless!

Harlequin Romance ®

Delightful

Affectionate

Romantic

Emotional

Tender

Original

Daring

Riveting

Enchanting

Adventurous

Moving

**Harlequin Romance—the
series that has it all!**

HROM-G

If you've got the time...
We've got the
INTIMATE MOMENTS

Passion. Suspense. Desire. Drama. Enter a world that's larger than life, where men and women overcome life's greatest odds for the ultimate prize: love. Nonstop excitement is closer than you think...in Silhouette Intimate Moments!